GUY ON THE
SIDEWALK

GUY ON THE
SIDEWALK

A novel by
Bharath Krishna

First published in India in 2016 by CinnamonTeal Publishing

Copyright © 2016 Bharath Krishna

ISBN 978-93-85523-21-2

Typesetting: CinnamonTeal Publishing

CinnamonTeal Publishing
an imprint of Dogears Print Media Pvt. Ltd.
Plot No 16, Housing Board Colony
Gogol, Margao
Goa 403601 India
www.cinnamonteal.in

GUY ON THE SIDEWALK

Prologue

My name is Jayawardhan "Red," and this is my story.

My introduction is incomplete without mentioning my fascination for the color red. As a kid, my love for red was so well known to people around me that it became my nickname. Even my ears liked the sound so much that when my friends called me Red they got a proud smile in return.

I used to make my mom and dad buy everything in red for me—red schoolbag, red lunchbox, red water bottle, red toys. I even wanted my underwear in red. Except blood, I loved all things red. If I wore a red trouser, a red shirt, a pair of red shoes, red glasses, and a red cap, like a cartoon, there would be no jaw-dropping at all in my neighborhood.

I graduated from high school, travelled to different places for higher education and work, and in the course of time, I matured from Red to Jay and started giving other colors a chance in my life. Red still tickles my fancy but eventually it faded from my name.

Part of my love for red could be attributed to my family's strong socialist leanings. My dad's belief in the leftist ideology, his frugal lifestyle, his love for the country, his confidence in the potential of India's youth and his sense of obligation toward society that he demonstrated throughout his life constantly pricked my conscience, urging me to match his legacy. But it couldn't stop me from going after a career in the US. At times, I wondered if I inherited just the color of his ideology.

In hindsight, his imprint may have been a big motivation for my choosing to return to India years later, leaving behind the life and career I struggled to achieve in the US, to discover who I was, where I belonged and what I was meant for in my short life in this big world.

This is the story of my fling with the hottest destination of the youth of my generation—America—and of my return to India and everything in between.

This story is a portrayal of a slice of my life dominated by my urge to confidently fight for what I truly desired while constantly being held back by the fear of unknown.

This story is neither an inspiration nor a tragedy, neither a success nor a failure, neither a drama nor a comedy. This is just my story—as it happened.

Yours,

Jay

1

September 19, 2013: If I had the habit of writing a diary, I would have marked that day in red.

Sipping hot coffee and smoking my favorite Marlboro Lights one after another, I sat in Venkat's backyard for I don't know how long, after walking there straight from the bed. While several unrelated thoughts passed through my brain, I sat there staring into the adjacent woods distracted sporadically by morning joggers and dog walkers, feeling the warmth of a bright sunrise along with a slightly cold breeze, playing occasionally with my iPhone. The couple of times I went inside were to refill my coffee cup.

"Jay, you woke up so early," Venkat said, disrupting my morning calm as he pulled the glass backyard door open. Dressed in formals and ready to go to work, Venkat stood in front of me with his hands in trouser pockets.

"I couldn't sleep well last night. I have one full fucking day in the flight anyway," I said, stubbing out my cigarette in the ashtray.

"And you don't have a problem with sleeping in the flight," he said.

Venkat took the ashtray filled with cigarette butts, emptied it, brought it back, and placing it on the table, he said, "There's another car at home if you want to go out somewhere or do some last minute shopping."

"I guess I'll just stay home today," I said.

"Okay."

"Venkat, are you disappointed that I am leaving? Do you feel whatever you did for me is wasted?" I asked the question I should have asked him when I first conveyed my decision to move back to India.

"What do you guys want for breakfast?" Venkat's wife Tulasi broke in as he was about to respond to my question.

"I'll eat something in the office. Did Diya eat breakfast?" Venkat asked about their daughter who had just started her school.

"She drank milk. I am packing bread toast for her. Jay, what about you?" Tulasi asked.

"I don't feel like eating anything now. I'll have something later," I said.

As Tulasi closed the backyard door, Venkat said, "Yours is a gutsy move, Jay. I'm proud of you. Very few people can do what you are doing. At least I don't know anybody who left America so easily without any hang-ups. Honestly, I am neither surprised nor disappointed. I knew this was coming even before you broke the news to me. I knew you weren't meant to settle down here."

"I'll miss this place though. It has been a wonderful six years," I said.

"Six years. Time passes so fast. I still remember that phone call you made from India. I was shocked to hear that you wanted to come to America."

"Yeah, I know. Sit down. Let's have a smoke, if you have time," I suggested.

"No, you carry on. I'll get going; I am already late. I also have to drop Diya at school on my way and be in the office by nine. These fucking status calls every morning you know . . . they shifted to nine o'clock recently. I guess they did it on purpose to force people to be on time," Venkat said.

"Especially desis," I said laughingly.

"Say desi girls, otherwise they will come to office directly after lunch. You know something funny, these Americans also started calling Indians desis. The other day during team lunch, our manager was saying that everybody in the team is a desi except him," Venkat said.

"Really? He might be an exception. I don't think many of them know that word. Even if they know, they'll not dare use it openly," I said.

"Desi is not a derogatory word," Venkat said.

"Not until somebody brings legal charges. This is a sue-happy country; anybody can sue anybody here just like that," I said.

"Haha, true, but our guys will not dare go to that extent. I'll get going, Jay. See you in the evening. We'll have our last smoke together in America then. Bye," Venkat said, walking into the house.

I waved at him with one hand, lighting a cigarette with the other.

Venkat and I grew up in the same neighborhood in India, and we studied together for the most part. I knew him from school days when he used to fight with other kids for petty things, and sometimes for no reason at all. Being the shortest and the weakest kid of our class, crying used to be his powerful weapon to win fights. By the time we started college, he changed a lot; the crying kid grew into a calm and confident man, and surprisingly, he grew taller than me. He has been the same simple, systematic and straight-forward character throughout school and college, and even today.

After college, Venkat and I opted for different careers. He chose to try his chances in IT and landed in the US and I chose management and stayed back in India, only to get in touch with him years later when the US bug first bit me. He has been my point man for everything since then.

9:00 a.m.—Nine hours left for my flight.

After living in the US for six years, I was moving back

to India for good that day. I was flying from Venkat's place, Charlotte, to Chennai via Abu Dhabi.

I didn't know what God's plan for me was but I was definitely not going to India on a vacation. I had wrapped up everything in the US both professionally and personally to return to India with more hopes than plans. I had enough experience with planning and failing in the past that I wasn't too anxious about not having a perfect plan in place. The only plan I had was to tweak my plans as I surged forward.

As I finished my nth cup of coffee and was about to finish my nth cigarette that morning, my phone rang.

"Good morning," I greeted Siri rather loudly in an effort to sound normal.

"Good morning." She tried to be normal too but couldn't alter her voice rendered bleak by repeated sobbing and lack of sleep in the past few days. As the day of my departure neared, Siri and I had often been on long phone calls with each other, sometimes all night.

The vacuum I was going to leave in Siri's life concerned me, but the purpose was much bigger and the calling was much stronger than one individual and one relationship.

"When did you wake up?" Siri asked after a brief pause.

"Just now," I lied as I wasn't in the mood to explain why I hadn't called her since getting out of bed more than an hour ago.

Siri expected a call from me every morning immediately after I woke up, but I usually need some time for myself before I open up to the world, and more than ever on that day. There were occasions when she caught me "liking" a Facebook post or being available online on WhatsApp before I called her.

"I thought so. You were at the party till late last night, that's why I didn't want to disturb you," she said.

"Liking" a Facebook post before calling her was unpardonable to Siri. Luckily I didn't do it that morning. The

WhatsApp thing could be defended to some extent; I could say I woke up and randomly checked my phone and went back to sleep. But it would be ridiculous on my part to say that I woke up and "liked" some stupid post on Facebook just to make someone feel good and slept again. Considering the ever-growing Facebook craze, some people might as well be doing it.

"I know you just woke up. Have some coffee, I'll call you in some time," she continued.

"I am already having coffee. No problem, we can talk," I said.

"You said you woke up just now, liar." She caught me.

Whenever Siri called me a liar, I used to clarify and try to convince her that I was not lying. I figured out later that "liar" was one of her frequently used words. When she really was pissed off because somebody lied to her, she would stress the word in a serious tone—*lliaaarrr*.

By the time I could respond, Siri ended the conversation saying, "Okay, I am walking to my cube. Let me login first and call you back. I am already late." She sounded as if she was running late to office for the first time in her life; truth is, she was almost always late. Being late and apologizing with a big artificial smile as if she had accomplished something great was one of her style statements.

I could hear her fast breath as she walked and talked. I visualized Siri walking briskly to her desk through the halls of her office and through the aisles between the open cubes, in her choicest attire—jeans, flat shoes, short sleeve or sleeveless top under a cardigan, signature off-white handbag hanging off her right shoulder, steel tea mug in her left hand, thick rimmed glasses on her narrow face perched on her sharp nose and her hairstyle which she frequently alternated between letting it loose and tying into a ponytail.

The company Siri worked for was perhaps one of the few

in New York City that wouldn't insist on formal dressing, and she exploited the lenience to the core. She spent at least thirty minutes every morning to pick a dress from her vast collection scattered all over the closet and bedroom. It didn't matter if she took a shower in the morning or not, she made sure that she was always dressed well and smelled good.

Most of my time in the US was occupied by Venkat and Siri. Without both of them, the economic downturn of 2008–09 would have kicked me out of the country like it did to some Indian software engineers. With all the debt I had amassed, courtesy of my graduate studies in the US, if I had left the country then, it would have taken a miracle for me to recover financially. Emotional distress would have been an additional bonus. But for Venkat and Siri, I would have told this story a few years back in a totally different tone. I wished several times that I could win a lottery to repay them, and even that wouldn't be enough.

I didn't feel like taking a shower so soon. I prepared another cup of coffee and came back to the backyard and sat there lighting a cigarette.

In the past few days, my conversations with Siri were filled with crying and consoling from both sides. Good that we started crying for each other sooner, as my departure from the US neared we both overcame the grief and started embracing the inevitable. But once in a while, the disillusionment of losing each other overwhelmed us. How could I return to India leaving behind someone who was a big part of my life for more than five years without leaving any scars? There was no formal relationship between Siri and me to call it a breakup. We had a different equation with each other. I guess some relationships don't cease to exist just because we cannot describe them. They remain beyond the capability of our understanding and the power of our vocabulary. Most of those relationships die when people try to define them instead of accepting and enjoying the mystery surrounding them. Siri and I never attempted to give our relationship a name, and that could be a big reason for the excitement we felt of being with each other that didn't diminish with time.

The phone ring kind of nudged my lost self. Siri again.

"Okay, tell me. How was the party last night? Did you have good time?" she asked as soon as I picked up the call.

Before I responded, I paused to clearly hear the sound Siri made when she drank tea, imagining how she would bend forward with closed eyes and make a typical sound that created, by all means, a very ungraceful scene. I would have hated if anybody else did that but Siri was an exception. More than the weird sound she made, I liked her boldness to do so even when people were around. Odd is beautiful, sometimes.

"Mmm, tell me," Siri broke the pause after a fresh sip.

"I am lost in the sound you make when you have tea," I said, with a smile in my voice.

"Stop it, Jay! You have been doing it for the last five years. How will you hear this sound from tomorrow?"

"The same way I am hearing it now, over the phone."

"Five years, Jay, can you believe it? I feel like I met you just yesterday," Siri said, her voice turning little emotional.

I didn't respond. I didn't know how to respond. Any response from my side would drag both of us back to the sad topic of my return to India. In the past few days, I made every effort to talk to her about everything else as I knew the consequences of talking about us—reminiscing about the time we spent together, how it would never be the same again, endless sobbing, cursing the helplessness, consoling each other, leaving it to God and accepting the destiny, more or less in the same sequence.

"Jay, are you sleeping?"

"Haha, no."

"Okay, tell me about the party," Siri asked, changing the topic. Probably she sensed my reluctance to talk about the past, or her curiosity to know about the party dominated. Last night, Venkat had arranged a farewell dinner for me along with friends who lived in and around Charlotte.

"Yeah, it was okay," I said, without going into the details.

"Just okay?"

"No, it was good."

"Where did you guys go?"

"P. F. Chang's."

"Again? Don't you guys know any other restaurant in the town? It's a good place though. What did you eat? Let me guess let me guess! Definitely dynamite shrimp, right?" Siri said, followed by her trademark laugh—loud, long and full of life. Sometimes her loud laugh forced me to pull the mobile a little away from my ear. Of late the life in her laugh had faded; otherwise it was not possible to imagine her not laughing with almost every sentence she spoke.

"Yeah, last night was shrimp night, Siri. I had dynamite shrimp and shrimp fried rice."

"Who all were there?" she asked.

"Did you have breakfast?" I tried to wean her away from the party discussion.

"No, I got tea from home. Tell me about the party first. Who all attended?" Siri asked, her voice insistent.

A mug full of tea was Siri's breakfast and pastime in the train during her commute to work from Jersey City to New York City. When she ate breakfast, which she did very rarely, she ate at around 11 in the morning when people were almost ready for lunch. And when she had breakfast, she would skip lunch for that day. She wouldn't pay half the attention to her eating habits that she paid to her grooming.

I knew Siri will not leave me until I satisfied her curiosity about the dinner last night, so I started listing the attendees.

"Oh, Geeta!" Siri intervened to make fun of Geeta's honeyed accent as soon as she heard me utter her name. Out of the entire group, Siri was interested only in Geeta. Somehow they became enemies for no apparent reason the first time they met.

Geeta and her husband Varun became friends with Venkat through his wife Tulasi as Geeta and Tulasi happened to have been classmates in India. Somewhere along the line, Geeta and Varun became my acquaintances too.

Siri only knew about the people at the dinner party as much as I told her about them. She hadn't met any of them except Geeta. Once, I had to request Siri to accommodate Geeta at her place when the latter visited New York City for a job interview. Venkat and others knew remotely that I had a friend named Siri, but nothing more, which often made it difficult for me to talk to Siri when I was around them.

"That's a big group. Did Venkat spend his one month's pay on your farewell?" Siri continued with her questions.

"Not that much. It was just a dinner, nobody in the group drinks except me," I said.

"I wish I could be there for you, Jay."

Siri wouldn't have been with me last night. For a moment she must have forgotten that we agreed on not making my departure an emotional burden for both of us and a spectacle for others. That was also a reason for me to take the flight from Charlotte instead of my place or her place.

"Okay, I need to run for a meeting. I am already late. I'll call you back after my meeting, okay? Bye." Siri hung up, again in a hurry and again for the same reason—she was already late. I never understood why hurrying thrilled her so much.

I felt as if I had just woken up and walked into the backyard. It was almost 10:30. While I wanted a slow passage of time that day, it was running like that girl who ran like a racehorse on the treadmill, making loud noises that reverberated throughout our apartment complex gym. I wish time had passed that fast when I was in the office. At work, breakfast to lunch felt like a lifetime and lunch to end of the day felt like two lifetimes.

I took a break from my endless coffees and cigarettes and walked into the house.

"Jay, do you want to eat something? You didn't have breakfast also," Tulasi asked as I entered the kitchen to leave the coffee cup.

"No. I'll have lunch directly. Don't cook anything, we'll go out. Let me take a shower and come back," I said.

"Why go out? Are you tired of my cooking?" she asked jokingly.

"No, no. We'll go out for my last lunch; it's my treat," I said.

She smiled, and said, "Okay."

I proceeded to the restroom for my last American shower, which was one of the several "last time in the US" feelings I had been experiencing—last night, last dinner, last day, last shower. More often than not, my bowel movements ditched me on big days, and what could be a bigger day in my life than that day? I gave it a pass and brushed my teeth and got into the shower. A little odd, but I would miss the American restrooms a lot. Unlike the dry and spacious restrooms there, I would be stepping into damp and narrow bathrooms in India.

2

Siri probed into last night's dinner party so much that I inadvertently relived the entire event during the shower.

We were at P. F. Chang's, one of my favorite Chinese restaurants in the US—chicken noodle soup, lettuce wraps, dynamite shrimp, fried rice, and a perfect finishing with delicious tiramisu.

Water jets on my body, coupled with Geeta's images from last night's dinner, were exciting me. Her ugly attitude, however, knocked down my arousal. Whenever I remembered Geeta, her beautiful face was almost always accompanied by her nasty mindset that turned me off instantly.

Without caring much about the company, I ordered for my favorite Glenlivet double on the rocks. Everybody in the group toasted to me with their favorite non-alcoholic drink.

For most of the dinner, I, rather my return to India, was the central point of the discussion. There was a long debate on whether returning to India will work out well for me, as if staying back was still an option. In a way it was, but I was past the contemplation phase.

Moving back to India was one topic that dominated conversations among Indians during get-togethers in the US, closely followed by comparisons of what others were getting paid. Most never actually returned, but they loved to argue about it. The dinner party that night was no exception. Everybody at the table vented their opinions on the subject.

If it were a slightly aged group, the discussion would have

extended to bringing up children in the US vis-à-vis India, houses and mortgages, and green card and citizenship, and if it were a little younger crowd, cars, casinos, and college debt. Ultimately, comparison between America and India was an obvious thread that ran in the conversations among the NRIs.

The good part about last night was that nobody drank, and hence no big drama, no histrionics, no crying, no vomiting, no regretting later for what happened, and no blaming it on alcohol. Arguing over returning to India naturally inebriated Indians, so not having alcohol didn't stop people from having fun, with no puking involved. I played the role of a good listener during most of the dinner. Animated conversations on the topic mattered to all those who never returned, not to me. I was already in India. I just had to transport my body physically.

Most NRIs would have started their journey to the US not with the goal to stay there permanently. Even while doing so, they argued that they wouldn't. They desperately aspired to have it both ways—American dollars and Indian nativity. America has something more than just dollars that kept Indians there, away from their homes. Folks who lived happily in the US without conspicuously making a statement about missing India constituted a minor percent. Some acted up the "missing India" thing to be in sync with the majority and escape being the odd ones drawing unwanted attention. While it should have been the other way around, missing India was considered cool among NRIs.

In spite of being neutral inside and polite outside about my return to India, undesirable provocation was not always avoidable. Last night was no exception.

"When are you coming back to America, Jay?" Varun asked, with his trademark awkward smile.

Geeta always boasted that she fell for Varun's smile the

first time she saw him. If she was truthful, I pity her taste, and if she lied, I appreciate her for being a nice wife.

I guess Varun tried to defend his staying on in the US by taunting me. "I am sure, Jay, you will come back in a year," Geeta joined her husband, predicting my future like a prophet.

I didn't respond to them, just nodded my head, shoving a lettuce wrap into my mouth.

Frustrated with my purposeful disregard, Geeta said, "What's there in India? I believe America is a better place for us and for our kids."

I prepared myself to go easy on them and started sharing my thoughts respectfully. "I'm not sure if America is a better place for us, but definitely it's a great place for our kids. They have the advantage of American opportunity coupled with Indian parenting. I'm sure Indian kids here will do miracles when they grow up. I'll be happy to cheer for them from India. But I cannot stay here thinking of my kids who are not born yet. There are more Indian kids in India than in all other countries put together, America included. What about them? It's a choice between continuing to live here since we were lucky enough to be exposed to a better world and trying to make the place where we belong a better one."

"Do you think we belong to India just because we were born there?" Geeta asked.

"There are more reasons than just being born in India. The country and the people are responsible for what we are today. We owe them something. When our motherland is lagging behind compared to its potential, for whatever reasons, I believe we have a responsibility to rise to the occasion," I said.

"You should have never come here then," Geeta made a derisive comment, looking down as if she talked to her plate. Seldom did Geeta look at me directly, probably because she was ashamed of how she behaved or because she knew that I understood her better than anybody else. She looked down even during a pause in the conversation.

"I wouldn't have understood what sets the most developed nation on earth apart from countries like India if I hadn't come here. I wouldn't have got an opportunity to turn inward and realize where I belonged. I wouldn't have been able to decide how I would like to mold the rest of my life. Most importantly, I wouldn't have got a chance to vouch for India to the extent of leaving behind a life in America."

"Oho, Jay, you are overflowing with patriotism," Geeta said, with a wry smile.

"I have a problem with using that word so casually. Our villages, our neighborhoods, our country, and our people never figured in our career plans. It has always been about us and our families. None of us here are even close to be called patriotic," I said.

"You should write dialogues for movies," Geeta said.

"My journey will be no less than a movie story, Geeta," I said to everybody's smile.

Geeta was addicted to a mean disregard for everybody in the world except Varun who escaped her scourge by virtue of being her husband. I didn't know if he understood that even a donkey in his place could have been Geeta's object of love. I knew Varun briefly before he married Geeta. He was not such a stupid man before marrying her as he was after. Over time, he seemed to have lost his identity and reflected his wife more than himself. He behaved like a male version of Geeta. I wondered sometimes if that was who he essentially was and if Geeta was instrumental in bringing out his natural self. As husband and wife, they complemented each other so well, at least in public, which made me believe that marriages are truly made in heaven.

That night Geeta was too cautious not to allow even a speck

of "return to India" thought to seep into her husband's mind. I could see the dark feelings vividly on her face in spite of the bright makeup. To Geeta and many Indian women like her, it was a choice between unlimited freedom and limited family in the US and vice versa in India. Why would Geeta want to deal with Varun's family and conform to social expectations when she could do nothing and be happy on her own with a simple NRI tag?

"What's your plan, Jay, seriously? What are you planning to do in India?" Varun asked. He better confirmed that he was serious otherwise usually he was funny.

"I'm going back to India with some savings, enough to sustain myself for a year or so. I'll figure out something when I go back. I can always take up a job and do something similar to what I am doing here, but I'll see if I can do something on my own first. I want to spend some time with my parents and my sister's family before I even think of doing something," I said, probably vaguely but honestly.

"So, you are going back to setup a business?" Varun asked.

"That's not the primary goal. Since I am making a big shift, I would like to take it slow and figure out something that I will enjoy doing. I could have gone with a job in hand from here but I chose not to. I would like to use this as an opportunity to explore possibilities in India, and that includes the possibility of setting up a business, like you said. I am more inclined toward doing something on my own than getting a job so that I'll have the flexibility of adjusting my time and efforts for my other interests and social causes rather than working just to make a living and living just for myself."

"India has changed a lot, Jay. I see a change in people's attitude when I go there every year. It's all about money and politics. People don't have qualms about doing anything to make it big. In fact, that's the scary part about India for me," a friend in the group chimed in.

When NRIs cribbed about India changing a lot, I wondered what their expectation was. That the country should be frozen in time until they come back?

"India has always been like that. People have been seeing a lot of money of late because of the economic boom. Everything is booming there you know. . . real estate boom, software boom, foreign money boom. I guess with money, the level of manifestation has increased. And unfortunately, that's spreading unchecked in a politically bankrupt country like ours," I said.

"Prices of tomatoes and onions are also booming. My mom talks about that every time I call her. People in India are showing a lot of creativity in cooking dishes without using tomatoes and onions it seems," Venkat said.

"Don't exaggerate," Tulasi interrupted him.

"That's really a big change in India because the prices of tomatoes and onions can decide the next prime minister of the country," I said.

"Haha, that's true. I am sure you'll be successful in whatever you do but you need to be careful, Jay. Prepare a solid ground for us also. Hopefully we'll join you sometime in the future," another friend said, reiterating the general apprehension NRIs had about adapting to India.

This time, I just smiled.

Nobody who visited India recently said anything like I felt good about this in India or I felt good about that in India. For people who were used to a structured life in America where common man's life doesn't get affected by any disruptions or corruption on a day-to-day basis, India would be a big change. Most of the current lot of NRIs went to the US for master's straight from their undergraduate colleges and started their careers there. They haven't experienced the real India. Indians in India are used to certain inadequacies, which hit them in a big way especially when they look through their American lenses. People also tend to exaggerate a bit. Unlike them, I did my MBA in India and worked for three years before going to the US. I travelled through the length and breadth of the country for education and work. I knew what people meant when they said India has changed a lot.

"Would you still have gone back if you were earning two times or three times what you are earning right now?" Varun asked.

I didn't respond immediately, not because I didn't have a ready answer but because I was thinking of a polite way out so as not to spoil the mood of the party.

"I might have given it a thought, but I would still have gone back to India. Here, we all work in similar kinds of profiles and earn almost the same kind of money. In fact, I can save more than anybody in this group if I want to because I am single. But I still chose to go back. It's not about the money," I said, taking a pause from chewing the dynamite shrimp.

"We don't spend all our lives here either," Varun said sarcastically.

Sometimes I felt Varun stress-tested my views; I thought positively about him for a change.

"Some of you might come back to India at some point, probably to retire or when you are kicked out by the US government for some reason. But I want to spend an active part of my life there. To me, moving back is not a career decision. It involves deep-rooted attachments. I'll not argue that all NRIs should follow me; I know it's an individual decision. At the same time, I don't mind if in the future, I stand as an inspiration for some of you here," I said.

After a brief silence in the group, I continued, "The more I stay here, the more it would be difficult for me to go back. And there is a lot of pressure from my mom to get married. Staying here, I don't want to give the impression to a woman that she is marrying a would-be American citizen. I don't want to sell my NRI status."

I invoked the marriage card to stop Geeta and Varun from irritating me further, though I didn't have plans to marry anytime soon. I completed my Glenlivet with a large gulp. The scotch scorched my throat just like my comments must have scorched Geeta and Varun's ego, especially because everybody in the group knew what I meant. Geeta landed in the US as a dependent after marrying Varun by paying a huge dowry. After searching for a wealthy bride for about three years, Varun had settled down with Geeta because she bid the highest amount.

"You can tell your would-be wife that you have plans to move back to India, like we all told our wives. And the girl will marry you anyway because Indian girls are used to hearing every guy say the same thing. Nobody believes that an NRI would ever return to India," Venkat said. His comments brought some laughter to the table.

As I looked around for the waiter to order another drink, a little under the influence, my eyes diverted to Geeta—her face, her curly hair, her bright red top, the patch of fair skin between her neck and her low-neck red top, and her deep neckline. Geeta had a good eye for colors, even Varun's dressing sense improved after marrying her.

My eyes wouldn't have diverted to her neckline if, every now and then, she didn't adjust her top, which barely covered her breasts. She was having a tough time between flaunting confidently and covering up completely. For an Indian woman, Geeta wore a lot of revealing outfits. I enjoy skin show from girls I don't know; with girls I know superficially, I would be caught in a dilemma; and with girls I know well, I don't appreciate at all. I have unambiguous double standards on this subject.

Why would someone like Geeta come back to India

where she wouldn't get to wear such dresses? Women like her stop their husbands from returning to India for the sake of frivolous freedom they enjoyed in the US. I'm not sure about guys, but most Indian girls there were far above their native country standards. Unbridled freedom in the US stimulated their suppressed fascinations which they often misconstrued as a modern women's individuality.

To be fair to Geeta, why should she come back to India if she was happy in America? But then why was she constantly engaged in defending herself for living in America?

While the group talked on the same return-to-India shit, my cell rang. I excused myself from them for a few minutes to attend the call from my mom.

As soon as I came back, Venkat asked, "Jay, do you want another drink?"

I ordered another Glenlivet double and joined the conversation.

"Jay, don't drink too much. You don't want a hangover on your last day in America," Tulasi chuckled.

"One double when I have to drive, two doubles when I don't have to drive. This is a fixed quota," I said with a smile.

"We will miss you, Jay. Best of luck with whatever you do in India. Don't forget that we are here for you if you need anything," said Tulasi.

I smiled back to her and nodded. Venkat and Tulasi had always been among the first people I approached for any support ranging from personal to professional to financial.

"I am still unable to believe that you are leaving," Tulasi continued, with a shiver in her voice and tears shining in her eyes not filled enough to roll down.

"Seriously, Jay, how can you leave America just like that? You are making us feel guilty," Venkat intervened.

"That's not what I meant," Tulasi said, looking at Venkat seriously.

Honestly, I had a difficult time leaving behind a comfortable life and a prosperous career and some good relationships I had developed in the past six years. But when was the last time my heart chose an easy path?

It was not as easy as it is depicted in the movies, to wake up one fine morning, pack the bags and say good bye to the US and land in India. I went through all the combinations of impulsive, compulsive, moral, social, rational, and strategic thinking before I arrived at the decision of moving back to India, and ultimately I realized there was no decision-making model that could be applied to this case. With a sense of duty coupled with real, even though little, love for India in spite of its anomalies, and little courage to face the country in spite of its aberrant socio-political structure, anybody can do it. India is after all the native country to all the NRIs in the US and that's precisely why they are called non-resident Indians. Most of them have lived the first twenty years or so of their life in India. Ironically, they feel extra careful planning is needed to return to India than for leaving for another country.

I even heard about websites and discussion forums dedicated to talking about plans of returning to India—when to leave, how to leave, what to do after moving back, how much money would be needed to relocate. How many of those active participants actually returned to India would be another interesting topic for discussion.

Most of the friends I met and talked to recently had a mix of emotions for me—some were sad that I was leaving, some wished for me to succeed in my endeavors in India, some wished me luck to be able to do what they had just been thinking of for years, and some were confident that I would go back anyway. Almost all of them suggested that I should not hesitate to come back to the US if I wanted to, which made me wonder why they were skeptical that I wouldn't be able to survive in India.

Nearly everyone bid goodbye saying, "You are on my Facebook anyway" or "You are on my WhatsApp anyway" as if Facebook and WhatsApp guaranteed relationships.

Finally, the dinner party last night ended like all other parties. No one in the group was devastated because I was leaving them the next day. And why should they be? It was my calling, my decision, my path, and ultimately my life.

3

I checked my phone as soon as I came out of the shower. Smartphones made life challenging, not easy to keep away from them for a long duration.

Two missed calls, from Siri and Mom. Talking to Siri was an ongoing thing for me, either I talked to her on phone or I talked to her within myself. I called Mom first.

"Hello, Ma."

"Jay, what are you doing? Are you done with your packing?"

"It goes on until I board the flight."

"Did you pack iPad for Chintu?" My mom was so particular about getting an iPad for my sister's son because all his friends had one and he was feeling left out. Gone are the days when kids used to ask for toffees and toy cars.

"Yes, Ma. I packed the iPad and chocolates for Chintu. And I am getting walking shoes for you."

"Who asked you to get shoes for me?"

"Haha, now you don't have a reason not to go for walks."

"This is not America. You know how much traffic and pollution we have outside?"

"No problem. I'll drop you at the park every day. That's my responsibility."

"You don't want to go to work or what?"

"I told you, Ma, I'm not going to get a job. I'll do something on my own. I can adjust my time for you."

"Then don't come to India. Stay there. You left a nice job

here and went to America, and now you are leaving everything there and coming back. Why do you do all this? Why do you make things complicated? I want to see you get a good job, get married, and be happy. No girl will marry you if you don't have a job," Mom said, raising her voice.

Marriage could be given the benefit of doubt since I knew many happily married couples including my mom and dad, but how could she equate job to happiness?

"Ma, marriage is not a priority now."

"What do you mean marriage is not a priority now? You are thirty-one already," Mom raised her voice even louder.

"Okay. We'll discuss these things when I come there."

"I know you'll convince me somehow, and your dad doesn't say anything."

"Ma, I said we'll discuss when I come home."

"Okay, did you tell bye to all your friends there?"

"I have been doing that for the last couple of months."

"You don't know how happy we are. We can't wait to see you," Mom said, becoming sentimental now.

"Just one more day, Ma."

I took a final look at my baggage, one of the several final looks in the past few days. I couldn't pack a few things, like my black suit that I had worn just once for a job interview, because of the weight limitations. I left them with Venkat. I might as well have donated them as they would never reach me in India unless I mailed them. Most of us try to reconstruct America in India and India in America, and hence nobody is an exception to space constraints. And to top it all, the airlines staff does not accept even a pound more than permitted weight. I generally appreciate stringent rules but I hate them when I am the victim of those rules. There used to be days it seems when American airports were not so particular about baggage weight and security check. Not anymore. After 9/11, everything became tough.

To move back to India for good, I made so many choices that it would be difficult and costly to unwind them. Apart from destabilizing a smooth life and successful career, I spent a lot of money on shopping and transportation. In addition to paying for the extra check-in bags, I already sent some packages overlooking the doubt I had about the people who would handle them in India. If for some reason I went back to the US, the NRI friends who know my story will have one more reason not to return to India. They would quote me indirectly as an example—"We saw people spending too much when they return to India as if they would never come back and they ended up in America within a few months." If I really do go back, the propelling reason would outweigh regretting the disruptions I created in my life and the money I spent on moving to India.

***

Tulasi and I went out for my last American lunch to my favorite restaurant, Panera Bread. I thought of what I would eat even before we started to the restaurant—broccoli cheddar soup and frontega chicken panini with chips and iced tea.

More than the menu I loved Panera Bread's ambience. The folks from nearby offices would crowd the place and take away its usual charm during afternoons on working days, otherwise most of the time it was occupied by college students working on their class work with their laptops and books spread on the tables and by older people having warm conversations. It was one of the few places I loved in America for having all three meals in a day on working days as well as weekends.

Panera Bread often reminded me of my conversation with Kalyan, one of my first roommates in the US. When I asked him about it during my initial days, his answer was, "That's not for us. We don't have anything to eat there." And the same

Panera Bread has become one of my favorite eating places. No fun in failing to experience what the place we live has to offer. At least people like Geeta faked American lifestyle. Every time she ate outside at a non-Indian restaurant, she would probably eat her favorite rice and yogurt with lemon pickle and with her hands when she goes home.

As Tulasi locked the house, Venkat called me. "Jay, what are you doing?"

"We are about to go out for lunch. What's up with you?"

"I just had lunch and came out for a smoke. Okay listen, Charlotte airport is not that busy. Why do you want to wait in the airport unnecessarily? It should be fine if we leave at four, okay?"

I kind of anticipated that call from Venkat. The time he suggested was almost one hour later than our original plan. Even if I had argued, he would have convinced me and so I okayed it. Venkat had a knack for planning and executing things perfectly well. He never wanted to be late, but curiously he never wanted to be early either. He always wanted to be on time, right on time. I was glad that he didn't say that we should leave at 5.

With his tendency to be exactly on time, it would be interesting to see how he would manage if he ever returned to India where uncontrollable factors control everything. Venkat just laughed whenever Tulasi and I made fun of his habit, but he never yielded. I guess he came out of his mother's womb exactly on the day and at the time predicted by the doctors, and he followed the same practice since then.

After lunch, I spent time watching TV and attending phone calls until Venkat came back from office. Tulasi bid me farewell without using loaded words as Venkat and I left for the airport. She stayed back at home since it was time for her daughter to return from school.

I chose Venkat as my chauffeur that day and his place to

spend my final days in the US for a reason. When I had only a broad vision but not the exact details about what I'll be doing in India, when I was listening to my heart over my head, and when I was doing something I believed was in alignment with the purpose of my life, I wanted someone by my side who accepted and appreciated my decisions irrespective of whether he agreed with me. I wanted someone who believed in me and had the patience to wait and see how my life would unfold. At times, I don't want to argue with people to prove my point and that day was one of those occasions. Moments before I left the country, I didn't want yet another debate on America vs. India. I wanted somebody who wouldn't question my decision and disposition in those final moments but allow me to be calm and live the journey by myself. Though I was susceptible to get panicked and even get delayed because of Venkat's fondness to be exactly on time, he was the perfect person I had in my mind.

Venkat was well settled in the US with a stable full-time job, big single-family home he had recently bought, and a happy family life. Anyone in his place was highly qualified to give me a long spirited lecture on the virtues of living in the US. But, being not-so-judgmental for an Indian, I was sure Venkat wouldn't, and he didn't.

Venkat was different from the other NRIs who desperately defended their stay in the US in an effort to balance the inner conflict between their responsibility and belongingness to India and their inability to return to India for various reasons. He believed his choice was good for his career and family. He had unapologetic plans to live in the US for years to come, which was contradictory to what I was doing. I didn't know whether he will return to India later but he never allowed the thought to rob him of his time in the present. He wasn't one of those paranoid desis who lived physically in the US and mentally in India. To me, he was a good example of how best people could lead a life away from their native country.

During the entire ride from Venkat's house to the airport, he kept talking about trivial things while I was lost in my own thoughts. Luckily he didn't stop talking to check whether I listened to him.

Venkat hugged me and bid a mild but not cold farewell after I checked in my bags. "Alright, Jay, take care. Call me when you reach Chennai. Convey my regards to your mom and dad."

I waved goodbye to him and walked toward the security check.

I passed through the security line fondly looking outside through the glass walls thinking how beautiful a country America was. The people in the line and the airport security staff, their smiling faces and their cordial gestures were already making me nostalgic.

I had been constantly getting calls from Siri that I wouldn't be able to attend until I reached the gate. Though known as a glorious trait that many people proudly proclaimed on their resumes, I am very bad at multitasking. Forget multitasking, I cannot even handle dual-tasking. I cannot even talk to people and simultaneously do small things like handling bags. To me, multitasking is equal to no-tasking.

After reaching the gate, I got my favorite Starbucks coffee and called Siri from the phone number that would disappear in a few minutes. Would this Starbucks coffee also be my last one? I hoped they expanded faster to every corner in India.

Life's experience and age did not give us enough strength to wish each other good luck with a smile. Although we both felt moving on from each other was not an option, I wondered if it was practically possible to keep up the relationship from a long distance. We were grown enough to understand that once I took that flight, practically everything would change—our lives, aspirations, priorities, everything.

It was uncertain whether Siri and I would get to see each other again, and whether we would even be willing to face each other if we had the opportunity. I hoped that sensibility would prevail and allow us to accept that time changes and everything changes with time. I would want our relationship to evolve, consciously on our part, into a realistic friendship and we both continue to contribute positively to each other's life without any hang-ups. It might seem like a demotion compared to the association we had shared with each other in the past five years, but it would still be an intelligent extension of our relationship and practically the only viable option, the other two extreme possibilities being getting locked up in a marriage for which we didn't fit into each other's plans and completely avoiding each other which would be a tragic end to a beautiful relationship. I left it to time with the hope that I wouldn't lose Siri.

I talked to her until there was nobody left in the line at the boarding gate.

"Siri, I need to go now."

"Are you leaving, Jay?"

"Take care, Siri. You should understand that you need to sound good for me to be happy."

"You are not just leaving by yourself, Jay. You are taking part of my heart with you. There is no replacement for you in my life. You know how the heart pounds faster just before the ride starts at Six Flags? But when we realize the inescapability we accept and go through. Don't worry, I'll be fine."

"Okay," I said, though I didn't like the comparison.

In a world where masking has become the new original, finding someone whose presence makes us unmindfully original is a blessing and that was Siri to me. In fact, there will be no replacement for her in my life too. Like always, she called it out loud before I did.

"I knew that this day was coming, and I was prepared. But

I am unable to control my emotions. Even I didn't think I would feel so weak. Sorry, Jay, I couldn't give you a cheerful farewell," Siri said, crying like a child.

"Drink some water," I said.

After a small water break, she said, "I don't want you to get delayed. Take care of yourself, Jay. Don't forget that I am here for you for anything, okay? Don't be arrogant about your plans in India. Take your time to settle down and be yourself. I am sure you'll be successful."

"Okay, Siri, take care. I need to go now. There is no one left in the line." I had to end the call while she was still weeping, which wasn't easy to do. I could only hope that Siri would return to her normal self soon.

What good is a relationship when we can't make compromises in our plans for it? I would have fallen for that logic a decade back and put my relationship above everything. But as we grow older, I guess self-actualization prevails over self-sacrifice. We don't have college-kid-like passion anymore to forego our dreams for others. Siri intended to stay back in the US as much as I wanted to move back to India.

If not being able to get married is not a blot on love, I love Siri.

4

The flight looked like a mini-India.

As soon as I found my aisle seat, I greeted the Indian gentleman sitting next to me, "Hi."

He looked at me from top to bottom without caring to reply. He didn't even smile. His rigid demeanor, the combination of his formal dressing and sneakers, like an Indian government officer, reminded me that my journey to India had started.

In my mind, I called him Mr. X.

I was already missing the American cordiality—simple polite things such as "Hi, how are you?", "How are you doing?", "Can you please…", "If you don't mind…", "Thank you!"—all with a pleasant smile. For all those niceties, we have just one answer—the great Indian stare. Many Indians criticize Americans of their plastic smile. If it's plastic, so be it as long as it makes life easy. Over time the plastic can become real once people realize the warmth it can bring to social life. In the last six years, I had gotten used to the American courtesy which had an effect on my mood; it made me happier. And in the flight, Mr. X's attitude also started affecting my mood, in the opposite way. His demeanor was quite unwelcoming as if I was soliciting at the entrance of his house.

As I searched for cabin space, pointing to my shoulder bag that I placed in the leg space of my seat, Mr. X said, "Put that bag in the upper cabin; it will be difficult to walk."

What the fuck? Did he really think I'll leave the bag there like that? I had barely settled down, and he watched me as I looked for a flight attendant to help me find cabin space for my bags. He didn't have patience. He was only concerned that my bag might block his way or his wife's way who was sitting to his left. He hadn't even bothered to greet me before pointing to my bag. Was he trying to overplay his assertiveness in front of his wife in an effort to fit into her "my husband is king" mold? There was not much change back home. The kind of meanness Mr. X was displaying was familiar to me.

God didn't listen to my prayers to bless me with a seat next to a young Indian woman. I definitely wouldn't have got bored with her fake American show off. Instead, God gave me the opposite—an old Indian man. The only thing common between what I asked for and what I got was "Indian" and needless to say that I was experiencing it.

"Do you want to step out now?" I asked Mr. X. My impatience with him showed in my tone.

He shook his head in disbelief. He must have thought that I would keep quiet. He was a little annoyed because his wife also got the message.

Standing at my seat, I saw a male flight attendant coming toward me. He looked Indian. I was right; the name on his badge read Arun.

"Sir, carry your bags to the front and see if you have space there," Arun said.

What the fuck? Another Indian in quick succession pissed me off. Did his *Indianness* dominate his professional decency? Was the universe conspiring to tell me that my decision to move back to India was not right?

You too, Arun, being a flight attendant? Your profession is supposed to be the epitome of customer service. How do you think I should carry my bags to the front when some people are still boarding the flight in the opposite direction and many who boarded haven't settled down yet in their seats? Can you not at least give me the information whether there is room for my bags in the front? I wished Arun could hear what was going on in my mind. To my luck, another flight attendant, not an Indian this time, came to me before I even responded to Arun, and offered to take my bags to put them in the cabin space in the front, if I didn't mind.

Why would I mind? In fact I was glad. That's being a flight attendant, Arun, learn, asshole! Again I wished he could hear what I thought.

After handing over my bags to the other flight attendant, I settled down in my seat and looked casually at the faces in the flight I'd be living with for the next few hours. I have a liking for aisle seats which have more space to stretch legs and better view of the people. I would rather let people bother me as many times as they wish than get struck with claustrophobia by sitting in the window seat.

I closed my eyes for a few moments and took a deep breath to relax my agitated mind. I didn't want to lose my spirit even before I landed in India. I remembered my dad's words. "You cannot really hate everything here in India," he had said. "It is what it is. You should accept a few things and keep pushing forward." His message started sinking in now. Dads are right, sometimes.

"Hi," I greeted Mr. X when we looked at each other coincidentally. This guy should have used deodorant; it's a long journey.

"Hi," he said.

This time he didn't have a problem responding while keeping the seriousness on his face intact. He started talking to me in our native language, as if it was written on my face that I belong to the same state. In India, states are demarcated not just by physical boundaries but also by languages. Not sure if that was a strategy not to let any two states talk to each other and team up against the central government.

"I wanted to tell you that you can adjust your bag there," Mr. X said apologetically, pointing to the opposite cabin.

"Oh, I am sorry, sir. I have other stuff also; I was looking for a bigger space," I said.

I guess I misunderstood Mr. X and Arun as I was too guarded to face India. I needed to loosen up a bit.

Looking at the pizza box I had placed on my lap, Mr. X asked, "Can you bring food on the flight?"

"Of course. Whatever we purchase after the security check, we can carry into the flight," I said.

"Oh, I didn't know that. This is one good habit I see in America, people don't throw food away," he said.

"You said it right, sir. Indians learn to respect food after coming here. Even I wasn't like this in India. I never carried leftover food from restaurants there. Somehow we are indifferent to food wastage. These guys here will be shocked to see the dishes we proudly serve at marriages and throw the large amounts of leftover," I said.

"Not much has changed in terms of restaurant food, but now we have people who take the leftover food in marriages and other functions and distribute to the needy," he said.

"Really? That's good to hear. But I feel there needs to be a fundamental shift in our thinking. We need to stop wasting food through overeating and over-serving. It's a grave sin to waste food in India when so many people go to bed every night on an empty stomach," I said.

"That's right," Mr. X said, nodding in agreement.

Sensing that the person sitting in the window seat was looking at me I turned my head.

"Hi," I greeted Mr. X's wife.

"Hello," she mouthed soundlessly and turned her head away. That was probably her way of giving me permission to continue the conversation with her husband.

"Are you going on a vacation?" Mr. X asked me.

"Yeah kind of, a long one. I am coming back to India for good."

"Why? Visa issues?" he asked. When people who knew me well didn't believe when I told them about my decision of moving back to India, how would a stranger believe?

"No. I stayed here for six years and I am completely satisfied. Now I want to live in India."

"Really? So, do you already have a job in India?"

"No. I am going to take a short break and figure out things."

"You must have made good investments in India?" he asked inquisitively.

"I didn't get enough opportunity to earn big in America. I came here as a student," I said.

"Are you married?" Mr. X tried to quickly figure out the personal, professional, and financial implications of my choice.

"No, I am not."

"Then you have a lot of time. You should have stayed here some more time and made some money," he said.

"I feel I am already late, sir. I planned to be here only for a couple of years. My stay got extended because of the recession and slump in IT jobs."

"My son also said he will return after a couple of years when he came here. Now I don't think he'll return anytime soon. He doesn't have time to come to India even once in couple of years. My daughter used to say when their family gets a green card they will not have visa issues and can visit India frequently, which didn't happen either. In fact, her India visits have reduced. I guess we cannot blame them; they are handicapped by several compulsions here. We have come to terms that both our children will settle down here though they didn't say it directly. We'll keep visiting them as long as our energy permits," Mr. X said, with a tinge of unhappiness.

I listened to him without making any comments so as not to incite him against his children.

After a pause, Mr. X said, "At one point, my daughter wanted to come back for her twin daughters. She was scared of the open culture here. Now, not just her, but I also feel America is far better and safer place than India. Even culture-wise I cannot confidently say that India is better. My granddaughters learn classical music and play tennis here. Some of their friends learn classical dance and painting. I am not confident that they'll have such opportunities in India. Even if they are interested, the school education won't leave them with any time for extra-curricular activities. People get together to celebrate Indian festivals here and in India, we are celebrating festivals by watching TV."

"That's right, sir, I agree. We have a proud cultural legacy but not a culture in practice."

"I guess Indians really don't see America anymore as a place which is not suitable to raise children in beyond a certain age. Initially, when I heard this argument from my daughter, I thought she was defending her stay in America, but she has a point. I don't think they can live happily in India, even if they compromise on the money part, there are several other factors," he said.

Parents in India always want their kids to live near them. That is one way of showing their love for them. Now they think India is so screwed up that their kids should settle down in the US and have a peaceful life, and of course, not to forget to send them dollars.

"True, sir. The attraction here is beyond dollars," I said.

"Then why are you coming back?" he asked.

"Even my motivation is beyond dollars, sir. I was earning good money, but I felt I was not realizing my full potential here. I am unable to think beyond software jobs because of immigration compulsions. I feel restricted. Plus, I want to be there for my country and my parents."

"You should take care of yourself and your parents first," Mr. X suggested.

"That would be my first priority, sir. What do you do in India?" I asked.

"I am an engineer in the state electricity department. I have couple more years before retirement."

I guessed it right. Government officers in India have a typical look—always clean shaved and shirt always tucked in, even for morning walks; they probably go to sleep like that. That's a style statement they followed for some reason. The "I am something" demeanor they wear on their faces beats everything. Seriously, they are something in India; they can even overthrow governments. Once they get into government jobs, they are entitled to suck the government forever. Even God cannot take their jobs away. God can take their lives but not their jobs.

"I am impressed by you. But I am afraid you'll not be able to keep up the same fire when you start living in India. I want you to prove me wrong. Good luck," Mr. X said.

"Thank you, sir."

Mr. X turned to his wife as she looked like she was waiting to tell him something.

Feeling sleepy, I closed my eyes after the conversation but I didn't want to miss the free dinner. In a way, I paid for it in the ticket. Because I wouldn't be paying during the flight, it gave me the happiness of a free dinner. The first meal during the international flight has a special flavor, the free drink has an awesome taste, the word "free" has a magic. To me, it is absolutely necessary to have a drink during the flight to sleep, even when I am sleepy. Otherwise, the thought of not having a free drink doesn't let me sleep.

Having stayed in the US for so many years I developed an appreciation for free food. At first I was amazed to see the enthusiasm people there had for free food. Any seminar or meeting notice in the university campus carried the "free food" tag in bold font to draw attention. Over time I realized there was a valid reason for it.

Children in the US start working from an early age to earn their living and fund their education. They learn about money at a very tender age. To them, every penny is valuable and saving some money through a free meal is a big deal. Having fed by my parents and supported by them for everything until I completed college, I could not appreciate free food in the beginning. Kids in the US do not depend on their parents forever like parasites. Even parents there are not so obsessed with their kids, unlike Indian parents who try to protect their children from, according to their reasoning, the cruel outside world, and in the process convert them into social misfits.

I overheard Mr. X saying to his wife, "The flight will have to take off to serve dinner." I guess all of us were in the same boat, the hungry boat.

My random thoughts dimmed as I slowly slipped into a short nap before dinner. The past few days had been hectic for me, shopping, packing, meeting people, bidding goodbyes and absorbing their emotions, some real and some fake. I didn't realize when the flight took off but I promptly woke up when food was being served.

Mr. X looked at me and the beer in my hand a couple of times. Come on man, it's just a beer. Is he one of those champions of middleclass moral high ground in India? Sometimes I wonder if their apparent moral values are a way of concealing their unfulfilled aspirations and failures in life. While drinking is considered a big sin, quite ironically, alcohol industry in India rakes in millions of dollars. Even beer is not accepted as a casual drink in spite of such a hot weather. What would happen if Indians enjoyed the social freedom to drink? Probably the world would face a shortage of alcohol. Somehow habits and character are synonymous in India. So-called bad habits like smoking and drinking, even casually, automatically make a person bad. People who drink are partly to blame because they drink desperately as if they would not get another opportunity to drink in their life.

Mr. X's glare at my beer made me really worry about how I will be able to quench my passion for single-malt scotches and beers in India. I'll still go ahead and buy my favorite Glenlivet at the duty-free shop in Abu Dhabi and figure out things later.

I dozed off after a beer and dinner. The whole backdrop pushed me into an involuntary recap of the first international flight I took six years ago—how it all started and how it ended, and how the hell what was supposed to be a quick trip for a couple of years ended up in a six-year extended stay.

5

As a kid, my impression of America was a dream place that existed only in books, magazines, and peoples' imagination. The beautiful pictures of big houses, skyscrapers, bridges, lakes, landscapes and woods were literally unthinkable for someone who had so far seen mediocre surroundings in India. I vacillated between believing that a country like America really existed on earth and it didn't.

In my entire neighborhood, I knew just one lady who had visited America once for a few months to see her son who went there and never returned. The country was so alien to people in our neighborhood back then that America became her surname after her trip. A typical conversation about her almost always had a reference to her America visit.

"*You know Seethamma?*"

"*Seethamma who?*"

"*Seethamma. . . the one who. . .*"

"*Oh yeah, the one who visited America. Of course, I know her.*"

We kids used to have enormous curiosity to see Seethamma. We would wonder how the lady who visited America looked like. To add to the curious aura created by her visit to America, she rarely ventured out of her house.

One evening, after playing cricket, I ran into my house frantically searching for my mom in the kitchen.

"Ma! Ma!" I shouted.

"Why are you shouting like that? What happened?" I heard mom's voice from a distance.

"Where are you?" I asked.

"I am in the bathroom helping Madhu wash her hair. What do you want? Wait there. I'll come in a few minutes," Mom said so loudly that I could hear her clearly in spite of the closed door.

I could smell the scent of the shampoo and hear the water dripping from the tap into a half-filled bucket as I proceeded toward the bathroom.

"Ma, did you ever see Seethamma?" I asked, standing outside the bathroom.

"America Seethamma?" she asked.

The sound of the water dripping stopped. Mom must have turned off the tap because she knew I wouldn't leave her until I told her what I had to tell.

"Yeah."

"Of course. I talked to her today also. Why?"

I knew my mom was one of the few women Seethamma talked to. But that's not what I meant by my question.

"Today when we were playing cricket, the ball fell into Seethamma's house," I said.

"Why don't you guys play cricket in the school ground?" Mom yelled without letting me complete what I wanted to say.

"Ma, listen," I tried to stop her.

"People don't like it when cricket ball drops into their compounds. It could even hit them by mistake," she went on.

Mom almost always succeeded in deviating me from what I would want to say. Sometimes I would even forget what I had wanted to tell her to start with.

"Ma, listen, the issue is not cricket here. I climbed on the side wall of Seethamma's house to get the ball."

"Why did you climb the wall?" Mom shouted again.

"Ma, please listen to me completely."

"Okay, tell me then."

"I didn't know that Seethamma was in the verandah. She saw me on the wall and asked me, 'What do you want?' and I said I wanted the ball."

"Then?" Mom asked me curiously.

"I asked her for the ball and she gave it to me, Ma. She didn't say anything. She smiled also."

"Jay, what exactly do you want to say?"

"He has nothing to say, just talking rubbish," my sister Madhu yelled at mom for stopping her hair wash and talking to me.

"You shut up," I shouted at my sister. "Listen, Ma—"

"You shut up first, idiot," Madhu shouted back.

"Jay, go and get something to eat from the kitchen. I'll be there in a few minutes," Mom said, trying to calm both of us down.

I didn't go away but persisted with my story. "I saw Seethamma so closely, Ma. She is very fair."

"So?" I could sense the irritation in mom's tone.

"Did she become so fair after going to America?" I asked.

Both my mom and sister burst into a loud laughter.

"No, Jay, she was always like that. Fair skin, sweet voice, and a very good human being."

"All my friends were telling me that she became so fair after visiting America," I said.

"Stay at home from tomorrow. No cricket, nothing. You and your stupid friends," Mom shouted again.

I left from there immediately fearing my mom could really put a stop to my evening cricket sessions. The water dripping sound resumed as I walked to the kitchen to get some cookies.

That was America for me as a kid.

Added to the enigma that the country already was to me, my friends used to say astounding things. They showed enormous creativity in narrating stories about America without knowing anything about it. I used to listen to them sincerely with my mouth wide open and come back and ask my mom. Poor mom, how would she know about America when she didn't even go out of our neighborhood that often? But that never mattered to me. I would ask her anyway and test her patience.

Things, however, changed drastically by the time I completed my undergraduate college.

America was not only well within reach but was also the hottest destination for Indian youth. So-called intelligentsia in the country had already started complaining about brain drain as if India had the environment for intelligent brains to flourish.

***

March 12, 2002: Last exam of my undergraduate program.

My classmates looked at me unbelievably as I walked briskly toward the examination hall. That was the only time I had walked enthusiastically to write an exam in the past four years. I stopped at a distance from the entrance of the examination hall and eagerly scanned the crowd. I was the only one around with just a pen in hand. Everybody else was crazily flipping through the books doing some last minute cramming for the exam.

I spotted what I was searching for, rather who I was searching for—Jhansi stood leaning against a wall with one leg crossed over the other, deeply engrossed in her class notes.

I walked up to her through the crowd and stood beside her. She looked at me and gave a smile and quickly turned to her notes.

"We'll meet for dinner at seven at Rainbow," I whispered rather loudly, reminding her of our plan to go out for dinner on the last day of our exams.

Jhansi gave me a hawkish look for my insensitiveness to the situation. But she was thoughtful enough not to embarrass me. "Okay, do well in the exam first," she said, looking at her wrist watch. "It's almost time for the exam, I'll see you later."

For all other students, exam was the most important activity that day, but for me, it was dinner with Jhansi. I stood there admiring her from behind as she walked toward the exam hall. Dressed in plain white churidar-kurta with a multi-colored mosaic chunni draped around her neck, her plaited long thick hair dancing on her back to the rhythmic music of her silver anklets, Jhansi slowly disappeared. Like a heroine in a typical Bollywood movie, she didn't look back after walking a few steps. She didn't care whether I was still looking at her or not. She probably switched me off as soon as our conversation ended and switched on the exam side of her brain.

Generally students came to exams with puffy eyes and oily faces, but I never saw a speck of exam tension on Jhansi's face. Exam, no-exam, class, lab, outing, movie, dinner, she was always the same. The freshness of her face and pleasantness of her smile were always intact.

After the exam, as I walked to the most happening place on the campus, the college café, a few early birds from the exam joined me. I generally completed the exams faster than most other students. Working hard in the exam hall was not my thing. I knew what I knew and that was it.

"Jay!" I heard Jhansi's voice louder than usual from behind.

All of us looked back.

"Hi guys, how did the exam go?" she said, looking at everybody.

"Umm... It was okay." The same disinterested murmur from everybody in the group.

One of them asked, "Jhansi, how come you are out of the exam hall so early today?"

"It was an easy exam," she said, with a smile. Generally, she utilized the complete time even for easy exams. She must have made an exception that day since it was the last exam.

As Jhansi walked up to us, one of the guys in the group said, "Okay, Jay, we'll catch up later," and walked away as I stood there for her. Rest of the group followed him.

"What's up, hero? I saw you were thinking very hard during the exam. Were you planning what to eat in the dinner or what?" she asked laughingly.

I just smiled.

"Jay, couldn't you wait until the exam was over, huh?"

"Yeah, but I thought you would forget. I wanted to remind you," I said in a low voice. I was not shy, I was proud of what I did. Jhansi was my first priority, nothing else mattered.

"Come, let's celebrate the end of our exams. Lets' have tea," I suggested as we approached the café. Jhansi was not a frequenter of the café but I asked her anyway.

She looked at me, and said, "We are meeting for dinner today. You'll be bored in the evening if we spend time together now."

"I am never bored with you. What will you do in the dormitory anyway? We'll have tea real quick and leave."

"Every time you say quick tea, we end up spending almost an hour. Now what does this real quick mean? Couple of hours or what?" she asked.

"This time, I promise."

"What? That it'll go on for a few hours?" Jhansi walked into the café without waiting for my answer. "I hate tea here. They charge so much and can't even prepare good tea," she muttered as we took the table in a corner.

Reaching the end of undergraduate college was making me emotional about the campus, unlike Jhansi who looked detached. She was already looking forward to joining her new university in the US. While Jhansi's attachment to the campus was mostly with classrooms, laboratories, and library, I had lasting memories with every nook and corner of the campus. I had an attachment with every wall and every tree in the campus and every place in the town. Whether on the campus or in the town, I had unforgettable memories with Jhansi from the past four years.

Sipping the tea, I said, "I don't feel good when I get a feeling that we don't belong to this campus anymore."

"We belong here for one more month," Jhansi laughed. "All joking aside, I feel the same way. These exams and applying to universities is keeping me busy. I don't know how I would have felt otherwise," she added.

"But you never looked like you have an emotional attachment with this campus."

"Should I cry to show my emotions?" Jhansi asked, looking straight at me with a smile.

I admired her straight talk in the beginning. Over time, I was eager to see her emotional side more than her stiffness but she remained the same. She was a better friend to me than she was four years ago, and I was definitely her best friend and her only guy friend on the campus, but I wasn't sure if I knew her more than I did four years back. Not making enough progress on that front was making me uncomfortable.

"No, don't cry, that doesn't suit you. You look good emotionless," I said.

I was pleasantly surprised to see Jhansi laugh out loud at my comment, unmindful of the crowd, which was so unusual of her. Normally, she smiled without even showing her teeth. She had a smile bigger than a usual smile and a laugh smaller than a usual laugh and that was the most emotion she showed.

She loosened up a little as we reached the completion of our undergraduate program.

Jhansi had a knack of not getting into topics she didn't want to talk about. In spite of my jab, she didn't care to defend herself that she had an emotional side too. Anybody else in my place, out of confusion about who she was exactly and what went on in her mind, would have pushed hard to understand those soft spots of her personality that she always avoided exposing and would have lost her by then.

"How is the application process going?" I asked.

"Very good, I am in a better position to apply for this fall itself. Most of our classmates are planning for next spring," she said. Beating everybody around gave immense kick to Jhansi which she barely tried to hide. But she was not a crook like students who did well academically. She was a graceful college topper.

"Good, you are continuing your topper status in this too."

"Not like that. I already have my GRE and TOEFL scores. I don't want to waste time. If everything goes well, I will not have much time between completing my project here and flying to the US," she said, taking my praise in her stride without blushing.

"Did you get good scores? Enough to get into good universities, get scholarships and all?"

"Yeah, I have decent scores. I would have scored better if only I were as good as you in English," Jhansi said, with a playful smile, picking up the tea cup. She waited until the tea got cold and by then I would have usually drank at least two cups.

"What English?" I just laughed it off.

"Don't think I am joking because I am smiling. I am serious. I thought about you several times throughout my application process. I really like your thoughts and the way you put them across. You have good communication skills."

"What good is communication without content?" I said but I took the compliment, after all, it came from Jhansi. I was overwhelmed.

"Content is easy to gain with little effort, Jay, but communication is an inherent talent. Very few people like you are blessed with it, and you are not using it properly. You should get over your stupid friends and focus on your career at least now," Jhansi said, getting into her preaching mode. I was never comfortable talking to her on her favorite topic, career.

"I should really thank you for your help. Without you, I would have struggled a lot to write the SOPs and answers to those stupid questions in the university applications," she continued to shower me with praises.

"I just edited the skeleton information you provided, that's all," I said, trying to be modest.

"Yeah, now you got the point. Content and communication both are equally important. Universities see what we write. They don't know who we are; they don't see us," she said, mocking what I said a minute back.

"Okay, I agree," I said, smiling.

"What's your plan next?" she asked. "You haven't applied to universities abroad, and you haven't applied to colleges here also. Don't say that you are going to stop your studies."

"No, I am not stopping my studies. At the same time, I don't want to hop from one degree to another without a purpose. I don't think these degrees are adding any value to me, or I should say they are not motivating enough for me to put in serious efforts. Either I should have complete dedication to what I am doing, like you, or just quit and look for something I really like," I said, not exactly pointing to my future plans.

Jhansi kept listening to me silently, sipping her tea. It was like an interview for me.

"I want to do MBA and diversify from science to management stream. Once I complete my project work here, I'll explore options," I continued.

"Why can't you start exploring those options right away? I don't know much about MBA. You'll definitely succeed in whatever field you choose, but you need to focus. Don't waste time. What are the prospects of—" she stopped, and smiled looking behind me.

"Hello Jhansi!" I heard a classmate of ours greeting her loudly, disturbing our conversation. I didn't have to turn back to know who that sucker was. No matter who, I hated being disturbed when I was with Jhansi. She glanced at me and understood my irritation but she showed her usual composed self.

"Hey, how are you? How was the exam?" Jhansi waved to that sucker as he approached our table.

Exams were a big topic, naturally, since we were writing our final year exams. That sucker not only disturbed us but also sat with us, uninvited and unwanted. He was one of those guys on the campus who wondered why a class topper like Jhansi hung out with someone like me who was known for all other reasons except studies. Honestly, sometimes I wondered about that too.

"Hi, Jay," that sucker greeted me as he sat down.

"Hi," I responded in a dull voice. I tried to be normal but I couldn't. I looked at both of them, and said, "Okay, you guys carry on. I'll see you later."

"You can have another cup of tea," Jhansi said, teasing my habit of having one cup of tea after the other. I didn't know if she understood but sitting in the café to me was not about the tea, it was about being with her.

I just smiled at her comment and walked to the back of the café. Obviously she knew that I would leave. She knew that I hated all the dogs on the campus except her.

We called all the academically studious and socially awkward students on the campus as dogs, equating their cramming habit to barking of dogs, and they shared some common characteristics. They neither knew nor cared about anything except studies, they cared more about scoring marks than friends, they were never late to classes, they never bunked classes, they were never attracted to girls as if they had erectile dysfunction, academics to them was a cut-throat competition, and in spite of all their conspicuous uncool characteristics at display they posed like cool dudes that made them even more despicable.

Girls who belonged to that group also had some distinct features. Whether they looked beautiful or not, they dressed up well, they talked to boys only when they needed some help, and behind every move of theirs, whether they cried or smiled, they had a hidden agenda.

Jhansi was an active dog too but she was my pet. She was the only one in that group who commanded dignity in the campus. She balanced between her dog friends and me so well, even though we didn't fit together. She never talked badly about any of her dog friends with me and she never let them talk about her friendship with me. All of us knew where to draw the line but Jhansi was the one who actually enforced it.

6

The café was my favorite spot on the undergraduate college campus and the back of the café was almost like my perennial hangout. I used to spend hours on the benches and chairs there, chitchatting with friends over countless teas and cigarettes and laughing to friends' jokes on practically everybody in the campus.

As I went to the back of the café, which was almost always filled with cigarette smoke interspersed with loud conversations and filthy words, surprisingly I saw no one except Venkat sitting there smoking alone.

"Hi, Venkat. How come I don't see anybody here today?"

"Cricket, boss. I would have also left if you had come five minutes later," Venkat said.

"Cricket? Watching or playing?" I asked.

"Playing. See, boss of cricket is here and they are playing cricket there," Venkat said jokingly.

I just smiled.

Almost any time of the day, a group of students either watched cricket on TV or played cricket in the college playground. And on the day we wrote our last exam, the playground must have been filled with crowds.

"Seriously, Jay, there's no fun watching cricket without you playing. Why are you not coming to the ground nowadays?"

Both Venkat and I knew that Jhansi was the reason for me not having time for cricket. He wanted to hear me say it.

Venkat pushed the cigarette packet toward me as I sat

with him. He was one of the few guys on the campus who purchased cigarettes in packets. Most of the students bought one or two cigarettes loose or just borrowed from generous hearts like him. Heavy smokers like Venkat and I didn't have an option but to buy cigarettes in packets.

"What's the plan tonight, Jay?" Venkat asked as I lit the cigarette.

"Rainbow. I am going out for dinner with Jhansi."

"Jay, can I tell you something?"

I knew it would be something related to Jhansi. Venkat was the only person who had the liberty to talk about Jhansi with me. I didn't allow my feelings for Jhansi to become a trivial topic for others to talk about, at least in my presence. I too never felt comfortable talking about Jhansi with anyone except Venkat. He was my emotional outlet, the only person with whom I opened up.

I nodded, telling him to go ahead.

"You should tell Jhansi about your feelings for her without any further delay," Venkat said.

"Something is stopping me, Venkat."

"What is it? Fear of rejection?" Venkat asked.

"Could be. I don't want to lose her," I said.

"You'll lose her anyway if you don't open up, because I don't think Jhansi will take the first step. After all, she is a girl. In a few months, she'll be in America and you'll be here which will make things even more difficult. If you share your feelings with her now, you'll know clearly what she thinks about you. I am sure she will not find another Jay in her life."

"My point is simple, Venkat. Jhansi is an utterly straight girl. She will not leave the campus without telling me if she shares the same feelings."

"Jhansi is an exception, I know. But girls are girls in these matters, Jay. What if she is thinking the same way you as you?

What if she doesn't say anything before she leaves the campus? What if she says goodbye to you as a friend?"

"I'll keep my feelings to myself," I said.

"What good is that?" Venkat asked.

"She should have understood by now what she means to me. She is decent but not innocent. In the last four years, I never got the impression that she had the same feelings for me as I have for her, and that's probably what's holding me back. Loving Jhansi in itself is a pleasure for me. Expressing it, getting accepted or rejected are just milestones."

"But don't you want to take your relationship to the next level?"

"I really want to but . . ." I didn't know what to say.

"Jay, some of our friends think Jhansi is just using you. You do so much for her. You were with her at every step since her first day on the campus when she came to this town from Bangalore. She owes a large part of her success to you."

"She would have been successful anyway, she is a go-getter. She may or may not be willing to take our relationship to the next level but I don't doubt her friendship. Leave others, what do you think about her?" I asked him.

"I don't know much about her. I never cared much about these dogs. She has always behaved like a lotus leaf, she floats without getting wet. You are the only friend she has on the campus. If you observe her, she is always on her own, very rarely you spot her with other people. She came all the way from Bangalore to this small town because this college has good ratings. Nothing makes her happier than success in her career. It's admirable to see her have the same passion for her career even after four years. I am not sure if you figure in her long-term plans."

I kept listening.

After a small pause, Venkat asked, "What is that you like in her, Jay? She is not a stunning beauty also." He had asked me that question numerous times in the past too.

"I don't know why I like her so much. I don't know exactly when it started but by the time I realized I was already in love with her. I only know that initially we were around each other regularly because of adjacent roll numbers. Maybe I was attracted to her no-nonsense approach to things," I said.

"You look strong outside, but you are very emotional, and Jhansi is pleasant outside but rational to the core. Platonic love versus practicality. Haha!" Venkat summed up.

We laughed, lit another cigarette, and left.

I admired Jhansi for her ability to be detached with the world around her, but not with me. Was she indifferent on purpose so as not to get distracted from studies until we completed college? Or did she not appreciate my recklessness toward career though she liked me as a person? If her career was her priority, then let it be. I didn't want to push myself hard into her scheme of things. It was up to her to decide whether it was career first or Jay first, or at least both career and Jay together.

I didn't have an urgency to decide something then and there. When it came to Jhansi, I had immense capacity to wait without losing hope. The feelings I had for her were not a burden that I needed to offload hastily. I wasn't sure about the future of our relationship, but years later when I look back, I would like to fondly reminisce that I conducted myself with dignity with Jhansi and not with desperation.

I walked to our hostel, casually reflecting on my last four years.

Three passions dominated my undergraduate life—Jhansi, cricket, and smoking, in that order. Everything else was just a simple part of my routine.

To me, college meant Jhansi. The certificate of completion was just a perk. I slept with her thoughts and I woke up with her thoughts every day, and that continued for four years with increasing passion. End of the day was like a downtime for me since I had to wait one full night to see her again. Holidays were hell. Jhansi made me realize human memory is a virtue which I used completely to store her images when she was not around.

As Venkat said, Jhansi was not so popular among boys in our college for her beauty. But to me, she had no comparison. No girl in the campus displayed Jhansi's richness, both in looks and conduct. Masked by the definition of beauty in the traditional sense, either all boys in the college failed to see her elegance or I was so mad about Jhansi that I liked everything about her. It wouldn't be easy for guys who are used to thinking with their penises to appreciate her. Even if few of them liked her later, I was already her good friend, and that acted as a barrier for them to come closer to her.

Jhansi had a distinctive dress sense. Unlike most girls on the campus, who were either over-dressed or under-dressed, she always wore perfect color combinations of churidars, chunnis, kurtis, jeans, and matching sandals, bangles, bracelets, earrings, and bindis. If she was not so serious about her academics, she would have made a great designer. The same old silver wrist watch she always wore used to disappoint me but then I came to know one day that that watch was gifted by her mom when she left Bangalore for her undergraduate studies and she felt like her mom was with her whenever she wore it. Once something is linked to sentiment, there is no room for argument. I fell for the sentiment and I started liking her watch too. I generally didn't recollect anything that I didn't like in Jhansi when I thought about her.

Venkat used to ask me sometimes how I liked her zigzag teeth and her deep masculine voice. To me, her teeth brightened her smile which I longed to catch a glimpse of and her voice amplified her strong personality which I yearned to hear.

Every time I liked a girl since childhood, I felt my liking for her will stay forever but the next girl replaced her very easily. But something prompted me that Jhansi's place in my heart will be irreplaceable. She steadily anchored my heart for four years. As long as we didn't talk about career, we were the finest friends on the campus. To me, she was my first real love, my would-be wife, my everything as far my imagination took both of us. And to her, as far as I knew, I was a good friend. At the most, I was her best friend but I was still a friend. She liked something in me and I liked everything in her, which kept our friendship going for four years.

Can a boy and a girl be friends forever without thinking about the next step in their relationship, especially at that age? Even if that's a possibility, I wasn't prepared to accept that we both were meant to be just friends. I didn't want my relationship with Jhansi to die out as just another college love affair. I wished to see it transcend to the next level artlessly, even without having to use those three beautiful words "I love you".

The word love lost its purity anyway with guys in colleges using it as a surrogate to convey a range of feelings—I like your dress sense; I am obsessed with your beauty; You look sexy; I'd like to talk to you; I admire your diligence in studies; I like the fact that your dad is rich; I like your presence; I'd like to go out with you; I want to sleep with you; I fantasize about you when I masturbate; I need a girl to boost my confidence; I need a girl to pass time; I'd like to try what it would be like to be with a girl; I generally look at you when I am bored in the class; I am left with no girl except you on the campus.

It could mean anything except love in its true sense. Often college love happens to be the starting point of a boy-girl relationship while it should be the ultimate step of commitment between the two. I have no statistics to prove, but if there were a contest, love will win as the most abused word in English language in India. Girls too played their due role in exploiting it for mean purposes.

Where had those authentic relationships disappeared that inspired the coining of the word love originally? I felt I needed a better word for Jhansi, for the word as it is currently used could never justify my feelings for her. I put a hold on my thoughts of Jhansi as I reached the hostel and saw a few friends there.

Those of us who hung around in the dormitories, playground, and college café proudly called ourselves lions, against the dogs who could be spotted in the library all the time.

After our final year exams, we were permitted to stay on the campus for a month to complete the project work. Most students never left the campus in that one month. The dogs used the college library facility to prepare for GRE and TOEFL and apply to universities abroad, and others prepared for graduate entrance exams in India. Almost nobody stayed on the campus doing nothing like Venkat and me.

Large part of my disdain for the idea of going to the US for master's was the kind of people I saw in our college who took that route. Come final year, all the dogs were aspiring to go to the US. It was amusing to see that all the dickheads on the campus had the same career goal. It was as if all of them formed a union and declared—We, the assholes of this college pledge hereby to go to the US at all costs and keep all the information regarding our efforts within this group only. Internet was not that popular and accessible in India back then that added to the false advantage they had. They behaved as if they were the chosen few by God for graduate education in the US. Open competition to them was a dirty word.

The whole atmosphere in the college gave me the impression that master's in the US was meant only for those who were fit for nothing in India. It was like watching corrupt cops again and again in the movies and developing a kind of aversion to that profession. I hated dogs and hence I hated going to America. I was indeed happy that brain drain to the US was like a natural cleanser for India. Let America bear with those jerks.

Venkat might have thought love blinded me, but Jhansi truly was an exception in that group.

For most part of our final year in college, Jhansi was busy applying to American universities for master's. Even while helping her write some parts of the applications, it never crossed my mind that pursuing master's in the US could brighten my career prospects. I was so inclined to staying in India even though I wasn't sure what I was going to do. To me going to the US for master's appeared like a defensive thought, an escape from Indian reality motivated by greed for money. Given India's potential, I believed people going to the US were not flying to the US but fleeing India.

***

While going to the US for graduate education was the trend in colleges, there was another category of people who were in queue to the US via H1B, the famous non-immigrant work visa. Contrary to what it said, most of them ended up becoming the US citizens later. Practically anybody was eligible in that category, even those who didn't complete their college education in India, not legally though.

"Mad" would be a sophisticated word if anybody looked at the people running after computer institutes even in small towns. It made sense to me if computer engineers did that, and not any Tom, Dick, and Harry. Interestingly, all the Toms, Dicks, and Harrys who followed that path successfully landed in the US, taking advantage of IT field's not-so-strong entry barrier. They did it so successfully that the so-called smart guys in colleges who looked down upon them felt left behind, only to follow them later.

IT jobs in the US changed the equilibrium among Indian youth. Suddenly, bright students in colleges, who opted for jobs and graduate programs in India, lagged behind in earnings. With the inflow of dollars, studiousness in colleges didn't carry much value in terms of earning potential. Slow, steady, and methodical approach, which did wonders for students academically, left them disappointed in the open world. IT revolution reduced the university certificates to pieces of shit.

Though this trend started when I was doing my undergraduate program, I didn't realize the intensity of the mad rush. The one computer course that was part of our undergraduate curriculum was a nightmare to me which also contributed to my reluctance to accept IT as a career option for a long time though several dumbasses I knew were minting dollars. I don't know how many of them even knew that IT meant Information Technology. That was the quality of supply available to match the demand for computer literates in the US back then. People good in their own fields stayed away from IT initially, and hence people who did not fit into any other field grabbed the opportunity. Eventually, most people at some point in their careers tried their hands at computers. Reason? Money, big money, the kind of money professionals never saw before in India.

I refused to recognize IT as a career option and America as a destination just because of their earning potential at that time. My conscience didn't allow me to follow the herd of sheep running after money in the name of career. I wanted to build a career and make money while doing something I relished, rather than run after money and fool myself that an extraordinary career was in the making.

7

I called up Jhansi to inform that I'll be there at her hostel by 9. Though I wanted to go out for dinner with her that day, we couldn't as she was busy packing her stuff and saying goodbyes.

I was in disbelief that that day had come. My mind was blank. Jhansi was leaving for Bangalore, and she had no reason to come back to the college campus again unless she wanted to meet someone. The association with the campus was practically over. Many students had already left the campus in the last couple of days after completing their final project work.

Four years of undergraduate college life was over in a jiffy. The first day on the campus was so fresh in my memory that I felt like I joined the college just yesterday.

There was no progress in our relationship. We were still good friends and obviously I was not happy with that status. I was not ready for a life without Jhansi by my side.

Was she waiting for me to say it first? Was she really looking at me as just a friend? Was she thinking that I was thinking about her as just a friend? Was she occupied with her career more than anything else? Was she thinking that the world was so small and we could keep in touch? I had only questions, no answers.

For reasons unknown even to me, I didn't want to be the first to come out. I wanted her to know about my feelings somehow. I wished for a miracle to happen. I handled my relationship with Jhansi so delicately that I feared spoiling the wonderful memories I had with her by acting like an insecure stupid on her last day on the campus. I was sandwiched between my feelings for her and my inability to express. Until that day, I hadn't seen a tinge of sadness in Jhansi about leaving me, which warded off even the remotest possibility of proposing my love to her.

I took a quick shower and reached the girls' hostel with a cab. Jhansi was already waiting outside with her bags.

So many bags? I wondered how she fitted them in the hostel room. Were girls' rooms bigger than boys'? Surprisingly, a huge number of girls came out to bid farewell to Jhansi. I thought she didn't care about anybody and nobody cared about her. It could be out of admiration than out of friendship. She didn't go on a hugging spree and make a show of emotions like how girls usually did. Jhansi never hesitated to show her preference for her space and she was the same on her last day too.

As we got into the cab, Jhansi said, "I'll miss this place, Jay." Her elegant smile was missing but she looked composed.

"Yeah, four years is not a small time," I said.

"It's not just about time, but the big changes that happened in my life in these four years. When I look back, I'll be proud to think that this college laid a solid foundation for my career."

Was the college just about her career? In a way, she was right. Colleges are meant for us to find the right direction in life, not to find life partners.

After a long silence, Jhansi said, as if she was done with framing her thoughts and ready to speak, "Keep in touch, Jay."

I smiled and nodded.

After another brief moment of silence, she continued, "Jay, you have been my support structure all these four years. You are the only person I am close to in my life, apart from my mother and sister."

I didn't say anything.

"Come on, don't be so calm, Jay. It doesn't suit you," she said.

I substituted my loss of words with a smile.

"When are you leaving?" she asked.

"In a couple of days."

"Do you want to be the last person to leave the campus?"

"Haha, no. I'll leave after Venkat submits his project work."

"Okay. What is Venkat doing after this?"

"He is planning to get into the software field. He'll join some course in Hyderabad."

"Oh wow. That's a big shift."

"Yeah."

"I know that's a growing field right now, but you don't do that. I am not sure if people getting into IT from our stream will go too far in their careers. They might make good money temporarily, but career is not just about money. We'll spend large part of our lives with whatever path we choose now, and it's important that we make careful decisions. You don't do that, okay? Do something concrete in your life, think long-term. I know you have plans to do MBA. Put in all your efforts. I believe it will work out well for you," Jhansi said.

"Okay." After a couple of minutes of silence, I looked outside, and said, "I guess we reached the bus station."

Excluding her pep talk, our conversation was unusually ridden with too much silence. Even after we got out of the cab, we kept silent for most part standing at the bus station. When the bus arrived, I helped Jhansi put her bags in the trunk and accompanied her into the bus.

"Alright Jhansi," I said, after she confirmed her arrival with the bus operator.

"What alright? I am coming down with you. We still have time. The bus will not start now."

"Okay," I smiled.

"Can I ask you something?" Jhansi asked as we got down the bus.

"Please don't ask me anything about what we studied in the last four years. I forgot everything after the exams," I said, mocking her love for academics.

"I am not that obsessed with studies, Jay. I try to be good at what I do. Is that an offence?" Jhansi said in a serious tone. I guess the joke didn't go well with her.

"I was just joking, Jhansi. What did you want to ask?"

"Nothing."

"No, ask. I am sorry, I take back my words. You can ask me about academics also, okay?"

For the first time that night, I saw her smile genuinely. "Why did you do so much for me? Since my first day in college till today, you were there for me for everything. Many times you did things for me even before I asked. I don't know if I can ever repay you, Jay," she said.

"Because I love you, Jhansi," was the straight, simple and right answer.

Instead, I said, "I might have been there for you on a few occasions but you did everything for yourself, Jhansi, which you would have in any case. You don't owe me anything."

I wasn't happy that we were talking so normally in such an extraordinarily emotional situation. But I was helpless. I didn't have different words for different levels of emotions in my vocabulary.

"I'll miss you, Jay, more than anything and anybody here. I'll definitely not find someone like you who I can count on anytime," she said.

The bus operator's announcement of the bus leaving in a couple of minutes broke our conversation.

Is that it? Is it over?

"I think I should leave now. Take care, Jay, keep in touch,"

Jhansi said, extending her hand to shake mine. That was the first time I felt the warmth of her touch and spotted a little sadness in her eyes.

"Take care, Jhansi. I can't believe that I'll not see you from tomorrow. Best wishes!" I said, holding her hand.

"Bangalore is not far. It's just a change of place."

She had been saying "It's just a change of place" thing often of late, to console me I guess. It wasn't about how far Bangalore was but how drastically things would change as soon as she stepped out of the campus.

"Call me as soon as you reach home," I said.

"Sure, I'll disturb you tomorrow morning. Take care. Focus on your career first, rest everything will be okay," Jhansi said.

She took a few steps back, smiled with tight lips waving her hand, and then turned back and walked toward the bus. She looked back and waved at me once again while stepping into the bus and waved one more time through the window after settling down in her seat. The bus drove away as Jhansi was still waving. I just lifted my hand unable even to move.

I stood there like a statue as the bus disappeared in front of my eyes. The bus didn't stop after a few minutes, and Jhansi didn't step down and come to me running and crying to hug me and say "I love you, Jay, I love you. . . You are my life, Jay, you are my life. . . ."

No, it didn't happen.

I came back to my senses and lit a cigarette to blow my sorrow out. Late in the night, instead of taking a cab, I chose to walk all the way to the college, smoking and thinking.

Earlier in the evening, Venkat had offered to come to the bus station to accompany me back to college. He presumed that I would be emotionally drained. Probably he knew what would happen, rather he was sure that nothing miraculous would happen. He was concerned about me as a friend, though he knew that I was mentally strong and prepared for the occasion.

Venkat stood at the main gate of the college, waiting for me. He came to me, put his arm around my shoulder, and said, "Jay, tell me if something exceptional happened. Else don't worry, it's just another day."

It was not just another day for me. It was Sunday, April 14, 2002—the day that would be etched in my heart forever.

I laughed, and said, "Let's go to the train station."

Venkat knew what I meant by that. The only bar in the town that served liquor 24/7 secretly was near the train station. Sitting over beers and midnight biryani, we spent time talking about our future plans.

"When are you submitting your project work?" I asked.

"Tomorrow. Everybody else submitted in time except me," he said. The deadline to submit the project passed but Venkat had taken special permission as he had to visit his ailing grandfather.

"It doesn't matter; the project is just a formality."

"Yeah, it doesn't matter until someone is detained for not submitting the project on time, and I don't want to be the first one in the college. Haha."

"What next?" I asked. I had a hint about his plans but wanted to know if there had been any developments recently.

"My brother is pushing me to get into software, like I told you earlier. He has sent me some contacts in Hyderabad. He is planning everything for me here from America."

"Okay. Don't you think it would be difficult for us having come from biology background?" I asked.

"That's what my concern was initially. I have finally decided to give it a shot after a lot of persuasion from him. IT jobs don't need much mathematical background. It's simple logic, and with some training, anybody can do it. At least that's what my brother said. He always says even housewives do software jobs there. What I understood from him was that there are some non-technical profiles in IT which we can do easily with some training. I'll know only when I get into it."

"The path could be different, but finally you'll land up in America too," I said.

"More or less. I guess nobody gets into IT without an eye on America. Wait and watch, Jay, all these dogs who boast so much in their university applications will end up being software engineers. I am not positive about Jhansi, but rest of them," Venkat said, with a mischievous smile.

"But what good is that except for a few extra dollars?" I asked, ignoring what he said about Jhansi.

"Jay, take my case. I don't have a clear inclination toward anything, either to continue my studies or to pursue a job. Why not get into IT where at least I can earn better?"

"But don't you feel guilty that you are just going with the flow?" I asked.

"That's exactly the point here. When I don't have a firm direction, the question of guilt doesn't arise. I don't know about the future but right now this option looks good, and I don't have a better alternative in my mind. Trust me, a large percent of people fall into this category. And a large percent of this large percent will never get to know what they are passionate about in their lifetime. They just go with the flow," Venkat said.

"Don't we need to take a pause and think at least?" I asked.

"You are right, but that's an unusual step. People generally feel insecure to stop and do nothing to take an objective look at things. They don't feel comfortable not being part of the flow. And right now, I am one of them, haha."

"Makes sense," I said, though I had a different perspective.

"Join me, if you are also interested. We'll do it together. We have my brother to support us. I know you want to do MBA but this is also an option. Perhaps you could get together with Jhansi in America," he said, and smiled.

"That would be another half-hearted attempt, Venkat. Right now, I am not convinced about getting into the software field."

"But what after MBA? Nowadays people from all streams, and even MBAs, are getting into IT, like all rivers finally merge into an ocean," Venkat said.

"Yeah I know. Software and America have become a craze. My idea of studying management is not for a job. I am looking forward to acquire some skills and launch something on my own in future. Even if I get a job, I wouldn't be continuing for a long time," I said.

"Okay. Let me know if you need anything in Hyderabad. I'll be there for a few months, until I take the flight to America, haha," Venkat said.

"Okay. And again, that's not how I want to get into Jhansi's life, by running after her wherever she goes," I said, answering his earlier comment.

"I know, Jay. I was just joking."

I drank beer after beer and smoked cigarette after cigarette that night. We spent the entire night at the bar. It was almost sunrise by the time we reached the college.

On our way to the dormitories, I asked the hostel office staff not to hesitate to wake me up when I get a call from Jhansi. For a moment, I even thought of waiting near the phone to pick her call directly.

I couldn't sleep well in spite of not resting the entire previous night. After some on and off sleep, finally I woke up late in the morning and went to the hostel office wondering why nobody had come to inform me that I got a call from Jhansi. I couldn't believe my ears when they said I didn't get any call. I checked with all the staff in the office including the watchman. I didn't doubt them, but I checked the phone call register also because I didn't want to doubt Jhansi. I knew those guys noted down the incoming phone calls and messages promptly in the register even if they couldn't inform the students. I went to the computer room and checked my email. This time I really couldn't believe my eyes—no email from Jhansi. The bus would have reached Bangalore early in the morning. She must have reached home several hours back.

Was she angry with me? Did she expect me to man up and express my feelings first? Should I have taken the lead being the guy? Or was she more rational and practical than what I understood of her? Did she just switch off her undergraduate life and switch on the next steps of her career? But I wasn't just a small part of her undergraduate life that could be switched off so easily.

Random and unrelated thoughts bothered me for a while. There was very little that I could do by fretting. I had her Bangalore contact number, but I hesitated to take the liberty of calling her. I could have emailed her but I didn't feel like doing that as well. Was she not supposed to convey the message to me that she reached safely? Did she not already pass a cold vibe to me?

My world had changed completely in one night. Though I was reluctant to accept it, I understood it was time for me to get used to a world without Jhansi.

8

June, 2002: Target MBA, destination Pune.

I had a difficult start after leaving college. With Jhansi and Venkat gone ahead with their career plans and having left the campus, which was everything for me for four years, I felt lonely and found it hard to recover.

For no credible reason, I didn't have the slightest interest in keeping in touch with any of my undergraduate classmates. My disappointment with Jhansi translated, though unjustifiably, into a disappointment with my undergraduate college and friends. I was the only guy to choose the MBA path which further isolated me from them.

Most of the MBA colleges had already conducted their entrance exams, and for some others, the deadline for applications for that academic year had passed by. I was a little late but went ahead and picked the best among the available few colleges and joined promptly without wasting much time.

Different college, different city, different people—is this what life is all about, a constant wandering with ever-changing situations and priorities? When we are on the verge of believing that we are something or something is ours, God has a way of reminding us that we are nothing and nothing is ours.

Seeing Jhansi off at that bus station remained the last time I saw her and talked to her, but she continued to stay in my thoughts almost all the time. Jhansi's absence in my life made me unusually introverted. There were times when I struggled to cover it up when people caught me with a sudden smile on my lips thinking about Jhansi during class or lunch. Contrary to the impression my undergraduate classmates had about me, during my MBA days, people saw me as someone who spent a lot of time alone.

I completed my MBA with a dual specialization in marketing and finance. Unlike the leisurely undergraduate studies, MBA was hectic. It was over even before I could completely overcome the undergraduate college hangover. After MBA, which was the only planned move on my part, events like campus placement, management trainee period, and a couple of years of job happened without much conscious intervention from my side. Never did I think seriously whether what I was doing was what I wanted to do. The thought of entrepreneurship lingered in my mind, but it didn't reach a tipping point.

My withdrawal period didn't last long. After a couple of years in a job, I felt I had hit the aspirational ceiling. I wasn't happy that I was headed to living an ordinary life. Added to the feeling of under-achievement, monotony had set in. Work days repeated, weekends repeated, and monthly salaries repeated without much change.

That's when our company's annual conference happened in Goa. Annual conferences used to be huge events where the entire strength of the company dispersed across the country in diverse profiles came together to have fun for three complete days. Lengthy speeches by top management were boring though.

While others were enjoying in groups, I sat alone on the sands of Candolim Beach, sipping beer and watching the sunset over the sea, thinking about my career.

"Hello, young man," I heard the voice of the vice president of the sales and marketing team of our company.

"Hello, sir. I didn't see you coming," I said, putting the beer in my hand aside.

"That's fine, Jay. Relax. Nobody is a boss in Goa. We are here to have a good time," he laughed and sat beside me.

That was not true. In the name of having a good time in exotic locations, transfers, promotions, salary hikes, and sales targets for the coming year were decided in the annual conferences. Not exactly discussed and decided, but directly announced by the top management with nobody in the company showing any disagreement on the outside.

"I heard from your boss that you wanted to shift to the head office," our VP got to the point after the initial pleasantries.

"Yes, sir. I wanted to explore if there is an opportunity in the product management profile," I said.

"Why?" he asked.

"I have been working in sales for two years, sir. I would like to take up bigger challenges now. Product management will be the right profile to bring together my experience and abilities," I said, blurting out the jargon I remembered from my MBA.

"I agree with you, but you are too young for that position. Compared to the average age of the product managers we have now, you'll be younger by at least five years which might create a problem for me. I'd suggest you to be in sales for one more year at least. The area you are handling is just picking up, and you are the only person who can consolidate that market for us. That's good for your career also in the long run; it's important for you to be in direct touch with the market," he said.

"Okay, sir," I said, though I wasn't happy with his suggestion.

"Leave your career to me. I'll take care of you, okay? Focus on your job for the coming one year. I have bigger plans for you," he said.

"Okay, sir."

Our VP did his job of motivating me to stay with the company in order to protect sales figures from the region I was responsible for. But, for me the learning curve had dropped in my current profile, and I was not getting much personal time because of traveling. How could I tell him the actual reason? Not liking traveling was a sin in the sales and marketing line. Sales people either enjoyed or pretended to enjoy traveling.

"So, are you still reading books?"

He asked me this question whenever we met. He was one of the guys who had interviewed me for the job. More than half of the time during the interview, we discussed the book *Good to Great* by Jim Collins.

"Not much of late, sir."

"I know you need to travel a lot, but try to catch up with your reading whenever you can. That's one thing that will set you apart from others in the long run," he said.

"Okay, sir."

"Alright, enjoy your evening," our VP said as he got up, and left me alone.

Enjoy my evening? Really? As if he had given great news for me to celebrate.

Our company had experienced a huge attrition rate in the past couple of years. I knew our VP tried to pacify me in view of the attractive packages people were being offered in other growing fields like IT, banking, and retail. He might have had the same kind of pep talk with many of my colleagues as well to retain them with the company.

I was doing well in my current job, but I wasn't doing exceptionally well. I was lucky to have had an opportunity to work with wonderful people in the past couple of years, and our VP was one of them. But my path was different from working for him forever. I wanted to make him proud whether I worked for him or not. I admired the MBA graduates who were happy doing the same job year after year, but I wasn't one of them. I was looking for something different.

Meanwhile, in addition to bribing me with an attractive salary hike, within a month after the Goa conference, our VP selected me to represent the company at an international symposium on the latest technological trends in supply-chain management in New Delhi. Probably that was also part of trying to keep me with the company.

The symposium experience disrupted my already disoriented mind. The idea of emerging global platform powered by technology had struck me. Generally, symposiums and conferences were meant for enjoying good food and sightseeing, rather than taking home life-changing ideas. Contrary to my impression, insightful speeches on the latest global trends by practicing managers from renowned companies and professors from eminent management institutes across the world caught me unawares. They made me realize the depth of my business illiteracy.

The global business trends increasingly pointed to the blurring lines among countries economically, even though they might be thickening politically. While the world's largest economies, the US and China, constantly squabbled with each other for supremacy on the world stage, isn't China the largest foreign creditor to the US? Had the trade between India and Pakistan ever decreased in spite of not seeing eye to eye politically? Aren't companies increasingly employing more people and owning more assets in countries outside their countries of origin? Could the ever-increasing outsourcing trends in spite of political rhetoric be overlooked? Aren't companies increasingly looking at the world as one market instead of restricting themselves geographically? Going by the conjecture, isn't the world moving toward a no-barrier trade pushing patriotic sentiments to the back seat? Could I still afford to be in a silo especially when my aspirations were so high?

I returned from the symposium carrying the burden of embarrassment of switching myself off from the rapid advancements happening around the world while keeping myself busy with trivial stuff. My job was basically to sell desi products of a desi company to desi customers. The discussion on exploring other Asian markets for our products came up in every annual conference but was completely ignored later without any follow-up. What I was doing was not even close to what I thought I would do when I initially wanted to pursue an MBA. And the symposium reminded me of it.

The fact that I was inadequate to the outside business world was the worst feeling I took home, which didn't leave me for several days. I started looking at the past four years of my life, two years of MBA plus two years of job, with resentment for not adding value to my career. What a waste of time and money if the two years of MBA didn't prepare me for the emerging international trends and entrepreneurship. Was I just trained for a sophisticated blue-collar job? Is that what an MBA meant for? How would a young doctor feel if his education was good enough to sell medical equipment and drugs but not to become a doctor? How bizarre even to think?

Instead of hopping jobs for marginal salary hikes, I wanted to be clear about the overall purpose to which I could align all my efforts. After weeks of contemplation, I chose to go back to college to upgrade myself. It was not an easy decision. This time I aspired to be part of a program that would build on the management background I already had and place me in a global orbit. I started exploring suitable programs across the world. When I was ready to break all barriers, why should I confine to just India? The search process finally settled at a few universities in the Mecca of management, the USA.

The first thought of awkwardness that struck me was my hatred toward the idea of going to the US and people who had such plans back in my undergraduate college days. Had my life come full circle? Not really. I would have hated myself if I followed the crowd and ran after America when I was in college, without a clear agenda for my career. I viewed my plan as an act of self-improvement to realize my full potential. My commitment to my country was still intact. Didn't whoever went to the US say the same thing? But the difference lied in the levels of commitment that only time would testify.

The first name I recalled when I thought of someone in the US who could help me in my pursuit was Venkat. In spite of immense camaraderie we shared during our undergraduate days, we didn't keep in touch after Venkat left for the US. Since I didn't have his phone number, I emailed him with a one-line message "Need to talk to you" and left my phone number.

That very same night, seeing the US number on my cell, I guessed it could be Venkat. I didn't expect him to be so fast.

"Hello," the flat voice on the other side greeted me as soon as I picked the call. I felt like our CEO called me, it sounded so professional.

"Hello? Venkat?"

"Jay, man, I am having goose bumps hearing your voice."

"Same here, Venkat. I am happy to get in touch with you after such a long time."

"Why are you sounding so formal?" he asked.

"I am feeling the same about you," I said.

"Let's blame it on the phone. We are not used to talking over phone. Haha." His boisterous laugh was intact. The flatness in his voice I felt initially was gone.

"True."

"Did I wake you up? I knew it was late but couldn't wait to talk to you after I saw your email."

"No no, I didn't sleep yet."

"Okay, tell me. How are you? Where are you and what are you doing?"

"I am in Pune, working as regional marketing manager for BSTK home appliances. I look after the marketing activities of the company in the western region."

"Great. Sounds like a challenging job."

"Tell me about you."

"I am in Charlotte, Jay, working for Bank of America as a quality assurance team lead."

"Good. How is your brother?"

"He is doing good. I received your email just when I was trying for your number; look at the coincidence. Where have you disappeared? None of our friends has your contact number."

I didn't say anything.

"I have something to share with you. I am coming to India next week. Do you know why?" Venkat said.

"Getting married?" I said.

"Yeah, how did you guess that?" Venkat asked surprisingly.

"Congrats first of all. That's a prominent reason why NRI bachelors come to India," I said.

"Haha, true. Otherwise we don't waste money on flight tickets," Venkat said. His sarcastic sense of humor was also intact.

"How many days will you stay here?" I asked.

"Almost one month, Jay. This is my first India visit after I came to the US."

"Good, I can talk to you when you come here then," I said.

"Sure, but tell me what's the matter. For a moment, I panicked seeing your one-line email. Are you getting married too?" Venkat asked.

"No. I am planning to come there," I said hesitantly, probably because of the overt repulsiveness I had in college for the idea of going abroad.

"America? Great! When? Is your company sending you?" Venkat asked casually.

"No, on my own."

"You too, Brutus? Haha, are you serious?" That was a loud laugh before his voice turned serious.

"Yes."

"But why now? What's your plan exactly?" Venkat asked, this time not so casually.

"I want to come there for an MBA with international trade specialization."

"Who is going to fund your education?"

"I'll have to try for financial assistance based on my GMAT score. If I don't get it, I'll have to shell out from my pocket," I said.

"It's very expensive here if you don't find some kind of assistance. I am really not sure if it's worth it at this point of time in your life. I believe you are doing well there," Venkat said.

"I know it's a big risk financially. But don't you think it'll benefit my career in the long run?"

"It depends on the program and reputation of the college. I know many MBAs who are working as software engineers too."

"Okay."

"Did you do any research so far?" Venkat asked.

"Yes. I didn't take the GMAT yet, but I have a tentative timeline for what I need to do, and I have shortlisted some colleges also. If everything works according to plan, I should be there for fall 2007."

"Really? I thought you just started thinking about it. Send me the details. Let me also talk to people here. This is a beautiful country and has a lot to offer, Jay. You should definitely come here, you'll gain a different perspective of the world. I am only concerned about the financial viability of your plan."

"Apart from financial risk, what other issues do you see?" I asked.

"Nothing, that's the only issue. You'll get visa easily. Student visas are not difficult. You have me here. I'll support you in every possible way. In the worst case scenario, we can find something for you in IT."

"Okay," I said, though I was not keen on IT.

"Send me the details first. I'll have some information for you by the time I come to India."

"Okay. Who is the girl by the way?" I asked.

"Her name is Tulasi. She is from a relative's family from my mother's side. My mother told that we used to play together in our childhood when I went to my grandfather's place during holidays, but I couldn't remember even after seeing her picture."

"Okay."

"When will you get married if you come here as a student now?" Venkat asked.

"Marriage is not that important, it can wait."

"I am going to get married in a few weeks, man. Don't make me feel guilty, haha." It had been a long time since I heard someone laugh like that.

"No no, I didn't mean that," I said.

"Any news about Jhansi? Where is she, what is she doing?" Venkat asked.

"I don't know."

"I asked a couple of our college friends about her. They don't know her whereabouts like they don't know yours, haha," Venkat said.

Jhansi topic didn't really enthuse me. By then I had

rationalized her absence in my life, though I didn't forget her.

"Alright, Jay, now that I have your contact, I'll bother you frequently. Convey my regards to your mom, dad, and sister."

"Alright. See you in India."

Couple of weeks later, I met Venkat in India. He came to Pune to see me. On the whole, he didn't think of my idea as dumb, but he didn't think of it as the smartest idea on earth too—to quit the job in hand and spend time and money on another master's.

While Venkat was still with me in Pune, after taking stock of what we knew until then, I made up my mind to go ahead with my MBA in the US plan, though I couldn't thoroughly vet the idea. From the moment I made the decision, Venkat was thoroughly involved in my preparations. We discussed the progress almost every day.

Based on several criteria like tuition fees, duration of the program, ratings and placements, I chose four universities which offered the specialization I wanted, two of them chose me, without offering me any financial assistance though, and I chose one of them.

Finally I was ready to fly to Austin, Texas, for a one-year MBA with a specialization in international trade for fall 2007.

While I was excited all through my preparations to go to the US, I was tense as the days neared. I was foregoing a lot in the present without a guarantee on what I would gain in future. The huge amount of money I was going to spend scared me. The repayment part worried me even before the spending part started. At one point, out of fear I even prayed to God to get my visa rejected because I couldn't voluntarily stop myself. But it didn't happen. I got my student visa in the first attempt itself. I prayed to God again that my flight somehow should get cancelled. It didn't happen either. Nothing worked in favor of stopping me; everything worked in favor of pushing me to the US.

9

I took the flight to America on August 15, 2007.

I thoroughly enjoyed my first international flight, not because I did something interesting but because I didn't do anything. I slept the whole time. The next thing I remembered after they served the yummy dinner as soon as the flight took off in Hyderabad was waking up in London.

By the time I reached London, I accepted that stopping my journey to America was not part of God's plan. I didn't know why I felt that somebody was forcing it on me in the first place.

Looking at the Indian crowd in the flight and during the layover time in London, I perceived myself as the odd one. I neither belonged to the category of college youth flying to the US for their master's immediately after undergraduate college in India nor the category of married couples with little kids who had been working there for quite some time. I was between both the categories which made me doubt whether going to America at that point was a smart career move or not. In any case, I wasn't planning to fly back to Hyderabad from London.

The layover time at London Heathrow Airport was refreshing with rich ambience, clean surroundings, wide internal walkways, and an assortment of shops on both sides. How could the place be so quiet and systematic in spite of being one of the busiest airports in the world?

Not as much as during the first flight, but for most part,

my sleeping marathon continued on the second flight also, from London to Austin. I woke up a couple of times to eat something. By the time I opened my eyes, when the plane landed in Austin, people were already getting down. I fetched my shoulder bag and followed them. For the first time, I felt standing up was so relaxing.

Seeing some papers in almost everybody's hands, I asked the white guy standing in front of me, "What are those papers?"

"Oh, thee—these things you need to fill out and—aah—mmm—submit to the immigration officer. Didn't you get them from the flight attendants?"

Why was he struggling so much to speak? "No, I slept throughout the flight," I said.

"No problem. You'll get them everywhere when you get down," he assured me, looking at the confusion on my face.

That was definitely not his first international flight, he knew things. "Okay, thanks," I said.

By the time I landed in the US, I had learnt to say thanks for every damn thing and sometimes for nothing. This time I meant it.

"No problem," he said, with a grin on his face.

Are they born with a smile on their faces? It has to do something with their genes, otherwise it's not easy to keep smiling like that always.

I got down the flight as the airhostesses stood on both sides near the exit door thanking and wishing the passengers with a big smile. I should be thankful to them for making my trip comfortable. So what if I paid for it? Nothing is guaranteed in India even if I pay. I didn't like the food in the second leg on my trip though. Probably they should include Indian menu, and why not when more than half of the plane was filled with Indians? I said thank you to the flight attendants in return and I meant it this time too.

I stepped out of the flight to a bright day that felt like Indian summer. I landed on American soil at around 2:45 p.m. on August 15, the Indian Independence Day.

I walked with the crowd toward the immigration counter thinking of Independence Day celebrations back in India. It should probably be renamed as India Formation Day or India Day or simply the August 15th. The word "independence" reminds me of being slaves once upon a time though it was true. Isn't it time to come out of the colonial mentality and treat the British Imperialist rule as a historical fact? I read about the oppressive British rule only in books but I witness a more sub-standard self-rule now in India. What's the point in celebrating Independence Days when we couldn't put the independence to proper use? At least as a kid I looked forward to toffees in school but as I grew older to the facts of society celebrating Independence Day made no sense to me.

I stopped at a point where people stood in queues. I looked around for men in uniform to get the immigration forms. Instead I saw a beautiful young lady in uniform who gave them to me along with a pen and a courteous smile. People in uniform were not scary in the US, unlike in India. Somehow uniform and cordiality don't get along well in India.

As I started filling out the forms while standing in the line, people behind me stopped and waited for me to move. I moved aside and signaled them to bypass me, which they did reluctantly. If it were India, no permission would be needed, people would do it anyway. Wherever people were required to follow a queue in India, they behaved like a hungry crowd fighting for free bread in a country drought-ridden for several decades. Some people hated standing in line as a matter of habit or prestige and others chose not to stand in line for the fear of standing there forever. On the whole, nobody stood in line in India except school kids who did it out of obedience to their teachers. Ironically, I saw the same Indians maintaining queues outside India. So, the problem doesn't entirely lie with the people.

Unknowingly, I was comparing everything I saw in the US to what it would be like in India.

The yes or no questions in the immigration forms were so obvious that even an idiot should know what to write so as not get into trouble. Things wouldn't have been so easy if they strip-searched bags instead of people. I cleared the formalities at the immigration counter and followed the directions toward the baggage claim. In addition to the easy-to-follow directions, the airport security and staff literally waited to help people, which was the best among the first impressions about America.

The bathrooms, no they call them restrooms in the US, could be spotted whenever and wherever people wanted to use. Finding washrooms in Hyderabad Begumpet Airport was almost like solving a puzzle, and when I found them after some hard work, the floor was so dirty that I didn't feel like carrying my bags inside. Getting the bags dirty was better than losing them altogether so I took them inside with me.

After collecting my bags, I was ready to get out of the airport but I needed to figure out how to let my contact in Austin know that I arrived. Close to the exit gate, I spotted a public phone. An old female security guard standing next to it understood that I was new to the country considering the smile she gave me.

"Hi, I need to use the phone. Where can I get coins?" I asked the lady, pulling a dollar note from my wallet.

"Oh, you want me to break the bill?" she asked, with a heavy accent.

Wasn't that interesting that they called currency notes as bills when the notes were supposed to be used to clear the bills?

She pulled out some coins from her pocket, and said, "I can give seventy-five cents for a dollar."

The awe for America that had built up till then dissolved. In India, at least I didn't come across people who made money on changing currency notes to coins.

I agreed and gave out a dollar bill to her which she took and pulled her other hand back before handing over the coins to me. Instead, she handed me her mobile, and said, "Don't worry about that phone; you can call from this one." That sounded like a win-win for both of us. I didn't have to experiment with the public phone there. What if the coins got struck in the machine without even using it, like the public phones in India?

I called my contact in Austin, Kalyan, from her phone. Luckily, he answered my call at the first try. "Hey, Kalyan. This is Jay. Your roommate Murthy asked me to contact you as soon as I come out of the airport."

I didn't know Kalyan directly. He was Murthy's roommate and Murthy was Venkat's brother's friend. It was a long chain of connections. Murthy didn't mind me staying with them for a couple of weeks until I found another accommodation close to the college.

"Oh yeah, Jay, I was waiting for your call. Murthy told me. Where are you?" Kalyan asked.

"I just came out of the airport," I said.

"Okay, which gate? Which terminal?" he asked.

I asked the old lady in uniform and gave the details to Kalyan. "You'll not be able to contact me. I am wearing a white T-shirt and I am carrying two black suitcases and a red shoulder bag," I said.

"Okay, I'll spot you. I'll be reaching there in a black Honda Accord," he said, and hung up.

I thought I should have asked him how much time he would take to reach the airport so that I knew when to start looking for a black Honda Accord. I asked the lady if I could make another quick call. She agreed without asking for another dollar.

"Hey, Kalyan, Jay again. How much time it takes for you to reach the airport?"

"Thirty-two minutes, thirty-three max."

Why was he so specific? Couldn't he give me a round figure like thirty minutes or forty minutes? Anyway, I let it pass.

I thanked the old lady in the uniform and walked out of the airport with my bags.

As long as I didn't step out of the airport, it didn't make much of a difference whether I was in London or Austin. Outside of the airport building the air was warm and fresh, and the surroundings clean and serene. I stood there on the curb looking at the people moving in and out of the airport, the hugging and kissing between them and the short and revealing dresses women wore which were beyond the acceptance of Indian cinema censorship. Toward one side, people stood in a queue for cabs. Why do these Americans love to stand in queues so much and Indians hate it equally?

I scanned almost every car that stopped near where I stood, staring at the brands that I never saw in India. Very few people owned big cars in India. In my neighborhood especially, I even knew the names of the people who owned costly cars, they were so few. Owning a car is a luxury in India but owning a luxury car is a real pain. Traffic is such a nightmare for car owners that it is incredibly difficult to drive on Indian roads without getting a dent on the car in the first one week of buying irrespective of how deft a driver is. Max two weeks, that's it.

After a little more than thirty minutes, an old black Honda Accord with a prominent dent on the front right side pulled over to where I stood. The right window came down and a man with a sluggish face and messy hair in the driver's seat bent toward right and literally shouted showing his forefinger, "Jay?"

His gesture and tone implied: Are you Jay?

"Hey, Kalyan," I waved my hand, confirming that I was Jay.

Kalyan got down and opened the dicky, no they call it trunk in the US. He looked like he came straight from his bed. No doubt he did; he was in his pajamas. He helped me put my bags in the dic. . . no, trunk.

As we got into the car, Kalyan signaled me to put on my seatbelt. Looking at my plight to pull the belt long enough to fit the buckle, since I was pulling the wrong strap, Kalyan said, "Just pull the buckle."

Truth be told, I never used a seat belt in India where it's not a general habit. Even if by chance some sophisticated folks wanted to use them, poor things how many people could they hold in one seat?

The inside of the car was spacious and comfortable but it was very messy with too many things scattered around. I bent down to pick the pen under my feet and searched for some place to keep it, which I couldn't find. Kalyan took it from me and threw it on to the back seat, and said, "I need to clean this. I am not getting time. How was the journey?"

"It was good. I slept well."

"You are lucky. It's like hell for me. I cannot sleep even for a minute in flights."

After a brief pause, I said, "Kalyan, I need to call my parents."

"You can use my phone." Kalyan pulled his cell out and dialed as I recited the number.

"It's ringing," he said, and gave the phone to me. He did all this while driving at almost seventy miles per hour. It seemed like the cars in the US managed themselves automatically once they were put in a proper lane.

"Hello." It was my mom's half-sleepy voice.

"Hello, Ma."

"Jay, did you reach safely? I couldn't sleep all night." Suddenly mom's sleep disappeared and her voice rose hundred times louder.

"I reached safely and my friend came to the airport to pick me up. I am on my way to his house."

"Good. How was your trip?"

"It was all good. I'll call you again later, Ma. I'll not call everybody now. You tell them, okay?" I told her the names of some of my friends and cousins who needed to be informed. Probably my mom wanted to know the details of my travel but I concluded fast.

My parents were not completely in favor of me going to the US. My mom was concerned that my America trip would delay my marriage, but she relented sensing my enthusiasm. My dad never accepted going to America as an option for better career but he stopped at the point of just suggesting without insisting.

"I need to make another call, Kalyan, to a friend here."

"Go ahead," he said.

I called up Venkat to inform him that I was on my way to Murthy's apartment.

"Thanks, Kalyan," I said, handing over the cell to him. His cell also looked like a medieval piece, like him.

"No problem. Are you feeling hungry, Jay?" Kalyan asked. "Let us stop by the Indian store on our way. I didn't have my lunch too; we'll pick some snacks," he said, before I could respond.

Actually I was very hungry. Good that he thought about it. How could someone not have lunch until so late? I didn't think he was waiting for me. I cannot skip any of the three meals in a day. To me, it's more psychological than physiological; the thought of not eating haunts me.

The highway, no they call it freeway in the US, mesmerized me—four lanes on each side with an assorted brands of cars, vans, and trucks zooming by at high speed. The scene in front of my eyes was like a high-end video game. It was a wonderful feeling to be in the car on that Hollywood movie kind of road. So there was no inconsistency between what we see in American movies and what we see in reality. Indian movies showed cars that never existed on Indian roads. The movies are so surreal that heroines woke up in bed with neatly combed hair and thick lipstick on. In a way that's acceptable if they didn't have sex the previous night.

I looked at the speedometer as we raced down the freeway. With closed windows, I didn't sense that the car was accelerating at close to seventy-five miles per hour, which was almost 120 kilometers per hour, which was unimaginable on Indian roads. Everything in the US was wowing me, except the old lady in uniform at the airport who bargained a dollar for seventy-five cents. In a way I should excuse her, she saved me from experimenting with the public phone.

"Did you eat something in the flight?" Kalyan asked.

"The first flight was good. I didn't feel like eating at all in the second flight. I didn't feel like drinking also," I said.

"Yeah, the second flight is tiring," Kalyan said in agreement.

Talking about food made me even hungrier. I wanted to eat something first. I wanted to go home and take a shower first. I wanted to clear my stomach first which I hadn't been able to do for two days. I wanted to brush my teeth first. I wanted to do several things first. Above all, I wanted to have a cup of coffee and have a smoke first.

I couldn't bring cigarettes with me as my parents were with me when I was packing my bags. Smoking and drinking are like a don't ask, don't tell agreement between parents and children in India. I wasn't sure if I would get my favorite Gold Flake Kings cigarettes in the Indian store there. I was also excited to have Indian snacks that we were about to buy.

Throughout the drive, Kalyan kept the conversation rolling with his questions ranging from my family background to my plan of coming to the US, making his comments once in a while.

"Why did you come here for graduation now when you were already working in India? Why do you want to spend money on a second MBA?" Kalyan asked, as if America was meant for unemployed Indian youth.

"This is not a regular MBA. It's a specialized program in international trade, which is not easy to learn on my own. And what could be a better place than America?" I explained this to so many people that I could answer the question even in my sleep.

"But you said you already did an MBA in India," he said, with a question mark face.

Kalyan apparently did not agree with the fact that someone from India came to America to feed it with Indian rupees rather than milking US dollars, that too for a second master's. If an engineering student didn't like his specialization after completing his undergraduate degree, will he do another undergraduate degree to compensate that? Probably that was what he wanted to ask but he didn't have enough acquaintance to ask me straight.

I might have been giving a false impression to people like Kalyan that pursuing a specialized MBA was just a reason to come to the US. If that was the case, I wouldn't have chosen such a costly route. Honestly, I didn't admit openly that part of me was attracted to the US, and who in India isn't? Until I got the visa approved, I wasn't sure about my plans but when I got it, I decided to give it a shot regardless of the outcome and my earlier reservations about the US.

Luckily, we reached the Indian grocery store soon and the uncomfortable conversation ended.

10

"This store is on the way to our house. We have big Indian stores near the downtown. Most Indians live there," Kalyan gave me an overview of the Indian stores in Austin as we entered into the Lotus Indian Grocery store.

I didn't know what downtown meant. I thought it was some small township a little outside the town, on the down side of the town, downtown, but hesitated to ask Kalyan. That was the kind of hesitation that several times landed me in situations when I felt, "Oh, I should have asked earlier."

Stepping into the store, I saw a stone-faced Indian girl standing at the billing counter who looked at us uninvitingly. Whether she invited us or not, we wanted to get the snacks. I followed Kalyan as he explored the aisles. The store was very small with just two aisles completely stuffed with Indian spices, readymade Indian snacks, vegetables, and Indian movie CDs in one corner.

Kalyan picked up some snacks and asked the girl at the counter, "Is the samosa fresh?"

She nodded indicating that they are fresh without saying a word. Is she in periods or what? Without a smile on her face, her attractive features looked deficient.

Kalyan asked me while packing samosas into a paper bag, "Do you like samosa, Jay?"

What a stupid question. Who doesn't like samosa, especially after eating those tasteless sandwiches in the flight?

"Yes," I said. "Do we get Indian cigarettes here?"

"No, that's why people get them from India. Most people here smoke Marlboro Lights, maybe that's close to Indian taste. We can get them at the pharmacy on our way, if you want. It's close to our apartment," he said.

Cigarettes and pharmacy? What a combination. The pharmacy stores in India might sell expired medicines, even fake medicines, but not cigarettes.

I looked at the stone-faced girl at the billing counter again before we left the shop. She was not looking at us. She was not looking at anyone or anything specific. I stepped out hoping to see her next time with a smile on her face.

Kalyan stopped at the pharmacy for cigarettes on our way to the apartment. Not having touched a cigarette for more than two days, I was craving a smoke. As soon as I got the cigarette packet in my hand, the chemistry in my mouth started changing.

Kalyan opened his wallet to pay for my cigarettes. "I have dollars, Kalyan. With great difficulty I exchanged rupees for dollars in India at two rupees less than the conversion rate. Let me use them," I said.

"Okay," he laughed.

In the next few minutes, we drove to the apartment. Even the local roads in the US were clean and smooth with well-maintained lawns and trees on both the sides. People maintaining their houses and cars well was understandable, but how come public places were maintained so well? I guess public places in America weren't meant for public dirt. Traffic signs placed at regular intervals adjacent to the roads constantly cautioned the drivers about something or the other without leaving them any reason not to follow the instructions. Every country has a way of controlling traffic I guess. Bumpy roads, pedestrians unmindful of traffic, vehicles coming from the wrong direction, and stray animals acted as natural speed limits in India. I saw Kalyan stopping at a red light even on empty roads. His car would have flown into the air from getting hit from behind if he did that in India. Nobody expects people to stop at the red light on an empty road here. Not many traffic lights worked in India in the first place, and even if they worked, people wouldn't pay attention to them unless cops oversee the traffic. After all, traffic lights are lifeless and cannot catch and punish people.

On the way, Kalyan continued making me familiar with the nearby places. It didn't matter to him whether I paid attention. As we entered the apartment complex, I started looking at the surroundings eagerly, after all, that was going to be my place to live for the next few weeks. The place looked pretty open with a huge parking space. In India, it would have been used to construct another apartment complex. Kalyan parked very close to the apartment's entrance so that we didn't have to walk too long with the bags.

Apartment 208, on the first floor—no, the second floor. In US, ground floor is the first floor. I followed Kalyan as we got out of the lift, no they call it elevator in the US. I appreciated Kalyan trying to get me adapted to the new place. I didn't like his straight-from-bed look though.

The apartment was so. . . dirty. The shabby look of the apartment dismissed from my mind the charm of American freeways, cars, roads, lawns, and buildings. Interestingly, both the gentlemen living in that dirty apartment were pharmacists by profession. Thank God, they were not doctors. They had almost recreated the typical Indian bachelor room in the US. The only missing part from the entire setting was underwears with holes spread on the chairs to dry.

"Keep your bags here for now, and you can use the bedroom to sleep. Generally I sleep in the hall," Kalyan said, pointing to a corner as we entered into the living room.

The mattress and bed sheets in the living room looked like they always remained there like common fixtures in that apartment, serving Kalyan for everything, not just for sleeping. The wall clock showed 4:30 p.m. I hoped it was working. The apartment looked smaller compared to a typical one-bedroom apartment in India, with a very simple structure—living room that extended toward the right of the entrance, kitchen toward the left, bedroom further inside to the right, and bathroom to the left.

Thinking about what to do first, smoke or shower, I decided on something else. I had samosas and asked Kalyan where I could smoke.

"You can smoke in that open space. Two Indians live in the apartment next to us. They and their friends smoke there generally. So don't worry, that's our place," Kalyan said, opening the apartment door and pointing to the open space at the end of the hallway.

"Okay."

"Every alternate apartment here has a patio; we don't have it. Of course, we pay 100 dollars less rent because of that," Kalyan said smilingly.

"This is even better." I was glad that I didn't have to walk all the way down to smoke.

The open space there looked like a common patio for the entire floor but dedicated to Indian smokers. I hoped Indians there purchased their own cigarettes, unlike my college mates in India some of who smoked their entire college life without buying a single pack of cigarettes. It was acceptable then in the name of friendship. I recharged myself by smoking in solitude. Two samosas and two cigarettes brought me out of the flight sickness.

Feeling too lazy to open the bags, I sat in the hall for a few minutes. After a while, when it was absolutely necessary, I started taking out my towel, clothes, toothbrush, paste, soap, all the things I needed to freshen up.

Kalyan looked at the scene, and said, "We have everything

in the restroom. Just use them. Take a shower and relax."

Did he really mean it or did he say it because he didn't want me to settle down at their place permanently? Whatever, I walked to the bathroom.

Surprisingly, the bathroom was neat. I guess Murthy took the responsibility of maintaining it and Kalyan seldom used it. Something was strikingly different and pleasant as soon as I entered the bathroom, compared to the Indian bathrooms though I couldn't recognize it instantly. One thing for sure was the shower curtain that separated the bath area from rest of the bathroom.

A huge mirror, clean wash basin, wide counter top, the entire area looked like three or four Indian bathrooms joined together. Being able to walk in the bathroom freely would be a huge luxury in India. Even in big individual houses, bathrooms are not paid enough attention. People save extra space for drawing room or bedroom instead of wasting it on a bathroom. Why waste so much space for a bathroom? Do we live there or what? But don't those few minutes in the bathroom in the morning set the pace for the rest of the day?

Turn the knob toward left for hot water and right for cold water—what a pleasure to have access to hot water and cold water anytime in the day for someone who came from a country where access to water itself is a big deal.

And then I sensed the difference—the carpet under my feet, the dryness of the bathroom was making me feel good. Except the bathtub part, the entire bathroom was dry. Seldom are bathrooms dry in India, unless they have not been used for a long time. Keeping bathrooms dry is not a habit somehow. Even the toilet seat is wet many times, and we don't have the luxury of using toilet paper to wipe since using toilet paper is a big joke. But seriously, why use toilet paper when America has no water scarcity? Preference for dryness at the cost of hygiene? Not a good idea.

The wide counter top beside the wash basin looked like an aisle for personal items in a grocery store with stuff scattered over the place—mouthwashes, toothbrushes, toothpastes, deodorants, perfumes, aftershave lotions, shaving foams. I didn't even touch the mouthwash. I tried it once when a cousin of mine brought to India and I felt like my teeth would dissolve and my taste buds would go numb forever.

I was brushing my teeth after a gap of two days, and the toothpaste I picked from there didn't foam. I made a note of the brand so that I wouldn't use it ever again. I should have got my favorite Close-up toothpaste from my bag. What good are toothpastes, soaps, face washes and shampoos without foam? After brushing my teeth, I sincerely wiped the water off the counter top, for the love of dryness.

What a relief to remove the clothes I had worn almost thirty hours back. I felt so relieved that I stood there for a minute looking at my nakedness in the mirror mounted on the wall. No other place in the world makes me feel as intimate with myself as a bathroom, especially when it has a huge mirror.

I stepped into the bathtub, again for hot water turn the knob to left and for cold water turn the knob to right. What a luxury getting the right mix of hot and cold water with just the turn of a knob and positioning it at right place. The Head and Shoulders shampoo and Dove soap were not new to me. The foam-less toothpaste was new to me and it disappointed. I took double the time I usually take for a shower. For the first time I felt like those folks who featured in the soap and shampoo ads on TV. After the shower, I reluctantly opened my bags to pull out the things I would need for the next few days.

"Hello!" I suddenly heard a voice from behind. It was a rather prolonged and loud hello. I looked back to see a lean, dark guy with prominent moustache peeping from the entrance with his feet outside and more than half of his body inside the apartment.

"New from India?" he asked, with a wide smile. The whiteness of his teeth was more prominent against his dark skin and thick black moustache.

I walked up to him, extending my hand, I said, "Yeah. Hi, I am Jay."

"I can tell from your bags. My name is Shankar," he said.

Without even confirming whether he hailed from my state in India, I started saying something in Telugu. "Wait wait, I don't understand Telugu, I am from Tamil Nadu," Shankar intervened.

"Oh, I am sorry," I said, and started talking in English.

"I live in the apartment next to yours. Come, let's have tea," he said.

"Okay," I accepted the invitation without thinking twice, since I was already craving for some drink other than just water.

Assuming that he worked as a software engineer, I asked, "Where do you work?"

My next questions would have been about his job profile and his company, which I didn't get a chance to ask.

"I work in a restaurant," Shankar said. My immediate thought was that he must be working in an odd job.

"I work as a chef in an Italian restaurant," he added, without giving me a chance to speak, and saved me from embarrassment.

"Oh wow! Meeting someone who is not a software engineer in America is a surprise," I said.

Shankar laughed loudly. He opened his apartment and invited me inside. "Did you come on H1B visa?" he asked.

"No, I came on F1, student visa."

He stopped suddenly and turned toward me. I could read his look. I knew what he would say next.

"You don't look like a student. I thought you came here for work," he said.

"Yeah, I worked for a few years in India. I took a break to join a college here," I said.

"Oh nice. You surprised me too. Generally I meet H1B candidates or engineering students straight from college. Best wishes, man, you took a bold step."

"Thanks." I tried to be confident though he scared me. I doubted my plans whenever people complimented me for being different or bold. I wondered if they were trying to be nice instead of telling me I was being stupid.

Shankar prepared tea for both of us, so fast like instant coffee, without giving it some time to boil. I wanted something to go with my smoke, so even his tea was okay for me. Shankar got me tea in such a big cup that I should call it a mug or jug. I would drink that cup full the entire day. He didn't fill it up completely otherwise I would have felt bad to throw it away.

I followed Shankar from the kitchen into the patio through his bedroom. Their apartment was of the same structure as ours, the only difference was that their bedroom led to a patio and ours didn't. The patio was already setup with two chairs and a table with a pack of Marlboro Lights, a lighter, and an ashtray on it—a perfect setting for smokers. Marlboro Lights looked like the choice of Indians in the US, as Kalyan had said.

Shankar and I sat there talking over a cup of tasteless tea and smoke. I was glad to find an Indian bachelor living next to my apartment as a smoking companion.

"You must be jetlagged. Are you feeling sleepy?" Shankar asked.

"Not sleepy, but I am tired. I slept most of the time in the flight, but still I am tired."

"Do not sleep now when you go back to your apartment. Control sleeping in odd times for a couple of days, and you will get used the time cycle here. Otherwise it'll take a long time for you to adjust."

"Okay."

The patio opened to an adjacent road where people were walking, some in pairs and some with their dogs. The ground was covered with layers of withered leaves of different shades, yellow, orange, green, red, and maroon as the fall season was about to begin. I wished several times during the time I sat there, we had a patio too. The extra 100 dollars rent would have been totally worth it.

"Okay, Shankar, I'll catch up with you later. Thanks for the tea," I said, standing up to leave.

"Leave the cup here," he said, pointing at the empty tea cup in my hand.

"No, let me wash this," I said, taking the cup with me.

"Leave it in the sink. You don't have to wash. I'll put it in dish washer anyway," Shankar shouted from the patio.

I didn't know much about the dish washer thing but I listened to him. I left the cup in the sink and let some water into it.

"Bye, Shankar. Should I close the door?" I asked rather loudly.

"No, just leave it," he shouted.

Leaving the doors open has an advantage, otherwise Shankar wouldn't have seen me and I would have missed the refreshing patio experience and Shankar's hospitality. His tea was awful though.

On the way to our apartment, I saw Kalyan outside the main door spreading the bathroom mats on the floor. Ignoring the fact that he was on phone, I asked, "What happened?"

He signaled something which I couldn't understand. I just nodded my head and went inside and opened my bags again lazily. To me, packing is okay but unpacking is a tedious job. I didn't know how long I would stay in that apartment. I pulled out enough clothes for me to get going for a week.

The apartment didn't even have a TV. Boredom in the house and pleasant weather outside invited me for a stroll. I waved to Kalyan to draw his attention hesitantly since he was on phone.

"I am going out for a walk," I said in a low voice.

"Okay, but don't go too far. You are new to this place and you don't have a phone also," Kalyan said, without caring to pull the phone away from his mouth. I would have hated him for what he did if I was on the phone with him on the other end.

11

"Hi," said an old lady in formal dress with a bright smile as I walked out of the apartment. She looked like she was coming back from work.

"Hello," said a young man carrying laundry with a serious smile on his face.

"Hey, how are you?" asked the postal guy dressed in formal shorts with no expression on his face and walked past me within no time.

People greeted me like they had known me for a long time. They had a natural and energetic vibe.

Through the parking lot I walked out of the apartment complex, which had no entrance gate and no security as if it was totally safe. I couldn't see why Venkat warned me so many times to be careful.

Standing outside the gate, I could see the mall Kalyan had talked about earlier, across the street with large crowds and noticeable energy. Toward the left, the road was straight, long, and endless and I found nothing interesting. I took the road to the right and walked through the shops with not very popular names, Mark's Barbershop, Best Mexican, and a few others. I saw McDonald's at some distance and that was something everybody knew. With separate walkways for pedestrians on both sides of the road, I wasn't worried about the traffic. I tried to remember the turns I took. Since I didn't have a phone, I didn't want to get into trouble by getting lost on my first day in the town.

By the time I came back from a refreshing walk, Kalyan was still on phone. Does he have any other work except talking on phone? I smiled at him and picked my cigarette packet and lighter and proceeded to the open space. Slowly I was getting used to Marlboro Lights in the place of Gold Flake Kings. I depended on smoking to beat the nostalgia for my family and friends back home.

I went straight to the kitchen from the common patio and searched for something to eat but couldn't find anything. Thankfully, just then Kalyan said, "We'll order some curries for dinner from outside and cook rice here, okay? Give me five minutes, I am almost done with my call."

I said, "Okay. Take your time." I should have stopped at saying just okay. I really didn't mean to tell him to take the time he wanted, I was already hungry.

I saw a laptop on the table near the corner of the hall with the internet cable connected, but I needed the password to use it, and again I needed Kalyan to get off the phone. Definitely the person Kalyan was talking to was not a girl, he was just talking plain with no excitement in his body language.

"Knock, knock," I heard Shankar's voice as I looked in the refrigerator once again though I knew we didn't have anything in it. I was already familiar enough to recognize his loud and squeaky voice.

"Hey, Shankar, come in," I shouted from the kitchen.

"Did you have dinner?" Shankar asked.

"No."

"Okay, great. This is chicken," he said, handing over a small box. "You eat chicken, right?"

"Yes, why not? If I have a choice I eat chicken only," I said.

"Why is it like this?" I asked as I opened the box. I could have chosen little nicer words.

"This is actually ground beef, not chicken. You eat beef, right?" Shankar asked me with a smile.

"No," I said in a loud voice.

"Haha, don't worry, I was just joking. This is ground turkey, it tastes just like fried chicken. You should try everything," Shankar said.

Anything fried was okay with me. Even if he had given beef or pork, I would have tried it. I was too full of Indian shyness to say no. I belong to that half of Indians who don't say no come what may and get screwed by the other half until they learn to say no.

Shankar waved to Kalyan who was on phone and asked me, "Would you like to have some wine?"

"Actually Kalyan said we'll go out to pick dinner. I'll join you sometime later," I said.

"Okay, no problem. Bye," he said, and left.

I didn't have problem trying wine, though I didn't know how it tasted, but I didn't want to blend jetlag with alcohol.

Finally Kalyan got off the phone and asked me, "Shall we order curries from Neetu's?"

"Yes." Neetu's must be the Indian restaurant he mentioned earlier. It didn't matter, I was hungry.

"Do you eat non-veg?" Kalyan asked me.

"Yes."

"Do you eat fish?"

"Yes."

"Neetu's is famous for Indian fish curry. Let's order one fish curry and one chicken biryani. We'll start as soon as we place the order. It takes about fifteen minutes to reach there, and by then, our order should be ready."

"Okay," I said and reminded Kalyan about putting rice in the cooker. I wanted it to be ready by the time we came back. I didn't want my dinner to get delayed.

"Oh yeah, we need white rice for fish curry and yogurt," he said.

"For fish curry and what?" I asked.

"Yogurt. Yogurt is curd," he said, with a smile.

"Oh, okay."

Kalyan placed the order, and said, "Get ready, we'll leave now."

He should be the one to get ready. I didn't know since how many days he was wearing the same pajamas and hadn't combed his hair.

"Don't we have to lock the door?" I asked as we stepped out of the apartment.

"No, generally I don't, and nothing happens," Kalyan said carelessly.

Things don't happen on a daily basis. But when they happen, the loss will be irrecoverable and what's the point in being careful after that? What's wrong in being cautious? I hoped I didn't lose anything from my bags. I spent a lot on shopping.

On our way to Neetu's, Kalyan said, "I was talking to a friend about the exam I need to take next month. He was giving me some tips. Already I have failed once, and I cannot afford to fail again."

I was right; it was not a girl. But passing the exam was not about taking tips over the phone. He needed to spend some time to study, which I didn't see him doing.

"Actually I am lucky that I can work here as a pharmacist by clearing this exam. There is a new rule that's coming up. Pharmacy graduates from other countries need to do a mandatory course in the US. They will not be able to work by just clearing the exam in future," he added.

Probably America had enough pharmacists already and it was time for them to change the regulations in order to stop the inflow. Our drive to Neetu's was dedicated to discussing on "Indian Pharmacists in the US: Past, Present and Future."

Pulling the car into the parking lot, Kalyan said, "Here we go. This is the great Neetu's. This is one of the best places in

Austin, but don't compare the food with Indian restaurants in India."

There was a separate counter for pick-up orders, the "to-go" orders as they called in the US. This time the Indian girl at the counter had a bright smile on her face.

Handing over the parcel to me as we walked out, Kalyan asked, "Jay, do you drink?"

"Yes."

"What is your favorite?"

"I am not really big on drinking. I drink pretty much everything. I don't have a preference. And you?"

"No," he said.

"No smoking and no drinking, all good habits," I said.

"Nothing like that. During my undergraduate days, I was somewhat interested but didn't have the courage to try. Now I don't even feel like trying," he said.

"Yeah, that's the time when people get into these habits. What about Murthy?" I asked. I wanted to know if I had company in the house without looking for Shankar all the time.

"Murthy drinks, but he doesn't smoke regularly. You don't want to be around him when he drinks. People don't expect it from Murthy but he is a nuisance when he drinks."

"Oh really?"

"Yeah. Good time pass but sometimes it is irritating," he said.

The spicy aroma of the food I was holding was so tempting that I couldn't wait to go home and devour it.

Kalyan picked up the bathroom mats left outside as we entered the apartment.

"What happened to them?" I asked.

"Actually you need to let the shower curtain inside the tub when you take shower. You must have kept it outside. Water dripped out of the tub and these things got wet," he said, carrying the mats inside.

I understood the situation completely. "Oh sorry," I said.

"Don't worry, I dried the bathroom floor and the mats are also dry now. That's the advantage with Texas weather."

By the time I used the restroom for a couple of minutes and came out, Kalyan was on phone again. I would be waiting forever if I waited for him to have dinner together.

"Shall we have dinner?" I asked.

"You carry on. Generally I have late dinner and study all night."

So that was the reason behind his eternal straight-from-bed look.

I started with chicken biryani, then biryani rice with fish gravy, and then white rice with fish curry, and then white rice with fish gravy and ground turkey, and finally white rice with curd, sorry yogurt. After such a large dinner, a dessert would have been perfect. The food from Neetu's was okay but not so great. Kalyan must not have visited India in a while and got used to places like Neetu's and started liking them out of compulsion.

As soon as I had the dinner, I rushed to Shankar's apartment. I never enjoyed the gap between the meal and a smoke. Surprisingly, the door was closed probably because it was getting dark. At 9:00 p.m. there was still some daylight. If fall was like this, will the sun ever set in summer in Texas?

I knocked on the door and heard a loud voice from inside, "Come in."

It was not Shankar's voice. I saw a new face inside as I opened the door.

"Hi," the guy watching TV greeted me.

"Hi, I am Jay. Where is Shankar?" I asked.

"Nice meeting you. My name is Dinesh. Come sit, I guess Shankar is in restroom," he extended his hand.

I sat there silently while Dinesh was glued to the cartoon show running on the TV. Cartoon at this age?

"Jay, had your dinner?" Shankar asked, almost screamed, as he came out of the restroom, breaking the awkward silence between Dinesh and me.

"Let's go sit outside," he suggested.

"What does Dinesh do?" I asked casually as we stepped out.

"He is also a chef like me. We completed our undergraduate program from the same college in India and worked for the same restaurant chain in Singapore and Mumbai. And then the employer sponsored our L1."

"What's L1?"

"L1 is also a working visa but works differently in terms of sponsorship compared to H1B. Only companies can apply for this visa for their employees to relocate them from offices in other parts of the world to the US."

"Oh, I didn't know about that," I said.

"There are several other visas also. The same kind of visa to the US applies differently to different countries. It's a complicated topic," Shankar said.

"For how many years you get this L1 visa?" I asked.

"It depends on how many years the company applies for. We came here for one year, we have six more months."

Shankar paused for a second to take a puff and asked, "How come you haven't heard about it? IT companies frequently send people here from India on L1 visa. It's like a bonus Indian IT companies offer to their employees."

"Oh, I don't know much about IT."

"You should know about IT. Who knows you might want to get into it in future? I heard many interesting stories about people getting into software jobs. Even some of my engineering friends suggested it to me. But I said no, I love my job. I know a retired military person who learnt some IT course and came to the US and is working now as a software engineer. He is from your state only, Andhra Pradesh," Shankar said.

Now Shankar has become close enough to joke on my state.

"Really?" I asked.

"Yeah, man."

"How is it like to be a chef in this country?" I asked very superficially to divert the topic from IT. Somehow I preferred a safe distance from technology.

"Huge opportunity and decent pay. This job is little different from others. People cannot become chefs just like that, like software engineers. It's a pain to stand in the kitchen for such a long time without having a passion for the job, leave alone skillful cooking."

What he said made perfect sense to me. I tried cooking couple of times in India, not easy. Anyone can make something to eat, but making something that everybody appreciates is not easy. And doing it every day as a job is even more challenging.

"Can you apply for visa extension?" I asked.

"Yes, of course. Even my company will be willing to do that. But I am not interested. In fact, Dinesh is planning to stay here. I like it here too, but my mother lives alone in India. It's my dream to start my own restaurant in Chennai. The city has grown cosmopolitan enough now to patronize a variety of cuisines from across the world. I can live in my own house with my mom and run my own restaurant."

"Great."

People like Shankar fall in a particular line of profession at an early age either according to their plan, or according to their elders' plan, or according to God's plan, or they are lucky to have found their passion in life at an early age, and it works out perfectly well for them. They escape dividing their energy and time on several things in life and dividing success also in the process. I wonder how they can ignore so many things happening in the world around them and be happy within their boundaries. It's not easy to have a mind to focus on one thing and a heart to be content with that.

"By the way, did you try the turkey?" Shankar asked.

"Yeah. It was good."

"I thought of not telling you that its ground turkey and was going to let you figure it out. But some people are very particular about their food choices, especially non-vegetarian food. So I didn't take a chance," he said.

"I don't mind trying new things. Turkey is a little hard to eat," I said.

"Yeah, it is, compared to chicken. To me, chicken is chicken. We can try turkey once in a while but cannot eat frequently like we eat chicken," Shankar, the chef, explained his take on chicken versus turkey.

"Let's have one more cigarette and go." Shankar pulled two cigarettes from the pack without even waiting for my answer.

We had one more smoke and walked toward our apartments. "Good night, Jay. I'll see you tomorrow evening again," Shankar said. Looking at the confused expression on my face, he added, "Generally I leave early for work, and I know you'll not wake up early until you get over the jetlag."

"Yeah. Good night. See you tomorrow evening," I said.

I entered our apartment and saw Kalyan still on phone. One day the solid matter between his ears will liquefy and flow out making a hollow barrel.

It was around 10 and I had to wait for Kalyan to finish his call to confirm where to sleep. I glanced through the books scattered over the laptop table for a couple of minutes, and when I couldn't control my sleep anymore, I asked in a low voice, "Kalyan, where can I sleep?"

"Bedroom. Both you and Murthy can sleep inside. I generally sleep in the hall," he said. I kind of knew his answer but wanted to confirm again. After all, I was a guest.

Kalyan saw me pulling the blanket from my bag, he said, "Wait I'll give you a comforter."

Comforter? I just followed him into the bedroom. He pulled out a thick blanket, a stuffed one, from the closet and handed it to me. Weather in Texas was not that cold but the cold ambience they created in the bedroom would require a comforter.

Kalyan set the AC in the room, and said, "Good night." He was on phone all through. I pitied the person talking to him on the other side. Kalyan being on phone most of the time was none of my business but somehow it was bothering me.

Lying on the bed, for a few moments I thought about my college visit the next day. I thought about my mom, dad, and sister for some time. Whether coming to the US was a right thing to do was a constant thought that didn't stop haunting me even after landing in the country. While random thoughts jumped from one to another, I didn't realize when I fell asleep.

12

I woke up from sleep with a jolt, feeling breathless.

I saw another guy on the bed, wrapped in a comforter like an Egyptian mummy. I walked into the hall and saw Kalyan sleeping there, also wrapped in a comforter. I would die of suffocation if I did that. To my surprise, the main door was not locked. Was it so safe in Austin that these guys left the door unlocked even during the night or was it because Kalyan was too tired to get up from his bed to lock the door after his phone conversations?

The morning sunshine was so bright that I closed the door instantly. The rays could have penetrated Kalyan's comforter and woken him up.

I went into the kitchen to make some coffee but not a single cup was in the cupboards. All of them were in the sink. When it came to morning coffee, nothing mattered to me. I washed a cup from the sink and used the microwave to make coffee without giving a damn about Kalyan's sleep. Poor guy, not sure when he had slept last night after taking tips from his friend over phone, he didn't move a bit in spite of all the noise.

I picked the cigarette packet and lighter and stepped out to start my day with fresh coffee and smoke. Good that I was the only smoker in the house, otherwise every time I wanted to smoke, I would have had to spend a few minutes searching for the lighter. At 9 in the morning it was piercingly hot. Texas was hotter and drier in August than India in its peak summer.

When I set out from India, I couldn't wait to visit my college, but I decided to go to my college a day later, on Friday, hoping to catch people in a happy mood. After spending some time in the morning sunshine, I went into the apartment to see both the pharmacists still sleeping.

I got ready to go out and have a look at the mall nearby. On the way, I saw a huge building on my left, with a prominent lettering, LA Fitness. I remembered the name from the papers on the laptop table. Such a huge building for gym? In Hyderabad that space would have lodged at least fifty software training institutes.

I checked out stuff in almost every outlet in the mall. I liked the fact that, except the sales girls, I could touch and feel anything in the shops. The sales reps didn't hound me whether I wanted their opinion or not. They just asked me to let them know if I needed any help and gave me the freedom to look around. They smiled when I left the store though I didn't buy anything. In India, first of all big malls where self-shopping was possible were not common. And in stores where it was possible, sales reps had the annoying habit of not leaving customers alone. If I didn't buy anything from their shops, they'll make sure to make me feel guilty with their frowns. They would have even charged entry fees if they could.

Every girl I saw in the mall was more attractive than most Indian heroines. Hot weather added to their beauty, not the weather as such but their clothing forced by hot weather. Even the skimpiest dress in India would cover more skin than the average girl's dress in Austin but the big difference lied in how they carried their outfits effortlessly without appearing awkward. They could probably stand naked and still not provoke people, unlike some girls from my college in India who could fully cover themselves and still draw the attention with their false shyness and sneaky looks.

It was very rare that I went for shopping and didn't buy anything. In spite of my intention of just passing time, I was tempted by the range of colors, designs, and touch and feel of the clothes. After window shopping for about an hour, I started exploring the options in the food court. I hadn't come out of the aversion toward non-Indian food that I had developed in the flight. I glanced through all the options there to see if I could find anything close to Indian palate and zeroed in on pizza, which was almost a universal food. I ordered a slice each of pepperoni and barbecue chicken, based on how they looked and a cold drink, no they call it soda in the US. After lunch, I went back to the apartment without covering the other stores. I wanted to show my face to Murthy before he left for work again.

By the time I went back to the apartment Kalyan was awake but was still in bed. Playing with his phone he was talking to Murthy. Dressed in khaki short and a navy blue tee, with neatly combed hair and a clean shave, Murthy stood in the kitchen preparing something. He looked neat unlike Kalyan. Going by the way he cut vegetables, he seemed systematic. On seeing me, he smiled politely without showing any unwanted euphoria.

After exchanging the initial pleasantries, he asked, "When does your college start?"

"I still have time. I have about fifteen days. I came early so that I could get acquainted with the place before the program actually begins."

"Okay, what course are you joining?" Murthy asked.

"MBA in international trade"

"Great, let me know if you need any help. I can give you a ride if you want to go somewhere. You can ask Kalyan also when I am not available. When are you planning to go to college?"

"Tomorrow."

"I have a night shift today and will come back from work tomorrow morning. I can drop you at the college as soon as I reach home. Where is the college, by the way?" Murthy asked.

After so much correspondence with the college, I had the address memorized. I recited it instantly.

"Okay. I don't have an idea about that place. Search on the internet if you have options to come back from college by public transit. Not many places are connected well here by trains and buses. It's not easy in Austin without a car," he said. "But that's fine for now; we'll figure out something," he quickly added, before my anxiousness about having a car erupted.

Murthy kept cutting vegetables throughout the conversation but he tried to make me comfortable. He seemed soft-spoken and helpful. Kalyan was friendly with whom I could have a casual conversation but he was more into his own world.

"I am preparing potato and eggs; we'll have lunch in a few," Murthy said.

"I already had my lunch," I said, a little embarrassed.

"Where?"

"I woke up long back. You both were still sleeping so I thought I would take a walk to the mall. I had pizza there."

"Okay, good, you already started exploring the place. Many people have a problem getting used to food here. How was it?" Murthy asked.

"Good. I had a slice of pepperoni and a slice of chicken barbecue. Both are good."

"Jay, do you know that pepperoni contains pork and beef?" Kalyan said, taking a break from his phone.

"Oh no. I didn't know that. And it didn't look like that also," I said, turning to him.

"Yeah it looks good I know, and tastes good also," Kalyan said.

"In fact, I liked pepperoni better than chicken," I said.

"Yeah, I know. I used to like pepperoni a lot. But after knowing what it is made of, I couldn't eat anymore. Try crepes next time, you'll enjoy. They taste similar to the rolls we eat in India, little more stuffed," Kalyan said.

Creeps? The name sounded weird but I didn't show my ignorance. Why should I when I have Google? And it reminded me that I needed to get the password for the laptop.

"Can I use that laptop?" I asked, looking at both of them.

"Of course. It's pretty much there all the time. I use it just once a day to check my emails that's all," Murthy responded. Sounded like that was his laptop.

"Can I have the password?"

"It doesn't have a password," Murthy said, with a grin on his face as if protecting it with a password was a waste of time. "But sometimes suddenly it shows a blue screen. You don't have to worry; just force shut down and start again. Be careful if you are working on some document, keep saving it frequently. When you get a blue screen, you lose whatever content you haven't saved."

"Okay, I just need it for browsing."

I sneaked to the laptop table through the gap between Kalyan's bed sheets and the wall. There was an email from the university asking me if I needed any help after I land in Austin, another one from the university Indian association to register for membership, and a few emails from friends wishing me good luck.

When I Googled, I realized it was not creep but crepe, a French cuisine. The picture looked like rolls, like Kalyan had said. I used to love chicken rolls at roadside stalls in India. I guess I had a replacement for them in the US.

I browsed through the Indian news websites eagerly as if India was missing me and people there were waiting for my suggestions to run the country. Actually I was already missing my family and friends. By the time I came to the US, I knew fairly well about America to endure any culture shock but little strangeness of a new place was there.

I replied to my friends' emails and closed the laptop. I didn't feel comfortable browsing so openly, not that I wanted to watch porn but I wouldn't even read a newspaper when I become conscious about people around.

I felt sleepy, pizza effect I guess. I flipped through the pages of a book I bought at Hyderabad airport, *The World is Flat* by Thomas Friedman, which didn't help either. Probably there is no big sedative in the world than reading a book. I wanted to control my sleep somehow and overcome the jetlag.

Looking at the Marlboro Lights packet I had placed on the laptop table, Murthy asked me, "Do you smoke?"

As if it was a crime. Or did I feel like that because I had the guilt of being a smoker somewhere in me? Whatever it was, I turned back, and said unapologetically, "Yeah, I smoke. I enjoy smoking."

"I smoke too once in a while, when I drink," Murthy said.

I was relieved. The guy who looked reckless on the outside doesn't smoke and drink and the guy who looked systematic smokes and drinks, interesting.

"Kalyan is a nice guy. He doesn't drink and he doesn't smoke," I tried to wean Kalyan from his phone.

"Nothing like that, Jay," Kalyan said, without taking his eyes off the phone.

I wanted to ask Kalyan what the hell he did on his phone all the time, but it was too early. Did he watch porn? No, it couldn't be porn for such a long time, otherwise he would have come several times in his pajamas by then.

"What can I do to pass time without sleeping in the afternoon? What are the options here?" I asked both of them.

"Internet," Kalyan said.

"I have some movies on my hard drive if you are interested. Or you can watch a movie online," Murthy said.

Movies are the next best sedatives to books. Looking at my not-so-enthusiastic face, Murthy said, "You have Barnes & Noble in the mall you visited in the morning. You need to walk all the way to the end; it's not visible from outside."

"What is that?" I asked. This time I didn't control my curiosity until I Googled it.

"Book shop. It's a huge book shop. You can sit there and read books for however much time you want. You can take the laptop and browse there, you have free wi-fi. There is Starbucks inside," Murthy said.

Sounded almost like an ad for Barnes & Noble. I knew Starbucks but what the hell was wi-fi? Whatever, to use that, Murthy said I needed a laptop which I was not ready to carry. So I ignored it for the time being.

I walked all the way to the mall again and reached Barnes & Noble—such a huge setup with such a huge parking lot for just a bookshop! The magnitude itself was a huge selling point for booklovers.

I hadn't felt happy about being a booklover among my outgoing friends during my undergraduate college days, which put a break to my reading habit. Those were the days when talking bullshit dominated talking book-shit. Luckily, the pseudo-heroism attached to "outgoing" didn't impress me later, and I started moving closer to books and away from jerks.

Inside Barnes & Noble was a gigantic space filled with thousands of books, clearly segregated and labeled by genres with customers buzzing around and assistants checking on them once in a while if they needed any help, and an in-house coffee shop with a convenient sitting place. I couldn't have asked for more. Why don't such places exist in India where shopping for books has never been an interesting activity.

I pretty much covered every nook and corner of the shop and picked *The Zahir* by Paulo Coelho, hoping that it would be as magical as *The Alchemist*. I handed the book to the beautiful white girl at the billing counter as my turn came.

"Do you have Barnes & Noble membership, sir?" she asked me.

"No."

"Would you like to have one? It is just $25 for a year and you get discounts on every purchase," she asked.

"Yes."

"Can I get your name, address, and phone number, sir?"

Except name, I didn't have any other detail she asked for. "I came to America as a student just yesterday. Can I give my temporary address? And I don't have a phone number yet."

She looked puzzled. It must be the first time in her life that she had encountered someone coming to Barnes & Noble a day after he landed in their country.

"I am sorry, sir. We need some id proof," she said hesitantly.

"Will my passport work?"

"Yeah, sure."

"But I don't have it right now. I'll take the membership in my next visit."

"Do you want to still get the book, sir?"

"Yes." I was in a hurry to start my new book, though I hadn't completed the one I was already reading.

"Thank you, sir. See you again," the girl said, with a big smile.

She was so cordial that any guy listening to her in India would have misconceived that she had fallen in love with him and really wanted to see him again and again. Make no mistake, from the flight experience and the stay of almost twenty-four hours in the country, I had realized that everybody there talked like that. People were naturally sweet, some more and some a little less.

I walked to Starbucks located on the other side of the billing counter for my afternoon dose of caffeine. I stood there checking the pastries and other stuff on display.

"Sir, are you in the line?" I heard a male voice from behind.

"No, you carry on," I told him, with a smile. I was not used to smiling for no reason in India. In America, people looked like they needed a reason not to smile.

Since I was used to tea in the afternoon, I ordered the only available option, TazoChai tea latte, and sat there browsing through the book I just bought. My eyes quickly wandered around the shop every time I lifted my head for a quick sip. My attention was drawn to the girl sitting diagonal to me a couple of tables away showing the side of her leg crossed on the other, through the slit of her long skirt that was so high that it could go no further up. Ogling has never been an interesting pastime for me. I don't know how girls felt but I get embarrassed on their behalf when boys stare at them. Probably guys were not so deprived in the US; I didn't see much staring there. Why did I look at her then? So was that slit meant for ventilation?

13

Murthy gave me a ride for my first visit to college as soon as he came back from work in the morning. His driving was as pleasant as his manners. My heart started beating faster as I entered into the campus, though it was just a casual visit. Probably it got used to that pattern from childhood—whenever I entered the premises of an academic institution my heart automatically worked faster.

I studied in the best of the colleges in India but none of them had a campus as picturesque as my new college—beautiful lawns dotted with splashing fountains, beauty amplified by bright sunshine, curvy roads that cut through the lawns, red and white flags alternately erected throughout the campus. I had visited the college website so many times that I could recognize some of the splendid buildings lined on either side as we drove in.

"Thank you," I said to Murthy stepping out of the car at the administrative building.

"No problem. How will you come back?" he asked.

"I'll take a cab. I couldn't figure out the bus connectivity online," I said

"Okay, but it might cost you a lot. Call Kalyan otherwise, he'll come and pick you up," he suggested.

"That's okay for a day," I said.

"Do you have money?" he asked.

"Yeah, I have enough," I said.

"Okay then, all the best," Murthy said. I felt like a kid

dropped at school by parents as he drove away.

The file I got from India looked a little big and odd in my hand compared to the backpacks generally students carried. I didn't see many students on the campus since it was a semester break. A few Indian students I spotted stood out prominently with their faces greasy and bellies protruding through tight tees. These guys should either work their asses off in the gym or wear clothes that conveniently covered their pot bellies. Other students looked either fit or chose clothes that fitted them.

I pulled the letter from my file that I received from the college with information about who I should look for when I visit the college. While walking toward the Business Management building, I thought about how best I could put forward my case to our course coordinator to obtain a fellowship, internship, teaching assistantship, campus job, or any damn opportunity to earn some money along with my course work.

After walking for about ten minutes and taking a few detours, I reached the office of our course coordinator—the name plate read Olivia Rosales. I walked up to the entrance and saw Olivia scribbling something. She raised her head and saw me when I was about to knock.

"Hello, my name is Jay, Jayawardhan," I said.

"Oh yeah, *Jeeayaawardaan*. Please come in. I am sorry. Did I pronounce your name right?" Olivia asked as I walked into her room.

I had to struggle to smile after hearing her pronounce my name.

"Yes, of course. You can call me Jay, like the letter J," I said, making it easier for her to remember and pronounce my name, and saving it from being murdered in future.

"Okay, Jay. I was thinking about you yesterday. How was your trip?"

"Yeah, it was great."

"Did you find accommodation?"

"Not yet. I am staying at a friend's place temporarily."

"Okay, is it close by?"

"It's some ten miles from here."

"Oh that's little far if you don't have a car. Many students live in the apartments across the road from the campus front gate. Let me talk to the guys in our department and see if they can find something for you."

"Sure, thanks Olivia."

"No problem."

Turning back in her chair Olivia collected the printout she gave while talking to me. Handing it over to me, she said, "You program starts on September third. Here is the list of the first semester courses and suggested books. I'll email this info to all the students anyway."

"Thank you." After a pause, I said, "Olivia, I was not awarded any scholarship or fee waiver. Can I apply for some on-campus jobs?"

"Oh you don't have a scholarship? I didn't realize that. Right now I am not aware of any opportunity in our department. I'll reach out to the professors and let you know. But let me warn you in advance, Jay, this is a structured program. You cannot pick and choose courses like in other master's programs. Apart from the classes, you'll have a lot of group assignments and homework that'll keep you really busy. I am not sure if you'll get time to work."

My hopes sank like the Titanic after hearing those beautiful words of reality from her.

"Let me see if I can find something for you," she continued. "Depending on your class schedule you'll have to figure out the timings with the professor offering you the job. Maybe a job in the computer room or library will be good for you so that you can work after your classes. They operate long hours."

A flicker of hope again.

"This is your email id right?" she asked, reading it out.

"Yeah, that's right. Do you want me to check with you sometime next week?" I asked.

"I'll update you. You are on my priority list now. I know how difficult it is to pursue master's without financial assistance. But I can't promise anything right now. There is huge competition out there for campus jobs."

"I understand that, Olivia. Thank you."

"I am not sure if you know this. You can apply for a fee waiver from the second semester. It'll be decided based on your performance in the first semester and the preference would be given to the students who don't have any financial assistance. Couple of students every year grab the opportunity. Instead of dividing your time, you can focus on your course work now," Olivia said.

Who will promise fee waiver for the next semester in spite of all my efforts during this semester?

On the whole, the situation looked tough but hopeful. I was a bit relaxed and started looking around in Olivia's office. It was a small room, very neatly maintained with her family pictures in the background. My eyes diverted to the openings between her tight shirt buttons. As if people would miss the show, she wore a red bra under a white shirt. When she was getting ready for work in the morning, was she not aware of what she showed to the public? The red lipstick on her Starbucks coffee cup that matched her bra was even more prominent. Women carrying lipstick in their hand bags is totally justified. They need to maintain a constant redness on the lips in spite of the coffee cups, water bottles, spoons and forks, and their boyfriends eating their lipstick every now and then. Not an easy job.

Since I didn't have anything left to talk, I stood up, and said, "Bye, Olivia. I'll wait for your email."

Olivia got out of her chair, stepped aside, and extending her hand, she said, "Bye, Jay. Welcome to Austin and I hope you'll like this place. Make yourself comfortable first. You have some time to worry about the program."

Shorter than me by a couple of inches, dressed in black formal pants, black peep-toe shoes, white shirt with the open top button, silky hair tied at the top of her head, big silver earrings, prominent multi-colored bangles on her right hand and a sports watch on her left hand, conspicuous folds on her face when she smiled, small eyes and an aquiline nose, typical Spanish complexion that looked like a mix of white like an American and brown like an Indian with a tinge of gold— impressive grooming though she didn't have captivating features.

It was almost lunch time by the time my meeting with Olivia ended. I went to the café in the student building to take a look at the options—Einstein Bros Bagles, Subway, Starbucks, Café Buffet, Taco Bell, Riverside Pizza, and few others.

For a few minutes, I stood there looking at the outlets lined in semi-circular shape, which together with the semi-circular sitting place with neatly arranged circular white tables, and exactly three red chairs at each table, made the whole café a circle. Red looked like the color of the campus.

I could see no Indian in the café. Was there any other place in the campus where Indian food was available?

Finally I chose to try the food with the longest queue, Subway—choice of bread, length of bread, choice of ingredients, and choice of sauces, very simple. American food is customizable to the core and hence fresh and tasteless, unlike the flavored, spicy, and yummy Indian food which cannot be prepared so quickly.

After lunch, I searched my pockets for the cigarette packet which I had forgotten to bring. Given the stringent regulations in the US, the guys working in the college café couldn't be expected to sell cigarettes secretly like in India. It was funny that I saw students smoking but they didn't sell cigarettes on the campus. Carrying our own cigarettes was allowed. It was like governments allowing manufacturing, advertising, and selling of cigarettes and running awareness campaigns worth millions of dollars in parallel.

I walked through the lawn from one building to another toward the exit gate. Texas might not record a temperature higher than that of Indian summer, but the heat was definitely more intense like hundreds of ants biting at the same time on my exposed skin.

I ended my first visit to college with a Frappuccino from the campus Starbucks.

***

September 3, 2007.

Dressed in a blue formal suit with a folder in hand, this time I carried a smaller one, I arrived on the campus on the first day of the program.

I was already waiting to get home to get into casuals. At least on the first day I wanted to stick to the norms, one of which was wearing a formal suit. What if I was asked to introduce myself to a group of professionally dressed students in a big auditorium? I didn't want to attract people's attention for not wearing a stupid suit.

Unlike my earlier visits, the campus buzzed with students that day. Formal suit was the etiquette only for management students I guess, others were dressed in all sorts of tees, trousers, sports shoes, and caps, with backpack as a common accessory.

I followed the directions Olivia had sent in the email to reach the place we were supposed to meet for continental breakfast. There she stood like a receptionist at a makeshift counter arranged near the breakfast area inviting the new students. She looked totally different that day in black skirt, black blazer, and a blue shirt inside, with no top button open and no peeping holes between the buttons. She had tied her hair with a hair stick with a prominent blue knob that matched with the color of her shirt. Her red lipstick and red nail polish were prominent against her black formals.

My earlier acquaintance with Olivia brought an automatic smile to my face as I approached her. After we greeted each other, she searched for my badge among the ones scattered on the table and handed it to me along with a red folder and a pen. "Here you go. Have breakfast and catch up with your classmates. We'll meet in the classroom G100 at 9:30. G100 is toward that side. You can see the direction board for classrooms when you take a right on that curve. G100 will be your classroom for the entire year, unless you have any special instructions," she said, pointing toward the classrooms building.

Olivia recited all the info in one go as if she crammed word by word like a school kid. Probably she had to do the same thing thirty times with all our classmates that morning. As I thanked her and walked toward the adjacent long table on which the breakfast items were neatly arranged, she called me back.

"Jay, I am still looking for your job. No luck so far. I'll let you know as soon as I have something for you," she said.

"Sure, thank you." That's exactly what I wanted to ask her before I walked from there.

"Did you find the accommodation close to college?"

"Not yet, Olivia. I didn't like the couple of apartments I visited earlier."

"Okay, check with your classmates who stay nearby."

"Yeah, I will."

"Alright, Jay. Good luck with your program."

"Thank you," I said, with a smile.

No proper accommodation, no fee waiver, no part-time job, and yet I was smiling, genuinely. Somehow, I stopped being desperate. The smile I acquired after landing in America started working from inside I guess.

Without getting into the queue, I took a quick look at the items arranged there in the name of continental breakfast— bread, bagels, croissants, butter, pastries, mixed fruit, coffee, and orange juice, I might have missed a couple of items. I got a croissant and coffee and found a quiet sitting place in the morning sunshine to enjoy my second breakfast.

I chose not to get into the greeting frenzy with anybody and everybody I saw there. If I hadn't done my MBA earlier, not being part of the high-energy group of people would have bothered me. But by then I was sufficiently self-assured to be myself.

I scrolled through the papers in the red folder that Olivia handed me—a small notebook and two stapled papers, one with the schedule for the day and the other with the weekly timetable for the semester and the list of professors. All those formalities were not new to me. I knew how management schools worked. I looked forward to the actual stuff. However, I reminded myself to be careful not to let my previous experience disengage me from the present.

While enjoying my croissant with coffee, I heard a loud male voice from my left, "Hey, good morning."

A short, round Indian guy with short hair and thick French beard was walking toward me. "Good morning," I said as he came close.

"Can I join you?" he asked, after he had already joined me.

"Sure." I moved a little to my right, showing my willingness for him to sit beside me, curiously thinking who he was.

"Hi, my name is Krish," he said in a fake American accent. His hand was ready for a handshake, dangling in the air as if he pulled it from nowhere like a magician.

I kept my breakfast plate aside, extending my hand, I said, "Hi, nice to meet you, Krish. I am Jay."

He shook my hand so hard that he shook my entire body, and he shook several times like how the premiers of the countries do on TV during state visits. He seemed to put into practice the theory that a robust handshake meant confidence.

"I believe you are in IT too," Krish said, looking at my red folder.

What the fuck information technology has to do with me?

"I meant international trade," he said, before my confusion took full shape.

"Yeah." Abbreviating just about anything has become a fad. Why would he come to me if he didn't know that I was part of his class?

For the next few minutes, we talked about where we were from in India. He was from my state but neither he nor I attempted to talk in our native language, it was kind of uncool to do so in America. The worst experience would be if he spoke in our native language in American accent. Since it was artificial, he couldn't maintain the same tempo throughout the conversation, very frequently he was falling back to Indian accent and coming back to the American accent. I wondered if all those efforts to fit in were necessary as soon as he entered the country without giving time for natural transformation.

"Alright, man, I'll see you in the class," Krish said, standing up. To my luck, he left me faster than I expected, giving me some time for myself before the class started.

"Alright, see you," I said.

One good thing about Krish was that he picked something to talk between the sentences I spoke without me having to worry about inventing something to roll the conversation.

When it was almost time for class, I walked toward the classroom building looking for G100 as directed by Olivia. I saw very few people walking alone. Most of them were in groups talking loudly as if they knew one another since childhood. I guess most of them were falling for their like-minded friends' efforts of mocking extroversion, following the popular belief that extroverts made excellent managers. Or were they naturally friendly and happy and excited? Whatever, I gave instant gratification a pass and walked to the class by myself.

14

Feeling a little conscious about the students already seated, I didn't get to feel the ambience as I entered the classroom. After I quietly went up the steps and took a seat in the second row from the top, I took a closer look at the brightly lit classroom that could accommodate double the size of our class, with semi-circular tiered seating and a huge green board.

Some of the students who were already seated were chatting with others sitting beside them and few others were looking into the red folder given to us that morning and the rest were doing nothing and looking nowhere. Krish sat opposite me and he was already into his work, bent toward the girl sitting next to him and talking to her making animated gestures.

The room was soon filled with my classmates. All the guys were dressed in black or grey formal suits and ties. In spite of all my efforts, I couldn't escape from being different with my blue suit. Somehow black is not a preferred color in India and that influenced my choice. The girls in the class, not many, were also dressed in formal coats and skirts or pants.

The clicking sound that resonated from the entrance of the classroom pulled my attention. A racy, saucy young woman, taller than me by at least a foot, with radiant eyes, tapering nose, and pony-tailed blonde hair, dressed in black suit, black shoes, and a red top under the formal coat that matched the folder in her hand, a perfect femme fatale entered the classroom with an upright but not stiff walk, a casual but not careless body language and a pretty but not provocative smile on her lips. With her height which gave her a kind of natural sensuousness, she would be the indisputable star of our class.

Almost everybody in the class got distracted to the sound she made as she walked in. Probably she asked for the shoes that made the loudest sound when she bought them. I glanced at her again when she settled down in the seat almost facing me. Her smile looked more like a facial feature than a facial expression. Hopefully, she would be able to maintain her beautiful smile as the course load increases.

At exactly 9:30, Olivia entered the classroom. After all, she was our course coordinator and she had to be on time to instill a sense of discipline in us. After she spoke some great things about the university in general and the MBA program in particular, she introduced herself. The job of a course coordinator sounded more on the administrative side, but Olivia was well educated with an MBA degree from an eminent Canadian university. She boasted as if she was born to be a course coordinator, which in a way was true. She created the same impression of genuine concern for every student in the class, fitting perfectly into her role like she fitted into her suit that day.

Formal introductions by the students followed Olivia's extempore. A total of thirty students in the class represented at least ten different countries across Europe, Africa, Asia and the Americas, and multiple majors and industry experiences. The sheer diversity of the class made me enthusiastically look forward to a great year ahead.

The class was then divided into six study groups of five students each on a lottery basis. Out of the five Indian students, three of us, the artificial Krish, a girl named Puja, and I fell into the same group. Puja looked decent with no major attractions or aberrations, and most importantly, no fake adaptation of the American slang. Apart from Krish, Puja, and me, Megan, a blonde from California who seemed quiet and reserved, and Amy, who looked like an Indian, Spanish, and American blended together were part of our group.

In the first round of introductions itself, Amy told us about herself, her schooling, all her odd jobs and regular jobs, her hobbies, her family, and her boyfriend who was as a Ph.D. student at a university in Dallas.

"So he will write all your assignments," Krish made a tongue-in-cheek comment that made Amy uncomfortable, which was evident from her half-smile and half-frown. She better get used to Krish's presence. She'll have to bear with him for at least one semester since students remained in the same study groups for a semester.

Megan looked reserved and Puja studious. The fact that she had a currently active professor boyfriend aside, Amy looked interesting. She seemed different from the other girls in the class—not slim, comfortable in her own skin, thick short hair tied back tightly projecting her broad forehead, big nose, bright golden skin color, voice like she always had a cold, joyful and ready to talk non-stop. Amy might hang on to her boyfriend at least during her MBA for obvious reasons but who cares. When did boyfriends stop girls from being interesting?

Within a couple of days, I fell into the typical routine of a management graduate. I started at 6 in the morning from Murthy's place, which became my permanent accommodation, and came back to home at around 7 in the evening, which included a couple of hours of commute by public transit. Apart from the class-work, we had homework and presentations for the following day.

The biggest motivation to continue to live with Murthy and Kalyan, though I could have saved substantial time by living near the college was my visit to check the apartments near college where mostly Indian students lived, through the references I got from Olivia.

I had never been to slums in India but after looking at the apartment, I thought slums wouldn't be that bad. It was cluttered with food, books, clothes, footwear and what not spread all over the place. The cigarette smoke inside was so pungent that even a smoker like me couldn't take it. I could have vomited if I visited the place immediately after I had eaten. Three people lived in a single bedroom apartment and they were looking for a fourth guy to reduce the burden of rent. I thought the first apartment was an aberration and went on to see the second one. Barring the cigarette smoke, the second apartment was as filthy as the first one.

Without financial aid, I couldn't afford the college dormitories or an apartment on my own but adjusting to those ghettos for the sake of being closer to college would be an everyday pain. Instead, spending a couple of hours on commute by sacrificing sleep seemed like a better idea to me.

I grew closer to Murthy in the short time I stayed at their place. He encouraged me to stay comfortably so as to not get distracted from studies and manage the commutation part. Especially after knowing about my date with the students' apartments near college, he was dead against me leaving their apartment.

I customized my bus ride to college and back to home to make good use of the time. I skimmed through Wall Street Journal during my morning commute which was a required read for our international economics class. I would be too exhausted to do anything productive during my commute back from college except ponder over the day that just ended. The best part of my trip was the layover time between two buses that I spent at Jack in the Box. I would get my breakfast there almost daily and in the evening, I would relax over Mocha Iced Coffee.

After reaching home, I would sit with Shankar for some time over his insipid tea and chain of cigarettes chatting over what happened at his work. Shankar was a chatterbox who wouldn't let me speak, and I didn't have a problem listening to his stories. That's probably why our friendship worked well.

Within one week of the start of the program, I got into such a frenetic schedule on weekdays that I started looking forward to weekends more than ever. I wondered how I used to work for six days a week in India. We had no issues with long weeks or long working hours. Probably slavery never went away from Indian blood though the British left us long back. People preferred submission and safety to risk and revolt any day.

Sometime during the second week, I went to Olivia and asked her not to worry about looking for a campus job for me in view of the attention the program demanded. That left me with pursuing a fee waiver from the second semester as the only way to redeem the money crunch.

Nearly one month into the program, I was totally occupied with academics. Within our study group, Amy and I formed a sort of sub-group. Sometimes I got a ride home from her as she stayed near my place. She didn't mind driving a couple of miles extra to accommodate me.

***

Theoretically, the right blend of individual aptitude and group savviness made successful managers, but practically, in the name of group collaboration management students fought for individual identity. Luckily in our study group, nobody except Krish was fond of putting individual above the group, and he didn't find enough support from anybody when he tried to do so.

As the semester progressed, the work load increased tremendously and our study group had to meet on the weekends also. On one of the several weekends we had met in the college to work on a group assignment, we took a short break after discussing passionately without making much progress. I didn't realize that Amy silently followed me until I stopped at the smoking zone.

"Accompanying a smoker during the break is not a good idea, Amy. They say passive smoking is more dangerous," I said, lighting a cigarette.

"I know. I wanted to have a talk with you. What happened to you? You used to be very active contributor in our group. Of late, you are calm and today I see the dullness clearly on your face. What's the matter?" she asked.

"You could see that on my face?" I asked surprisingly.

"Of course. I don't see you only in the class and group meetings. We commute together sometimes. I know you well."

"How can I deny when you are so confident?"

"What's the matter then?"

"It has nothing to do with the group. In fact, ours is the best study group in the class. Megan and Puja are studious and always willing to take extra load, and we have Krish to entertain us. You bring lot of practical insights from your work experience. And we have the bonus of getting a free opinion on our assignments from your boyfriend, haha."

"And we have a good presenter in you. The bonus part is not valid anymore. I am not on good terms with my boyfriend now."

"Sorry to hear about that."

"Oh, don't worry. That goes on between us. You didn't answer my question yet."

"I don't know if my worry will make any sense to you."

"Tell me anyway, I am your friend."

"I am disappointed with this program, Amy. This is my second graduate program in management, you know that. I opted for this program for its specialization. Except the international economics class, most of it seems like a repetition. I don't feel good spending so much money on a program that's not adding any value to me. I am also worried about the placements later. None of the Indians from earlier batches, you can think of them as non-American citizens, found a company that was willing to file for their work visa upon completing the program. Few of them who were super rich or sponsored by their companies went back to India. Among the guys who stayed here, some extended their studies into other majors, and most of them shifted to IT. I don't know how many of them paid full fees from their pockets like me. None of those consequences will be the desired outcome for me. What I am talking might not be relevant to all the Indians in our class since they have a fee waiver." I gave rather a long speech, but she asked for it.

"I guess you need to think with a clear mind, Jay. Don't you think you are mixing up too many things?"

"Let me simplify this for you. Basically three issues here— quality of the program, fees burden, and visa issues after completing the program."

"I really don't understand this visa stuff. Until now, I didn't even know that's an issue for you guys. As far as the quality of the program is concerned, we have just started. Generally in the first semester we have introductory courses, right?"

"I have seen the curriculum, Amy. There are some interesting courses in the coming semesters. It's not about the courses as such. I guess I am not happy with the learning experience on the whole. In a way, I wouldn't have bothered much about the money part if I was happy with the program."

"But are you serious that the MBA you did in India was better than this?" Amy asked astonishingly.

"Yes. Again there are all sorts of colleges and programs in India too," I said.

"That's interesting to know. So, what do you have in mind? I guess you are stuck anyway for a semester?" she said.

"I know. If I end up in a situation where I couldn't get into a management job after the program owing to the immigration compulsions, I am putting in so much time and money for nothing. By the time I complete this semester, I need to think through this more clearly. I am talking to people to understand my options," I said, throwing the cigarette butt.

"Okay, cheer up now. You have some time to figure out things. And who knows you might decide to continue in this program," Amy said.

"We'll see. Let's go, we took a long time. People will be waiting for us," I suggested.

"You carry on. I'll join in a bit," she said, walking toward the ladies room.

The group discussion went on for another hour. Amy offered to give me a ride back to home that day.

"What made you think that the quality of the program is not up to the mark?" she asked as soon as I got into the car. What I said during the break might have made her think about her choice of the program.

"Maybe I didn't put it in right words. Most of the stuff to me is repetitive." This time I tried a toned down version of what I said earlier in order not to disappoint her.

"No, you said something about the overall learning experience."

"There is no excitement in the program. What's being taught in the class, I guess we can learn on our own. They need to include more case studies, project work and guest lectures, throw more light on practical stuff like the way our international economics professor does."

"I guess it depends on the professor. When you talked about your unhappiness with the program, I felt really discouraged. I quit my job for this program and I am spending all my savings," Amy said.

"My situation is different than yours, Amy. I guess none of the things I said is relevant to you," I said.

After a brief silence, I tried to talk something different. "Leaving our program aside, I like the college education system here."

"Why do you say that?" she asked.

"Look at the average age of our class. It would be around thirty-five to forty. Look at the average age of Indians in the class, it'll not be more than twenty-five. Graduate education in India is taken up as a casual extension of undergraduate studies. People don't have to take the risks you guys take here, since funding in most cases is done by either government or parents. There is no encouragement for people to bring their work experience to college. Back to college is not a norm there."

"Is that the reason why so many Indians come here for master's?"

"Not at all. For most of us, master's is a legal and easy entry into America. It's easy to get a student visa since the universities here need money. Being a student here has advantages in the immigration process also. It's a win-win for both."

"That's a fine observation, but isn't it costly for you guys?"

"Yes and no. Most of the Indian students drift to cheaper colleges as soon as they land here. They work outside and make up for part of their expenses. Even if they don't work part-time, even if they have college debt by the time they pass out of college, it works out well for them financially in the long run, compared to staying in India."

"College debt is a big mess in this country. It runs into

billions of dollars; not millions, billions," Amy said, pulling the car into our parking lot.

"I know. At least you guys have equal opportunity in the job market. You'll not be pulled back because of visa issues," I said.

"Like I said earlier, that's a new dimension that I came to know from you today. Think about your options with a cool mind. You need to get good grades in this semester in case you choose to continue in this program, so don't lose your focus. That's all I can say," Amy said.

"Yeah, I know. Bye, Amy. Thanks for the ride."

"No problem."

No problem? I didn't enjoy the negative vibe the expression carried but I got used to it anyway. I started equating it with "you're welcome."

15

October 26, 2007: With the group presentation in the international economics class, I formally completed half-semester.

By then the euphoria of MBA in the US evaporated and my hopes for a successful management career in America almost hit a wall. I came to a firm assessment that the current MBA program could jeopardize both my short-term financial situation and long-term career prospects.

For that one night, I chose to completely switch off my brain from the disillusionment with the program and be part of the group dinner. Krish had proposed at the beginning of that week that our study group should go out for dinner on the weekend to celebrate the completion of mid-term evaluations. That was the first sensible idea that had come from him, and the group readily agreed. Curiously, the two non-Indians in the group suggested an Indian restaurant while Krish suggested an Italian place. Not sure if he really liked Italian or wanted to show off his high-class taste. For Puja and me, anything other than what Krish suggested was okay and we agreed on the Indian place.

Amy offered to give me a ride to and back from the restaurant.

"Hello, Jay. Wow, I like the perfume. What is it?" Amy asked, inhaling strongly as soon as I stepped into her car.

"Thanks, Amy. I don't remember exactly," I said.

"Do you have so many in your collection?"

"Not me, my roommates have."

Amy laughed, and said, "You don't have to be so honest, Jay."

"It's easy to be honest," I said.

"It's both easy and difficult," she said.

"It's easy on the whole. Going through the difficulty of being honest is easy compared to the difficulties involved in not being honest," I said.

"Haha. You are right but you could have said it in a simpler way," she said.

Amy looked stunning that night in her black sleeveless dress. When I got into the car, she took her matching black leather clutch from the seat to make way for me. She stretched to put it in the back seat, coming closer to me. I liked her musky smell, but didn't say it. I didn't want to sound like I was reciprocating the compliment as a formality.

As we drove to the restaurant, Amy asked, "Do you have a girlfriend, Jay?"

I was surprised by her question that came from nowhere. I guess she customized the topic of our discussion to suit the occasion. Usually she would ask me about some article in the Wall Street Journal.

"No."

"Did you have a girlfriend?"

"No."

"Didn't you ever have a girlfriend?"

"No," I said a little hesitantly, because I hadn't come to terms with the fact that Jhansi's part in my life was over.

"How old are you, Jay?"

"I am 26."

"That's unthinkable here, not having a girlfriend in 26 years of life," Amy said. "I had an Indian friend in college. I was surprised to hear about the arranged marriage system you guys have. Is it true that people get married according their parents' choice?"

India is like an animal in the zoo for these guys. Everything about India is a surprise.

"Things are changing fast in India, Amy. Love marriages are on the rise and divorces are also on the rise. Celebrities are into live-in relationships and people are not making a big deal of it. Very soon, ordinary people will follow the trend. We are catching up with the western world fast; it's just a matter of time. But most marriages are still arranged in India."

"How is it possible? I mean, how does that work? It amazes me."

Did she say that the arranged marriage system amazes her instead of saying it nauseates her?

"It has been working like that since ages. Marriage system in India is very complicated. Parents have a big role in shaping the life of their children and that includes marriage also," I said, without going deep into the topic.

"I am in a relationship with my boyfriend for the last three years. I am still not confident about taking the next big step," she said.

"That's the point here. In arranged marriages, people get into the relationship with a clean slate and minimal expectations. They work it out as they live together. Love marriages start with huge expectations that an institution like marriage cannot sustain. Honestly, in Indian conditions, there is not much difference between love marriages and arranged marriages, both happen with little or no understanding between the boy and the girl. In a love marriage, the boy and the girl make the choice with almost no information, and in an arranged marriage, parents choose the partner for their children with some information. Success in both the cases is a matter of chance. At least in arranged marriages, the boy and the girl are aware that they don't know each other before marriage and are prepared to accommodate each other."

"So you are cool with arranged marriages?"

"Haha. No. I am a management student, Amy. I am arguing both the sides."

"Haha. Good one. That was a good presentation in the international economics class today. You handled the questions very well," she said.

"Thank you."

Hearing the GPS say that we had reached the destination, Amy slowed down the car and bent forward to find the restaurant. GPS is such an amazing tool especially for people with poor topographic sense like me. We don't have to use our brain while driving.

"Yeah, this is the place. Let's try to find a parking spot. It's difficult on Friday nights. If not, there's paid parking behind the restaurant," Amy murmured as she scanned the streets around the restaurant for a parking place.

She parked the car a little far and as we walked toward the restaurant, Amy called up Megan to check if they were already in. Puja and Krish were also riding with Megan since all of them lived near the college.

Friday nights in downtowns showcase America at its best—busy streets, colorful lights, and jubilant people. I guess in a week only Friday is God's creation and the rest of the days are man-made. People wouldn't have half that brightness on their faces on week days.

"They started a couple of minutes back. It might take another ten minutes for them to reach here. Should we wait outside? It's good here. We have our table reserved anyway," Amy suggested.

"Yeah, sure."

"Do you have cigarettes?" she asked.

"Yeah, I carry them always. You smoke too?"

"Once in a while, not regularly. Today I want to relax completely. The last couple of months were tough. I had never worked this hard in my life," she said, laughing.

As we stood there smoking, I got calls from my mom couple of times. The rest of the group soon arrived and Amy joined them inside. I stayed back to call my mom. I wouldn't let my mom's calls go unanswered since she would be worried for no reason.

Despite Amy constantly reminding us to talk about something else during the dinner, we mostly discussed the performance of our group versus other groups in the mid-term presentations. We did quite well as a group, our coordination was perfect.

I had heard about going Dutch, but that was my first experience at it. After the dinner, Megan calculated the cost of what she ate and drank and her share of tax, and everybody followed her. We kind of went strictly Dutch. All others looked comfortable with it, so I didn't mind.

After pooling the money and handing it over to the waiter, we sat there talking for a few minutes about Indian food and Indian culture. Amy's assumptions were a little closer to reality, but to Megan, India is a sacred country, a land of spirituality and idealism. Her assumptions were not just different but completely opposite to what actually India is. That's what happens when people assume they know things by reading books. To be fair to them, how would Americans know about such a diverse country like India when even many Indians don't know completely?

After spending a good two hours at the dinner, Amy and I bid good bye to the other three and walked up to our car.

"Should we have a drink, Jay?" Amy asked on our way back to home.

"Now? After dinner?"

"It's not a drink drink. We'll just have a glass of vodka at my apartment."

"Your apartment?"

"Don't worry, I'll drop you back."

The dropping part was okay but her apartment? I didn't want to be in the news the next morning—Indian student murdered by a drunk American girl, or something of that sort. Amy didn't seem like that, but I wasn't comfortable with the idea. I was attracted to her, but I didn't know much about her. The scary part was that she invited me to her apartment without any hesitation, which I thought was not common for an American. Amy was probably more influenced by her Columbian mother than her American father. They say South American countries have cultural resemblance to India.

"Okay sure," I said, suppressing my doubts.

"But only on one condition," Amy said.

How can someone who invited willingly put a condition? I looked at her questioningly.

"You should use the patio to smoke, please," she said.

I thought she would say you shouldn't touch me after the drink, not that I had any hidden intentions. "Okay, even I don't like smoking inside," I said.

The discussion on Indian culture we had during our ride to the restaurant and during the dinner continued on our way back to Amy's apartment as well.

"Make yourself comfortable, Jay. I'll prepare the drinks," Amy said as we entered her apartment.

Her apartment was very appeasing. Things were so tastefully organized that I didn't find a single misplaced item in the house, exactly opposite to that of ours. Even the loose papers on the desk had the Barack Obama cup on them as paper weight, which reminded me of her blog on why America was ready to accept a black president but not a woman president.

Both Amy and I were avid followers of politics and loved to discuss it for long hours. Before Amy I never found an equally enthusiastic person with whom I could talk about politics. Generally I don't leave a word of political columns in the newspapers. In spite of being an MBA student, not once but twice, I wasn't naturally motivated to read the financial section unless I had to for academic purposes.

"Who do you think will be the next president?" I asked Amy casually while she prepared the drinks.

"Too late to talk about politics," she laughed.

Before I had time to feel bad about my badly timed question, she said, "I was just joking, Jay. There's never a wrong time for me to talk about politics. To answer your question, Barack Obama."

"You think or you wish?"

"Both."

"Why?"

"Several reasons, I cannot give a simple answer."

"Give me couple of them by the time you prepare the drinks."

"Obama is young and dynamic. He has been showing an extraordinary character on the campaign trail. I feel he has got the temperament to be the president," she said.

"I guess whoever wins the democratic nomination will be the next president. Republicans don't stand a good chance this time," I said.

"Exactly. And I think Obama will be the nominee," Amy said, handing over the vodka glass to me.

"How is it?" she asked, as I took the first sip.

"Perfect."

"Should we sit in the patio so that I can smoke?" I suggested.

"Yeah, sure."

"I like American politics. There is a huge debate going on among the candidates and among the people on issues that matter," I said as we walked to the patio.

"How is politics in India?" she asked.

"I don't see this much political awareness among people in India. Political campaigning is largely confined to cheap exchange of words among the candidates and parties, rather than focusing on real issues. People have gotten used to it," I said.

"But India is known across the world for its democratic credentials, right?"

"India is a loosely structured democracy. There is a lot of room left to the judgment of people in the high offices. With time there has been a decline in the integrity of the people, more so among politicians, and hence a decline in the governance. I should say India has a long way to go in streamlining its democracy."

"No wonder India is lagging behind in spite of huge resources and highly skilled manpower," she said.

"You guys think highly about our skills looking at the software engineers who work here. But the country on the whole is far behind on the human resource development front. Poverty and illiteracy are rampant in India. But as you said, we have abundant potential."

"Where did the country fail?" Amy asked, like she was interviewing me for a talk show.

I took a pause and lit another cigarette. The pause gave me time to frame my thoughts. "Several reasons, I can think of two mainly. One is corruption which is part of our daily life. And two, there is a huge deprivation of ideas on the part of Indian leadership. Most of the times, government decisions in India are thoughtless quick fixes rather than sustainable solutions."

"I like it here. It's been a long time since I have been so relaxed. Let me get another drink," Amy said, interrupting my speech.

I felt the same; it was a quiet and pleasant night.

Amy came back with the drinks and put them on the table, she asked, "Jay, are you getting late?"

"No. I am fine." Actually I was.

"You said you live with your roommates, right? What do they do?"

"Both of them are pharmacists."

"Yeah, you said that once. I forgot."

"What about your family? Do they stay nearby?" I asked her.

"My mother lives in the town. Actually, she offered me to stay with her until I complete my MBA, but I chose to stay on my own. I sacrificed free accommodation, Jay. Can you believe it? Haha. I love my mom a lot. She got divorced immediately after my younger sister was born and she worked so hard to raise us. She never married again. She is a lovely woman," Amy said, looking deeply into the drink as if she was seeing her mom in the glass.

"Can I have a cigarette?" she asked, after a moment of silence. "With you around, I am turning into a chain smoker," she said, lighting the cigarette.

"It's okay once in a while," I said. "What does your sister do?"

"She works as a school teacher. She lives in Dallas with her husband. She has two beautiful daughters. Her husband is a very nice guy. He is a real estate agent there."

I just had to ask one question and Amy would tell all she knew.

"Actually my mom went to Dallas today for the weekend. I am surprised she didn't call me yet; she might have slept already," she said, looking at her watch.

"I thought here parents don't bother kids after a certain age," I said.

"I guess my mom grew a little more concerned because we live close by. Again, it depends on the family. We three formed a close knit family after our parents divorced," she said. "How often do you talk to your parents? Do you have siblings?"

"I have a sister. She is married and has a new born baby boy. I talk to my parents and sister almost daily."

"Really?"

"Yeah." As we completed the second drink, I said, "I'll get going now, Amy."

"Oh, do I have to drive you home now?" Amy said lazily.

"Don't worry. I'll take a cab," I said.

"You can sleep here tonight if you are okay with that. You can sleep on the couch. I'll drop you in the morning, please. I don't feel like coming out now."

"Don't worry at all. I'll take a cab."

"I'll not let you do that. I'll drive you home if you want to go now, but if you sleep here that's absolutely fine with me."

"Okay," I agreed reluctantly.

"Great. Let's have another drink," Amy said, and went inside without even waiting for my response. She came back with the drinks, and asked, "Do you want to go to gentlemen's club?"

"What club?"

"Gentlemen's club."

"What is it exactly?" I asked.

"You don't know about that? Women dance naked—" Amy said, moving her feet and body lightly.

"Really?" I asked, suppressing my astonishment.

Amy's idea scared me more than it shocked me. She didn't feel like coming out to drop me at my apartment, but she was okay to go to the club. Logically things were not in sync. Wild side of women is good for movies but not in real life. My pulse rate picked up rapidly and all that I had drank till then vanished. If she was really that fun-loving and letting her hair down that night, it was okay, but what if she had a wild side that was dangerously wild? How could I judge that? My manly ego wouldn't allow me to just put on my shoes and run away.

"You should really go if you haven't been there," Amy said.

"Okay. But how can you go there?" I asked.

"Girls are not restricted. In fact, you'll see lot of girls."

"Really?"

My excitement dominated my hesitation that prompted my acceptance of the proposal.

We drove for about fifteen minutes to reach the club a little outside the town. With fancy lights outside and black muscular bouncers at the entrance, the place had a distinct look. As we stepped inside. . . Oh. . . My. . . Fucking. . . God. . . I couldn't believe my eyes. There existed an entirely different world that I didn't know of. Scantily dressed girls, most of them slim and some voluptuous, danced in colorful neon lights. Some wore two-piece, some just one-piece and a few others nothing at all, exposing their tight, smooth bodies. All of them were beautiful without any exception. All of them commonly wore pointed high heels as if they were meant for kicking the guys who tried to mess with them.

Amy ordered beers as we sat close to one of the several dance floors. I understood why she asked me to get dollar bills at the counter when we got in. She tucked them in when the girls approached us, and I started doing the same.

"At twelve o'clock, you get a lap dance for two songs at the cost of one song," Amy whispered in my ears.

"What does that mean?"

"You'll see," she said. "By the way, which girl do you like the most?"

"That one in red," I said, pointing to the girl sitting on the handle of a sofa little away from where we sat. The man in the sofa held her in one hand and a beer in the other.

"That one? Are you kidding?"

"I have a thing for red," I said, defending my fascination for the girl who looked the oldest among the group.

"So you just go by color of the dress? That's weird."

What good is a weakness if it is not weird?

The girl in red came to us responding to Amy's signal. After Amy whispered something in her ears, she was all over me. I felt shy for a while before I got comfortable.

Exactly at twelve, when the announcement was made, there was a hustle and bustle toward the back of the hall.

"You should try a dance with me. It's two for one," the girl in red asked rubbing her breasts against my shoulder.

I looked at Amy and she made a gesture with her hand to go. I followed the girl in red.

After the twelve o'clock special offer, Amy and I sat there for some more time and had a couple more beers before leaving. Discounting the lap dance part, which was good, I was fascinated with the ambience of the place. It was surprisingly calm and relaxing, contrary to what I had thought when Amy told me about it for the first time.

I had a good night's sleep that night on Amy's couch. I woke up early and went to the patio, which opened to an adjoining lake with still water reflecting the sun in it. Sitting on the patio, I felt like I was sitting on the bank of the lake.

A few minutes later, I looked back to the sound of Amy pulling back the patio door.

"Good morning, Jay."

"Good morning."

"Did you have trouble sleeping?" she asked.

"No, I slept well. I am good sleeper; I can sleep anywhere," I said.

"Why did you wake up so early then?"

"I am a habitual early riser. It doesn't matter when I sleep."

"Oh, my brain doesn't work properly without eight hours of sleep," Amy said, sitting on the other chair.

"Then go sleep for some more time. I can pass time here; it's beautiful."

"No no. I feel fresh, probably because of the vodka last night, haha."

Adjusting her thick hair which wouldn't listen to her fingers Amy gave a full view of her thick upper arms, shoulders, and underarms through the loose top she was wearing, and her smooth heavy legs crossed one over the other in the short printed shorts.

"I'll be back," she said, and went inside.

Right decision by her at the right time. I was already forced to cross my legs to hide the bulge in my pants. She came back with freshly washed face and hair tied back tight and with coffee for both of us.

"Should we go get breakfast? We have a nice coffee shop here; they sell good bagels. We can walk there. It's real close."

"Okay, let's go," I said. I wanted to give her some time before I asked her to drop me at home.

The breakfast at the local coffee shop was awesome. The experience of having breakfast was actually awesome. Great American ideas that changed the world might have popped up during breakfast in such morning calmness.

I proceeded directly to the patio for a smoke after returning from breakfast while Amy went to use the restroom.

I guess most Indians in the US who enjoyed morning sleep as much as I enjoyed the morning freshness never understood this part of American life. Worst are those who wake up early and think several times if they should spend so much on a breakfast by making a quick calculation in Indian rupees according to the current conversion rate. Ironically they conveniently ignore the conversion part when they get paid every fifteen days, which is several times more than what their counterparts earned in India for the same work. Invaluable American experience goes missing when people earn in dollars and spend in rupees.

In the past few months in the US, the college has been a great experience, shopping a pleasant experience, Barnes & Noble an overwhelming experience, morning breakfast an invigorating experience, smoking a refreshing experience, and interacting with people a cordial experience. It's difficult to recollect something called experience in a positive sense in India except being with family. If I wanted to have breakfast outside, just go, order, eat, pay, and get out; if I wanted to buy a book, just ask the shopkeeper if they have it standing outside the shop, pay, get the book, and get out; if I wanted to smoke in a fresh air I better quit smoking because India doesn't have fresh air.

Amy came and sat with me, folding her hands behind her head bending a little backward. "What are you thinking, Jay? It's a beautiful morning, right? I can't believe I asked you to stay back last night. I hesitate to allow even my boyfriend to stay all night," she said.

I smiled looking at her. Why does she do this? Even during our study group discussions, Amy's plump upper arm and underarm exhibition through her loose tops, especially when she folded hands at the back of her head which she did frequently, made it really hard for me to resist.

"What are you looking at? Is there something?" Amy asked, looking to her left, down her shoulder.

"I don't look at anything specific when I talk," I said.

"Oh really? But you are not talking now," Amy said, laughing.

She still didn't remove her hands folded behind her head. Was she playing around with me or she didn't care or she didn't know where I was looking?

"Okay, let me add another clause then. I don't look at anything specific when I talk and when I listen," I said.

She laughed.

After a pause, I asked her, "Can we go now?"

"Yep, what are you doing for the weekend?" she said.

"Nothing much, I'll just relax, will catch up with people in India. That's all. Do you have any plans?"

"No big plans as such. I need to go for a carwash and I might go to the mall for shopping, need to buy a few things. Do you want to join?"

"No, you carry on. Probably next time," I said.

"Okay, no problem. Will you wait for a few minutes for me to get ready so that I can go to the mall directly?" she said.

"Sure, take your time," I said, lighting a cigarette and offering one to Amy.

"Okay, last one for this weekend," she said, taking one.

After the smoke, I followed her to the kitchen for a cup of coffee by the time she got ready. As I stood there in the small kitchen space along with her to fill my cup, Amy came closer and gave me a light hug. "Thanks, Jay, I had a great time," she said.

I could smell her deodorant remnant from last night while I held her. I had to move my pelvis back as we hugged, to conceal my embarrassment.

As we unlocked from the hug, I said, "I had a great time too, Amy." The hug dried my mouth and my voice cracked as I spoke. My heart was beating faster. I needed some water.

Amy stepped even closer and kissed me. I was shy but not innocent to understand what it was. I kissed her back. Standing in the kitchen for next several minutes we kissed each other. It was kind of a coffee kiss, her mouth tasted like a diluted coffee. I rubbed her back with my hands on her loose tank top at first and then moved my hands inside, but didn't dare to bring them to the front. Amy nudged both of us into the bedroom without breaking the kiss.

We got undressed kissing each other when Amy stopped suddenly, and said, "Wait, wait."

For a moment, I thought she would say that she had a boyfriend. She quickly jumped out of the bed and came back with a condom pack which was hidden deep inside the closet. We both ignored her boyfriend for our convenience and started kissing again.

After a few minutes Amy pulled me closer and whispered in my ear, "Take out the condom, Jay."

I sat back on the bed and tore the purple pack and took out the slimy thing.

Amy saw me fumbling and asked laughingly, "What are you doing? Haven't you ever used it?"

"Actually, no," I said, with hesitation in my voice.

"Don't tell me you are a virgin," she laughed.

"Actually, yes," I said, with the same hesitation.

"What the fuck?" She sat on the bed suddenly, followed by a deep laughter.

Amy put her hand across my shoulder and looked at me unbelievably: *Really? Am I fucking a virgin?*

I smiled looking at her: *Yes, you are, though I am not sure if I am proud to be a virgin at twenty-six.*

"This is going to be interesting. Give that to me," she said, taking the condom from me, and guided me through the next steps.

As we both lay on the bed looking at the ceiling I wondered if Amy deliberately wore a red panty. I didn't think she had the energy and patience last night to change her panty for me. It could be a coincidence.

Putting a break to my thoughts, Amy asked, "How old are you, Jay?"

She had asked the same question earlier too, but I knew what she meant this time.

"Twenty-six."

"Fuck. I can't believe you're still a virgin."

"Not anymore," I said.

"True, haha." After a hearty laugh Amy turned toward me resting her hand on my chest, she asked, "Did you have grand plans for your first time, Jay?"

"No, I didn't. I am glad that you are my first."

Amy moved closer and we started kissing again.

Honestly, she didn't have to feel so privileged. Virginity in India is more out of deprivation than out of dedication. I wasn't sure about being glad, I just said it. Though I thought about it, sex before marriage was not something I craved for. Nor was I so particular about losing my virginity to my wife only. I was quite happy using my creative imagination. Once in a while, in a typical Bollywood movie style first-night scene, I fantasized about it—experiencing the first time after marriage with a shy and hopefully virgin Indian girl in the darkness and confusion of not knowing what we were doing. But it happened with a half-American and a half-Columbian woman during the morning sunrise. I guess nothing goes according to plan in life and now I knew for sure the list also includes losing virginity.

Sex meant only after marriage by default once upon a time in India and hence no plan was needed. Nowadays no plan is needed with virginity becoming increasingly inconsequential.

When I was already wildly promiscuous in my fantasies, what difference does it make to lose my physical virginity? If I had the opportunity of growing up in a free society like America, would I have been a virgin till then? Would anybody in India be a virgin until marriage? Would virginity be considered a trophy that people won after marriage? Is marriage all about virginity and sex? I used the best of my rational mind to feel good about the first experience I just had with someone I was physically attracted to, but with whom I hadn't spent enough time to have real emotional intimacy.

Once it was over, it was over. I changed my plans to go home and stayed back at Amy's place. Everything else could wait.

16

The Sunday night, after coming back from Amy's place, I called Venkat—no, not to describe to him about what I did with Amy that weekend but to talk about something more important.

"Hi, Jay. What's up? I was just thinking of you," Venkat said, picking the phone.

"Don't give time for your mind to think of me, just call," I said.

"Haha. I thought of calling you after reaching home. I am on my way back to Charlotte from my brother's place. I have some interesting news for you. Let me call you in an hour, okay?"

It should be something related to my college transfer, since that was the hot topic running between us for some time.

The MBA program already bled me off the little savings I had and was increasingly pushing me into debt. I wasn't sure when and whether I would have the pleasure of converting American dollars into Indian rupees, but the pain of converting Indian rupees into American dollars was killing me. Instead of getting the bang for the buck I was getting fucked up. I wouldn't get into a situation where I would stop my MBA for lack of money. In addition to having Venkat's support, I had the opportunity to avail education loan from Indian banks from the second semester, since they wouldn't trust me unless I completed one semester in college. If at all it was worth it was the question.

I wouldn't have cared much if I was doing the same MBA program in India. In the name of education, we were used to spending precious time of our lives in the confines of college campuses for the fear of losing in the open world. Financial dependency on parents was no big deal; we were cool with that.

More than anything else, possible visa issues distressed me. If I couldn't get into a management job after completing MBA because no employer would file for my work visa, I would be forced to try my chances in IT to recover the money I had spent on master's, in which case, I would have taken the costliest route to become a software engineer.

Two things were passing by just like that with my conscious notice and helplessness at the same time, time and money, but I needed to see it through.

Didn't I do this dissection when I started in India? No. If I waited until I had all the information, I would have never taken the flight to the US. I was aware of the risks involved when I started off and that's precisely the reason why I was open to the change of plans.

I could have gone ahead with the current MBA program because that was the goal with which I had landed in the US and hoped for things to fall in place somehow. But hope is not always a good word. It might sometimes push us to the edge of a cliff and just disappear leaving us on our own. I could have returned to India by writing off the money I spent in the first semester in Austin as a bad investment and restart my management career, which would have been a bold decision that boosted my self-approval. But I yielded to the fear of potential financial repercussions.

In the end I chose to abandon all other options for IT to make good use of being in the US. I chose to be a normal human being and be practical and opted for a less bold path. I chose to play safe, much against my will. I only hoped that I wouldn't forget the reason for changing my plans and get carried away in the flood of dollars and situational compulsions, like many fellow Indians in the US. I rationalized my continuing in the US thinking there could be a far more meaningful benefit beyond financial gain or loss, by merely going through what I was going through. Returning to India was always an option at hand.

With the decision to shift to IT field, lot of my preferences changed. When getting into IT seemed inevitable, then why hang around with a sophisticated tag of MBA? Why not do something in that direction sooner? Performing well in the current semester was not a priority anymore. Reputation of the college and quality of the program didn't matter anymore. Finding the cheapest route to IT was the target.

I started looking for graduate programs not loaded with intimidating technical stuff but with content enough to make my entry into IT possible. At least until the end of the current semester which was the middle of December 2007, I was struck in Austin but I needed to make some quick decisions. I needed to finalize an alternate program well before the current semester ended so that I could inform our university about the college transfer in time.

Colleges in America were so hungry for international students that every college I approached was more than ready to give me admission with full transfer of credits, which could also be the reason why I got my student visa in the first attempt itself. Some of them offered me a partial fee waiver as well. Coordinating with them was like bargaining with vegetable vendors in India.

Venkat called me exactly after one hour. "Hi, Jay. Just reached home. What did you do for the weekend?"

"Nothing much, how is your brother?"

"He is good. He gave an interesting option for you. First of all, how did the mid-term exams go?" Venkat asked.

"Yeah, we did well. They are group-based evaluations."

"Okay. Here is the thing. When you are prepared to get into software field, why don't you join a desi consulting company right away and continue your studies in parallel?"

"I don't know how that works." Honestly, I didn't understand anything he said.

"Even I was not aware of this option until my brother told me about it. I was casually discussing your issue with him then he mentioned about his colleague's younger brother who came to the US on a student visa like you. After a semester, that guy shifted to a cheaper college in Virginia, and he has been staying at a desi employer's guest house while attending college."

"If I move to IT, we need a desi employer anyway to get into a consulting job. I know that, but I thought that'll come into picture after completing my master's," I said.

"That's the way it works generally. And most employers do not entertain students before completing their graduation. I am talking about someone with whom we can work out things differently. And by the time you complete your college, you can get trained in IT and be ready for a job. You don't have to pay rent also. It'll save you a lot of time and money. Of course, the employer will squeeze everything back from you after you get into the job, with interest. We'll think of that part later. What say?" Venkat explained how the new plan works.

"Sounds like a great idea if it can be worked out. I don't see any issue," I said.

"We know someone who is already doing it. I asked my brother to get complete details."

"Okay."

Sensing the hesitation in my voice, Venkat said, "See, Jay, when you are deviating from your plan for whatever reason, what difference does it make what you study as long as it is related to IT and where you stay? Now our goals should be to take care of your future immigration status and get into the job market as soon as possible without spending much."

"Yeah, right. I was thinking something in the same direction. We need to verify the credibility of that college in Virginia before we request a transfer. In the meantime, I'll put other universities on hold without confirming."

"How many do you have right now?"

"I am coordinating with two universities in New Jersey."

"Even New Jersey is full of desi consultancies, but we don't know anybody there. I don't want you to go to any place just like that. This employer in Virginia is someone who my brother's colleague knows very closely. Its better we go through a reference."

"Where exactly in Virginia?" I asked.

"The guest house is in Fairfax, but I am not sure about the college. We'll have more details in a couple of days. How is everything else? Do you need money?" Venkat asked. That was a standard question with which he ended the conversation most of the times.

I didn't have to be skeptical of the idea of moving all the way from Texas to Virginia, especially because it came from Venkat. He was not someone who just threw ideas and left the fate of working on them to me. He always put himself in my shoes before he even suggested something to me.

There was a time when I thought of people running after IT jobs as crazy, and here I was adjusting all my plans with IT as the goal.

Despite all the confidence in Venkat, I slept that night thinking about the pros and cons of his seemingly out-of-the-box idea. After joining my current college, that was the first night I didn't think about my next day's class presentations before sleeping.

***

The following Monday, Amy and I met each other normally. The difference was that I had company for everything. She waited for me to go together anywhere on the campus—café, library, student lounge, everywhere. She started informing me even when she went to the restroom like a kid informs parents. I got a permanent ride to college and back to home, though that was not on my mind when I accompanied Amy to her home on Friday night. It would be childish even to think of it, but I really missed the Jack in the Box stopovers.

The episode with Amy introduced a new angle within me. Being born and brought up in the country that's known for its high cultural standards, I was surprised that I didn't even feel a trace of guilt.

The gentlemen's club experience dominated my mind for few days. Every girl seemed like one of those nude dancing girls. My eyes kind of turned into X-ray glasses and my imagination passed through whatever they wore.

Over the next couple of weeks, after obtaining complete details from his brother and a series of deliberations, I decided to go ahead with Venkat's suggestion.

Amy didn't get emotional when I broke the news, since she already had a hint of it. All she said was that I needed to put my career first. Olivia and my other classmates respected my decision and wished me good luck. Except Murthy, who felt I should stick with my original plans without getting deterred by obstacles, everybody thought my choice was practical.

Murthy said he admired my guts initially when he heard my story, and couldn't let me fall into the beaten track like most Indians in the US. His opinions resonated with me. His words made me listen to my faint inner voice more clearly, but I felt the obstacles I faced had the potential to evolve into a full-blown crisis. Finally, I chose to be pragmatic, I bended in order not to break, but not without building a sense of guilt within me.

Venkat took the complete responsibility of relocating me from Texas to Virginia. I spent the couple of weeks' gap between the completion of my first semester in Austin and joining the guest house in the first week of January at Venkat's place.

I called my mom on my first new year day in the US to reveal my change of college plans.

"Happy new year, Ma." It was rare that I got a chance to speak first after she picked the call.

"Jay, happy new year. What did you do for the new year?"

"Nothing much, I came to Venkat's place. We went out for dinner. And you?"

"We saw TV till twelve and slept. Madhu is here. Chintu is standing up; he tries to walk and falls down. He'll be one year old next month. Can you hear him shouting?" Mom asked. She probably brought the phone closer to Chintu, my sister's son; I heard his voice real loud. I regretted being in the US at times, I could have relished those family moments if I was with them.

"Yeah yeah. He has a loud voice like Madhu," I said.

"True," my mom said, laughing.

"What true? What do you mean like Madhu?" I could hear my sister shout.

"Ma, you should tell me when you keep the phone on speaker. Happy new year, Madhu."

I heard Madhu's voice indistinctly, probably she wished me back. I waited until the end of the conversation and asked my mom to put the speaker off to break the news.

"Ma, I am shifting to a new college from next semester," I said.

"Why? Talk to your dad. I don't understand these things." There was a sudden rush in her voice exactly as I anticipated.

"No, wait. You tell him. Don't make it a big issue," I said, calming her down.

"Tell me if there is any issue in the world that is big for you.

You said you selected the college because of the course. Why are you changing now?"

"Ma, I am going to a better college, okay?"

"Okay, but do you know anybody there?" she asked.

"Yeah. I have friends, and I have already found the accommodation," I assured.

"What should I tell your Dad?"

"Tell the same thing I told you," I said.

"Wait, you tell him. He is here. I am giving the phone to him," she said.

"No, wait. You tell him. Also convey new year wishes to him."

"Okay, be careful in the new place."

Most of my phone conversations with my mom end abruptly. At some point she tries to hand over the phone to my dad forcing me to hang up the call.

The transfer to the university in Virginia was smooth. They offered me maximum possible credits transfer so that whatever time and money I spent in Austin wasn't wasted. If I hadn't changed the university, I wouldn't have witnessed the beauty of the American education system. Choosing universities, transferring between universities, and shifting majors, discontinuing the programs and coming back to university later, practically everything was possible. Except the student loans issue, the education system was totally student-centric.

Why the hell is the education system so rigid in India then? I wasn't aware if anything similar to a college transfer or program transfer even existed in India when I was a student. It was like an assembly line in a manufacturing plant. If students made wrong choices, which they did more often than not, they couldn't jump off the assembly line. Their fate was sealed forever. In my undergraduate studies, I realized halfway through that biology was not my thing, but I had to wait until I completed it before changing to management.

With the prior information I had about desi employers and guest houses, I didn't have huge expectations about moving to Fairfax, Virginia. The guest houses were not even close to normal houses, nor were people treated as guests. They were like slaughter houses where the future IT professionals were prepared to be sold in the market. The word guest house was a total misnomer. The only parameter based on which they could be called guest houses was that they were free to stay. Some employers even paid for food partly, I heard.

Still, the concept of IT consulting survived and had been serving the IT industry in the US successfully because it is a win-win for all the players involved—aspiring employee, employer, vendor, and client. Employee is the guy who needs a job, employer is the guy who invests in the employee and sells him as a consultant for the right price and runs the payroll, vendor is the guy who disregards certain facts so as to hire a cheaper consultant, and client is the guy who thinks his job is over by hiring a consultant and expects the consultant to be an answer for all the IT issues.

The employers arranged training facilities in IT courses based on seasonal flavor in the market, with absolute disregard to things like competency, skill set, and interest of the job-seekers. Sometimes, by the time people completed their training, the course would have been outdated in the market and they would again be trained in another course, and the process continued until they were placed.

Whatever stupid IT courses I would be learning there at the guest house was next to the benefit of not having to pay rent. Two things that do not appear big but suck big time are monthly bills and interest on money borrowed. For now, I would be saving on my monthly bills.

17

January 5, 2008: Move to Fairfax, Virginia.

This time around I wasn't as much anxious about the college as I was about the guest house.

Our guest house was a big four bedroom house occupied by three people. One of them was Sumit, a tall and lanky guy with spiky hair and stubble. His round neck tees over blue jeans looked like they were hanging on a hanger. He was the reason I was there in the university and the guest house in Virginia. The other guy had recently come on H1B visa from India and was actively searching for a job. And a female lived in the basement about whom the two guys knew nothing except that she was a close relative of our employer, Rajiv.

Sumit showed me a bedroom, and said, "This is yours. Enjoy!"

How did I get a bedroom for myself? That was contrary to the impression I had about the guest houses.

"Enjoy yourself in this bedroom for now. More people will be joining by the end of January," Sumit said.

How did he know what I was thinking?

Like any other business, desi consultancies also had a flush and lean season. Their season started from January when fresh graduates pass out of colleges and job market resumes after holidays. In the name of getting a graduate degree in the US, when mediocre Indian engineering students pass out of mediocre colleges with so-called excellent grades, what other options do they have other than depending on such consultancies for jobs? Folks from Harvards and Stanfords are sold out in campuses itself, their return on investment is assured. For those who fall at the bottom of the ladder in terms of education, it doesn't matter anyway as they end up in gas stations or grocery stores and become independent business owners later and earn probably more than software engineers.

As I arranged my bags in the bedroom, Sumit knocked on the door. "Hey, Jay, do you drink?" he asked.

What a stupid question. "Of course," I said.

"Good. We are going out to get groceries, and we'll get beers also. Do you want to join us?" Before I responded, he said, "But you need to change your pink t-shirt, dude. People think we are gays."

Really? Is pink that untouchable? For a moment, I felt sad for the pink collection I had and sorry for people who attribute the color of clothes to personal choices in life.

"You guys carry on. I am little tired," I said.

"Do you want me to get anything for you?" Sumit asked.

"Hmm no. Do we have milk and coffee in the kitchen?"

"Yeah."

"Coffee is the only thing I need," I said.

"Okay, enjoy."

What did he mean when he said enjoy for every damn thing?

"You said you will stay back," Sumit asked, seeing me follow him outside.

"I want to have a smoke."

"You can smoke on the deck. You don't have to come down," he said.

That was a huge luxury.

I prepared a cup of coffee and walked on to the deck. While I stood there enjoying my smoke on a mild evening, the weird look of a short Indian girl in grey tracksuit and pink shoes, walking like she jumped with every step which didn't match with her looks, drew my attention. She looked slim with loose, long, sexy hair that bounced rhythmically with every step. She seemed to have a fine taste for colors. If the reason for her disgusting look at me was because I was smoking, that was none of her business. If she had those thick-rimmed glasses even during walking, she definitely wouldn't be able to see anything without them. I turned my head. A moment later, I checked if she was still looking at me when she looked at me again. I turned away my head again. I checked again, and by then she already walked past and was only visible from a distance. I have an instant turn on for girls with strong personalities, but not for headstrong girls, even if they are attractive.

Barring her weird look, the smoke on the deck recharged me, and I was ready for the new place. Cigarette is one of the best human inventions I guess. If and when I quit smoking completely, I'll not regret that I was a smoker once. I admire people who never smoked in their life, but I pity them for their loss of smoking experience.

Rajiv came to see me the day after I landed in the guest house. He might as well have come to check whether the guests were maintaining his house well or not. He assured me of my stay in the guest house until I completed my graduate program and gave a brief overview of the classes that he was planning to conduct when new graduate students join us by the end of January.

Rajiv had a pleasant personality, unlike the not-so-good opinion I had about the employer community. The employers accommodated us, trained us, placed us in jobs, and they drew benefits from us only when we got paid. And still we called them cheap. Isn't that funny?

Exactly two weeks after I joined the guest house, the honeymoon period was over. The guest house was flooded with a flock of seven guys and four girls from the same university in New Jersey. I felt aliens had encroached on my space as if I owned the guest house while my success lied in getting out of that place sooner. I adjusted my routine and tried to not get bogged down by the crowd. I used the guest house just to sleep and spent most part of my day either at Barnes & Noble or Starbucks or local gym if I didn't have college. Luckily I had access to all of them at a walkable distance from the guest house.

The day after the aliens' entry, Rajiv announced the schedule for training classes he was going to organize on some IT applications, which didn't make much sense to me. I asked Sumit, but being an engineer, even he didn't have an idea. I'll make use of the opportunity anyway, since Rajiv was not asking for tuition fee but I'd have felt good if I had a clue what the hell they were all about.

On day one, when our classes started, Rajiv gave a rousing speech like Barack Obama outlining his vision on how he wanted to extend proper training facilities, unlike other employers who just pushed consultants into the job market without preparing them well and left them on their own. He even arranged free snacks and coffee that day.

"Who is she? That girl with thick rimmed glasses. See those red Puma shoes?" I asked Sumit who was sitting beside me in the class.

He looked at me first before he looked at the girl: *What happened to you today?*

I was surprised to see her in the class. She was the same girl who had given me a weird look during her evening walk on my first day.

"She is the one who lives in the basement. Rajiv's relative."

"What's her name?"

Sumit looked at me again, and said, "Siri something."

"Nice name."

"But the girl is not nice, dude."

"Really?"

"Yeah, she is very rude."

Sumit sounded like he had got a nice thrashing from her sometime in the past.

Why was she staying in the guest house when she could have stayed in Rajiv's house if she was his close relative? Did she want to live independently? Using his guest house facility was not being independent; it was just being away from him that's all. Anyway, she was not invisible anymore as she was attending classes with us, and she was not exclusive anymore as four other girls joined our consulting company.

Since the classes were informal, people were in less than informal dressing. But her dressing was perfect—tight dark blue jeans, white top visible under her red cardigan and matching red Puma shoes. Her sharp nose, big eyes, thick rimmed glasses, and non-smiling lips added some kind of magic to the mystery surrounding her. She was conspicuously non-interactive with an I-don't-care expression on her face.

Will she recognize me if we happen to see each other?

Rajiv announced that he had arranged a separate apartment for girls, close to the guest house, which will be ready in a couple of days. That was kind of a perk to attract girls, which most employers didn't offer. I wondered if the mysterious girl would go along with the girls to the new apartment or prefer to stay in the basement.

Rajiv also announced that smoking and drinking wouldn't be allowed in the guest house.

What the fuck? Did she already complain to Rajiv about me? Is she the watchwoman of the guest house or what? These girls cannot hold anything. I thought she hated smoking in general. It was because I was smoking in Rajiv's house and Rajiv happens to be her relative, that's why?

Rajiv left it open for the trainer to take over after the introduction. The guys who taught us at the guest house were practicing software engineers. The trainer's fake accent and freaky body language turned me off even before he completed his first sentence. The more he tried to be cool, the more disgusting impression he gave. I hated his dressing—half-sleeve sweater on a full-sleeve thermal. What an awkward combination. Did this guy learn anything at all staying in the US apart from piling dollars in his bank account?

During the round of introductions, the mysterious girl confirmed her name as Siri in her loud and not-so-sweet voice. I fell in love with her name. She had done her undergraduate studies in computer engineering in India and came to the US for master's. She currently worked as a data modeler and wanted to become a software architect. Was she so inclined toward technical stuff? I thought most girls in IT were confined to peripheral roles.

Why the hell she was in the class then when she was so qualified? As soon as I thought about it, the trainer asked her the same question to which Siri said that she was there just to brush her basics. While leaving the class, I got to look at Siri closely. She gave me the same weird look. What the fuck? Again? Just for smoking on the deck?

With no prior knowledge about IT, I was totally lost in the class. I didn't care much on the first day, but I grew a little concerned on the second day when I didn't understand a single word in the class. I couldn't afford to go on like that forever. The classes in the college which were meant for grades and immigration status were easy, but the classes in the guest house which were supposed to land me in a job were hard. So America was not an exception to the irrelevance of university education. Then why the hell people complained about it so much in India as if only Indian universities were the most fucked up in the entire world? It looked like it's a global phenomenon.

I called up Venkat immediately after the class to share my problem.

"What's up, Jay? Had you dinner?"

"Yeah."

"What happened?"

"Nothing, Venkat."

"You sound dull."

"This IT thing looks like it's not my cup of tea, Venkat. It's so technical. You know I have hated math from childhood," I said.

"Software is not math, Jay. And you don't have to be an expert in technical stuff. Just learn the basics, and after you complete college, we'll find a functional position for you. If IT was difficult, so many dummies will not be working here."

"But the classes here make no sense to me."

"Fuck those classes. If possible, find somebody who can help you understand the concepts. Don't worry about coding stuff, okay?"

"Okay." Venkat's words gave some comfort to me.

"Take things slow, Jay, you have time."

"Okay."

"How is the guest house?" Venkat asked.

"It's okay, but too many people," I said.

"Yeah, guest houses are like that. They should actually be called whorehouses. Employers are like pimps who prepare us to get fucked by the clients. They say yes to whatever the clients' requirements are like a pimp and leave us in their hands."

I couldn't stop laughing at Venkat's comments. That's exactly how it worked.

"Since you are into software now, leave it to me. We have so many contacts here; we'll work it out," he said.

Venkat's pep talk boosted my morale, though it couldn't

completely dispel my phobia for IT. It was sad that I needed pep talks even at that age.

One take-home from my conversation with Venkat was to find someone who can help me. Sumit was an engineer and a good friend, but he was too chilled out to be of any help to me academically. I didn't understand how most guys in the guest house were not so serious about their careers. Were they under the impression that Rajiv will push them into jobs somehow? Or was I more worried about things than I should have been? Even if I discounted the age difference, which wouldn't be more than five years between them and me, I didn't remember being so reckless at their age. I didn't remember letting life just go by. But why did I care anyway? Because I was jealous that they came to the US at the right age and were not making proper use of time? Maybe.

On the third day of the class, I couldn't take it anymore. The trainer was going at full speed, assuming a certain level of understanding among the students. I couldn't even take notes. Except me, everybody had an engineering background, and most of them had done their master's in computers. Not that education guaranteed understanding, but having spent so many years in an environment related to computers, they were at least familiar with what was going on in the class. I badly needed someone's help to bring me up to speed. A special class with the trainer was unlikely. He probably would charge Rajiv extra to teach me separately. Those guys got used to charging by hours after going to the US for whatever they contributed, as if every hour of their life mattered. Even if he agreed, I'll not be able to take his fake accent.

A couple of the younger folks were good in the class, but I was a little egoistic to approach them. How would I get help when I didn't even ask? But still I didn't. My attention diverted to Siri who answered the instructor's questions when nobody in the class knew the answer. She waited for the kids to compete amongst themselves before she stepped in. But she looked unapproachable. Was she headstrong as Sumit said or was she just strong-minded? Even if he was right, I preferred approaching a headstrong woman to approaching childish college grads. The thought of asking Siri for help gave me an instant fright. What if she complained to Rajiv thinking that I was flirting with her? She had already complained to Rajiv about my smoking on the deck. Luckily Rajiv didn't do a police identification parade of all of us in front of her to point at the culprit.

I chose to disregard the misconceptions and fears and approach Siri assuming that she would be mature enough to understand my situation. I rehearsed what to talk to her in order to keep it strictly professional. I planned to talk to her when nobody was around, so that whatever would happen between us stays with us. If I got a dress-down by chance, whether people believed it or not, at least I would have an option to say she was lying, if that happened in private. In some corner of my heart, her intriguing personality was also a reason to approach Siri. Otherwise where was the need to consciously decide to keep it strictly professional?

I knew Siri went for evening walks, courtesy of her weird looks, which would be the best time to get hold of her alone. I waited on the deck the following evening and spotted Siri in the same grey tracksuit. The girl who sported colorful dresses to the class wore the same tracksuit for walking every day? Of course people don't own a dozen tracksuits, they are not underwears. That shouldn't matter to me anyway to ask for her help. Didn't I decide that I would keep it strictly professional?

I quickly stepped down and walked toward Siri so that stopping her and starting the conversation would be easy. I felt nervous as I approached her. My heart beat faster. I couldn't walk in a straight line. My smiling lips contracted looking at her non-smiling face as we looked at each other.

Somehow I pulled the courage to start the conversation as we came closer. "Hi," I said.

Siri slowed down and responded with a rigid expression on her face, "Hi."

"Do you go for walks every day?" I asked. That question was not part of the text I had rehearsed, didn't know where it came from.

She didn't answer. She gave me the same weird look and continued to walk. Was "weird looks" her major in graduate studies?

I called out to her when she almost walked past me, "Siri!"

She stopped and looked back.

"I know you. I stay in the guest house too," I said.

"I also know you. You are the same guy who was smoking on the patio the other day," she said.

"So, you are the one who complained to Rajiv?"

"What nonsense? Do you think I am a school kid?" The irritability was visible on her face.

"Sorry. Rajiv said particularly not to smoke or drink in the guest house in our first class. I thought you complained."

"Rajiv says that every time so that people don't spoil the environment in the guest house. It was not specifically meant for you."

"Oh, I was overthinking unnecessarily."

"That doesn't mean you can smoke in the house."

"I didn't smoke in the house, I smoked on the deck. Anyway, I stopped smoking there after you gave me a weird look that day."

"What?" she asked, with a scowling face putting one hand on her hip and adjusting her glasses with the other. I guess people ask "what" with strange expressions on their faces when they need time to react though they heard it right the first time itself.

"Nothing. Are you still staying in the guest house? Didn't you move to the girls' apartment?"

"That's none of your business."

"What?" I asked her in the same tone putting my hands on my hips, almost imitating her.

"I said that is none of your business," Siri repeated each word in the sentence slowly without any hesitation. She was really headstrong.

"I am just asking because we are in the same guest house. That's all."

"Bye." Siri started to walk.

"Wait, wait. I need a small help from you," I said, lifting my hand almost horizontally to stop her. She was so much shorter than me that she could walk freely below my arm if she wanted to.

"But you are talking nonsense," she said.

With every sentence she spoke, Siri tried to walk away. Was she in a hurry to go or was she just showing off?

"Why are you in a hurry? Are you worried that Rajiv will see us?" I asked.

"What nonsense? Look, I don't know who you are. I don't know your name. You are just wasting my time. I stopped as a matter of courtesy because you said you needed some help. I guess you are just—"

If I could remember her name from the class, why couldn't she remember mine? Or was she posing as if she didn't care though she knew?

"You stopped even before I told you that I need help from you," I said.

That angered Siri the most I guess. She started walking briskly. Quickly following her, I said, "Wait. I really need some help from you."

Siri stopped and looked back with both hands on her hips and an intimidating expression on her face which got magnified by her thick rimmed glasses. "My name is Jay," I said.

"Come to the point. What do you need from me?" she asked curtly. She was not even half of me in size. Why does she carry so much head weight?

"Okay, coming to the point—"

"Yeah, that's what I was waiting for," Siri said, smiling for the first time during the conversation. That's a good sign.

I realized that by then my hands were on my hips like she did, unknowingly. Is that contagious too like yawning?

"Whatever the trainer is teaching in the guest house is not making any sense to me. Courses they teach me in college are a waste of time, courses taught in the guest house only get me job, and you know that. Before I lose track completely, I want someone to teach me the basics. I want you to help me," I said.

"Very very funny," Siri said, smiling and shaking her head.

Can you please help me understand which part of that was funny? I didn't ask her though.

"No. I might have been funny earlier, not now." I tried to bring some seriousness to my face and tightened the grip of my hands on the hips to prove I was not joking.

"You have other guys in the guest house. Why don't you ask them?" she asked.

"Don't I know that? None of them are serious about learning. And you look like you have a good understanding of things. That's why I am asking you."

She looked down probably contemplating whether she should agree.

"Please, you don't have to do this handholding forever. I

need your help to understand the basics, that's all," I said, trying to tilt her decision to yes.

"There are some good websites which teach you basics that even school kids can understand," she said.

"So, does that mean no? Don't you think I know about websites?" I asked.

"But, I am not as good as you think, and definitely not good at teaching. Where do I teach you?" she asked.

Done. She just agreed.

"You can come upstairs or I can come to your room or we can go to Rajiv's office or we can go to Starbucks. There are many options, whatever is convenient for you."

"Do you want me to walk all the way to Rajiv's office to teach you?"

These girls I tell you. . . was that the only option I gave her?

"I am really not sure if I can be of help to you. I never taught anyone in my life," Siri said, adjusting her glasses.

"Don't think of this as a formal class or something big like that. Just share whatever you know. I am asking you because I saw your spark in the class."

"No spark nothing. It's just that I have some work experience, that's all," Siri said, with a little smile, unable to conceal her acknowledgement of the praise.

"Exactly. That's the main reason why I am asking you. You can relate the stuff better to practical scenarios."

Siri looked at me with a smile and shook her head.

"Okay. Since we have evening classes, we can discuss sometime in the afternoon after lunch from tomorrow," she said.

"Okay, great. Where?" I asked.

"In my room in the basement. That's the best option of all."

So Siri didn't move out with the other girls to the new

apartment. Not sure if Rajiv asked her to stay back in the basement as a caretaker.

"Okay, thanks."

"But don't make a show of it in the guest house," she said.

So that's what was stopping her from saying yes for so long. As she was about to leave, I asked, "Where do you eat? You never come upstairs to the kitchen?"

"This is your last question. I need to go get ready for the class. The basement is fully equipped, including kitchen. Okay? Bye."

"Okay. Bye."

Slender and short frame, sharp nose and big eyes, silky hair falling on her forehead, cheeks with not-so-conspicuous pimple scars, and the onset of wrinkles and dark circles. She didn't look like someone who landed in the US straight from the undergraduate college. Or did I catch her at the wrong time, with a sweaty face and without makeup? So what if I stopped her during evening walk, aren't girls supposed to look good and smell good all the time? Maybe she doesn't care. When she talked to me, her dark black, clear, and sharp eyes looked straight into mine without a hint of hesitation to expose her original face. Maybe her confidence was not dependent on her looks.

As I reached the guest house thinking about Siri and my classes with her, I saw Sumit at the entrance.

"What, hero?" Before I could say anything, he went on, "I saw you talking to her. You know that she is married, right?"

Siri was married? She definitely looked older but that was shocking. I tried not to react overtly. Why was she in the guest house if she was married? Sumit gave another twist to the mystery surrounding Siri, not that I cared. Didn't I decide that I would keep it strictly professional?

"I told you I was going to ask her for help," I said casually.

"She might have asked you to fuck off," he said even more casually.

"No, she agreed."

"Really?" he asked, sitting straight with a sudden jerk and looking at me. "But be careful, bro. She is mad," he said.

"Okay." I didn't feel comfortable talking to Sumit about Siri. And he didn't continue the discussion either.

"I am going out. Do you want cigarettes?" he asked, getting up from the sofa.

"Yeah, get me a pack. Are you not attending the class today?" I asked him.

"No. Rajiv conducts these classes round the year. Even if I learn now, I'll forget by the time I pass out of college. And who knows this course might be irrelevant by the time we are in the market."

I laughed with him, but I wished I could be that carefree instead of constantly being bugged by career related thoughts. But seriously, what else did I have to do in that guest house except prepare for a job?

I saw Siri coming to the class that evening a little late, perfectly dressed like always with hair tied back like a corporate woman. She played subtle variations without deviating much from her style. She wore different colors of almost the same kind of dress every day. Comparing her daily looks would be like playing around with a dress in an online store with different colors.

After the class, I was surprised that Siri talked to me first as we walked out of the class. "How was the class?" she asked, with a sarcastic smile.

I showed my hand zooming over my head indicating that it was beyond my understanding.

"Haha." I didn't know that Siri laughed too. But when she did, she laughed her head off. Her faultless, pearly teeth added extra shine to her smile, laugh rather. Did she flaunt them intentionally? No, such a prevailing laugh couldn't be planned and practiced. I could see an astonishing look on the faces of the people around us: *How come the mysterious girl is talking to him?* They might have thought even I was mysterious because I didn't interact much with people in the guest house except with Sumit. Wrapping myself in a comforter all day and babbling on about movies, cricket, and girls wasn't me.

"It's not that difficult. Don't worry. I'll help you out," Siri said.

"You are my hope. Give me your number," I said.

The pleasantness on her face suddenly disappeared. "Why do you need my number?" she asked.

"I'll call you before I come to your room for the class tomorrow."

Siri shook her head with a little smile. She didn't have much choice. She couldn't obviously say that I was welcome to her room any time.

I scanned her quickly from top to bottom out of curiosity but didn't find a single indication of a married Indian woman—no sindoor, no wedding ring, no mangalsutra, no toe rings, and no plump look.

Modern Indian women outsmarted traditions. They discard the symbolic stuff when they wear jeans and tees, and project the same things with pride with sarees as the combination goes well and adds to the overall look. To be fair to them, Indian culture prescribes these symbols which are kind of constant reminders of marriage to women only, with footnotes of scientific explanations. Incidentally, men happen to be the authors of all the ancient scriptures and the patrons of ancient wisdom, and why would they impose such sanctions on themselves? What a foresight did they show ages back that the power of women would be formidable that they wouldn't be able to cope up with if they were not restricted by a moral code of conduct, but how long? Aren't we already hearing the murmurs of the so-called guardians of culture about growing liberty for women? Didn't history time and again prove that oppression only led to secretly wild ambitions among the oppressed which in turn led to revolutions? Why would women be an exception?

Was Siri one of those married women who longed to cast off the symbols of marriage in the name of modernity or someone who refused to agree that marriage was not all about wearing some token ornaments or someone who didn't what to be known as a married woman as if it was an offence to get married?

I wasn't interested to take up the topic of Siri's marriage with her or with anyone. Didn't I decide to keep it strictly professional with her?

18

I knocked on Siri's door exactly at the time I had set up with her earlier in the morning. That day since morning, I was totally occupied with thoughts about my tutoring class with Siri.

Oh no! Siri opened the door dressed casually in light blue printed pajama and black sleeveless tank top. Didn't she know that bare upper arms triggered reactions in my body? But how could women be expected to keep track of such a bewildering range of men's fetishes?

"Hey, Jay. Come in."

Siri turned and walked inside, lifting her hands to tie her hair into a knot at the top of the head with no idea how much she was turning me on. As I followed her, I looked at her nape and a streak of thin hair that ran from the back of her head passing into her tank top, prominently visible against her fair skin. She should put on a shirt or a jacket or something immediately. Sleevelessness is no good for the class. At least she should stop lifting her hands so frequently.

"Sorry I didn't get a chance to shower, I was tied up with phone calls since morning," Siri said, picking her clothes spread around in the hall and thrusting them into the closet. Probably she was too conscious that she didn't take shower in the morning, I could smell the perfume from her prominently.

"I can wait if you want to take a quick shower," I said.

"No, it's okay. If I don't take a shower in the morning, then

I don't get the mood again until evening. Now I'll take shower directly after my evening walk," Siri said, abruptly turning back, without giving me a chance to look elsewhere. My eyes, which were on her bare back before, were now on her breasts, unintentionally.

The basement had a spacious kitchen, a bedroom, and a hall that can easily support a small family. Siri did not maintain it well with clothes books and other stuff spread all over the place. Surprisingly the kitchen was neat and clean.

"How do you know Rajiv?" I asked.

"Jay, shall we start our class?" Siri asked, with her hands on her hips.

"Okay."

"Rajiv is my elder cousin. His father is my father's elder cousin," she said.

"Oh, long distance."

"Not really. It's a close-knit family and we are all from the same place. We know each other very well."

"Okay."

"Shall we start now or do you have any more questions?" Siri asked, with a sarcastic smile on her face.

I wanted to ask if she was married but didn't, maybe some other time. "Yeah, we'll start the class," I said.

Too early to conclude, but her unguarded attitude was charming me. She didn't look like a girl obsessed with putting her best look forward, always.

"We can sit on those chairs and discuss," Siri suggested, showing the bar stools near the kitchen top.

"For now, don't even use the word discussion. I'll not be contributing anything. You teach me, and I'll let you know if I have any questions," I said as we sat there.

"I am calling it a discussion, because I don't want to call it teaching, haha." She had a really loud voice and the loudness amplified with her laugh.

"How does this software consulting business work?" I asked, before she started the class.

"Say IT, not software, okay? IT, Information Technology. IT is lot more than just software. We are working in IT industry and we are IT consultants, okay?" She stressed the word IT so many times that I wouldn't dare use the word software instead of IT, again in my life.

"Okay, IT."

"Good, now tell me what you mean by how it works?" she asked.

"I get confused with all the terminology that people use. How does a consultant like me land a job? What are the steps and who are the people involved?"

As Siri started saying something, pointing to the one hanging to the wall, I suggested, "You can use that white board. Did you hang it there?"

"Except my personal stuff, nothing is mine here. When I am not here, Rajiv uses this place for classes. That's why the white board is here," she said.

"Why do you stay here and how often you come here?" was my next question which I didn't ask but somehow she heard it.

"In fact I am not inclined to stay here, but I couldn't say no to Rajiv. He doesn't want me to waste money when I don't have a job," she continued.

"Okay."

"Let me use a book and pen. I'll not be comfortable using the white board."

"Okay."

Scribbling in the book, Siri said, "The starting point is the client's business need that can be successfully addressed by an IT application. Ultimately it's the business need that drives an IT project, and it's a business decision whether to go for an IT solution to address the business need. Right?"

"Right."

"There are n numbers of situations from where a business need arises. We can categorize them mainly into two areas, improving business efficiency and compliance with government mandates. Right?"

"Right."

"Sometimes the reasons are so trivial. A CIO changes and everything changes, and new projects are initiated. It's good for people like us because we have more jobs in the market. Haha." Same loud laugh.

"Okay."

"And the nature of an IT project could be an upgrade of an existing IT application, replacement of an existing application, modification of an existing application, or implementation of a totally new application."

Siri made notes as she talked. She had the handwriting of a kid, legible but not tidy. While I got distracted by her bare upper arms sometimes, I was with her on the whole.

"The process of selecting a suitable IT application by the client is an entirely different topic. We'll talk about it some other time. But understand that when the client is convinced that there is an IT solution that can effectively address their business challenge and when they are convinced of the financial viability of the solution, an IT project is conceptualized."

"Okay."

"Then you need to understand various stages of project implementation like planning, requirements gathering and documentation, coding, testing, deployment, maintenance."

"Okay."

"I guess business analyst profile suits you," Siri said suddenly.

"A friend of mine said that too," I said.

As she went deeper and deeper into the IT project

management and business analysis stuff, I interrupted, "I think I asked you something else."

"Okay sir, be patient. I'll come to that point."

"Okay."

Siri continued, "To implement an IT project, clients need qualified resources with specific skill-set to fill different positions at different stages of the project. When they do not have the resources internally, they hire people from outside for the period of the project on a contract basis and they are called consultants. Clients generally depend on their primary vendors to supply the consultants. If the vendors do not have them readily available which is the case most often, they broadcast the requirements to sub-vendors. Our desi consulting companies fall into that list of sub-vendors somewhere below the chain."

"Okay."

"That's how employers like Rajiv know about the profiles currently in demand, and based on the demand, they train and market us. That's why networking is the key in this field, and Rajiv is very good at it."

"Okay."

"These vendors, I mean the primary vendors get paid by clients directly, which they pass on to sub-vendors after retaining their margin. Every sub-vendor in the chain retains a margin, and that's why the longer the chain the lesser our pay. And our employers pay us on a percentage basis."

"Salary, right?" I interrupted.

"Did Rajiv say salary?" Siri asked.

"Yeah."

"He'll move you to percentage basis after six months I guess."

I could feel the lack of oxygen in the basement. "It's suffocating in here, right?"

"Yeah, it gets heated up faster here. Shall I switch on the

fan? I use fan even in winter to beat this heat, haha, funny right?"

What's so funny about it? I laughed with her anyways. Sometimes girls feel bad even if people don't laugh at their jokes. Siri didn't seem that silly but still I didn't want to take chance.

"Shall we go out for a walk discussing this stuff?" I asked.

"Go out where?" she asked, widening her eyes.

"We'll walk up to Starbucks, get a coffee, and come back."

"Coffee now? I just had lunch."

"No problem. Have cold coffee, I mean Frappuccino. It's like a dessert," I said.

"Coffee is coffee, Jay."

"Okay let's go," I said, standing up.

"Hello, sir, I didn't say I'll come out now."

"Okay, say yes now."

"Haha. Very funny."

Again I was confused if I should laugh because it was funny to her.

"I don't want to get dressed now. It's cold outside," Siri said.

"Just put on a coat. It's not that cold," I suggested.

Siri literally put on a coat and came out. Any other girl in her place would have taken at least half an hour to get ready.

"Jay, you are wasting my time. I need to prepare for my interviews also," Siri said, during our walk to Starbucks.

"Do you have any interviews scheduled?"

"Not right now but a few are close. Interviews are scheduled on a very short notice. We don't get enough time for preparation after they are scheduled."

"You look like you are passionate about this field. Are you so inclined toward technical stuff?" I asked.

"I love computers. I started my career as a programmer. I can pretty much handle any technical profile. I have a thing for math and science from school days." Siri's face brightened as she talked about her job.

"You are exactly opposite to me. As much as possible I avoid getting involved in technical stuff. I am from biology background and did my graduation in management," I said.

"You look like that," she said.

"What do you mean?"

"You can talk passionately without a point," she said.

"What?"

"I was just joking. I know nothing about management. I feel our project managers get paid for having coffee and talking bullshit. They don't understand a thing more than deadlines. How come you are into IT then?" Siri asked.

"It's a long story. But in one sentence, all for immigration status and job and money," I said.

"Sentence is one but the purposes are many, haha," she said.

"Yeah, but your impression about management is wrong, that's not what real management is all about," I said.

"I know. I was just talking about our PMs, they are also managers." I guess I would appreciate what she said when I start my career in IT.

Contrary to my first impression, Siri was casual and talkative. I thought she was quiet and rigid. Trying to put what I was thinking into proper words, I asked, "Why do you keep such a serious face in public?"

She stopped suddenly and put her hands on her hips and gave that typical weird look of hers, and asked, "Is there any relation between what I was talking and what you are asking?"

"No, but I just asked."

"Jay, this is the last time we are coming to Starbucks. I

don't want to waste time like this."

"It's just a simple walk for coffee. And we are not wasting time. We are talking the same things while walking, which we would have talked in the room. We came out because your room was hot."

"Aha!"

"So tell me," I said.

"Tell you what?"

"Why do you keep such a serious face in public?"

"I don't do it intentionally. I don't like to talk shit like these college girls, dresses they wear, dishes they cook, TV shows, and all. I need mature people to talk to. I am happy on my own, but I hate to get involved in childish stuff."

Siri was like me in this aspect, but I didn't say it.

As we reached Starbucks, I ordered a black coffee, and asked her, "What do you want?"

"Nothing."

"Take something."

"Why? So that you don't feel guilty that you made me walk all the way for your black coffee, huh?"

This woman is too straight to handle. "Not like that, but I'll feel good if you take something. Don't you drink coffee at all?" I asked.

"Very rarely. I am a tea person."

She looked at the glass display for a minute, and said, "Let me take a cookie," as if she was doing me a favor.

Siri offered half of her cookie to me as we walked up to the seating outside.

"No, thanks," I said.

"Don't worry, I'll not ask you to share your coffee, haha."

"I don't mind sharing my coffee," I said, taking the half-cookie from her.

"Yuck! I hate black coffee."

"Black coffee is for real men. Not for a girl like you," I made a friendly comment.

"Shut up."

Wow, shut up never sounded so sexy before Siri said it.

"Do you mind if I smoke?" I asked her.

"And smoke is for whom? Super men?"

"Haha, yeah."

"Yeah. What yeah?" Siri mocked making a face.

We sat outside Starbucks in the afternoon sunlight, enjoying a slightly cold breeze. Siri surprised me by not complaining a bit about my smoking.

"Why did you give that weird look the first day when you saw me smoking on the patio? I thought you don't like smokers," I said.

"I don't like smokers even now. That day I looked at you thinking who the new face in the guest house was, that's all. And by the way, I didn't give you a weird look."

"Oh that's the way you look naturally at new people?"

"Shut up."

"I saw you from a distance that day and thought you are one of those straight from college girls," I said casually.

"What do you mean?" Siri asked, turning toward me.

"I mean looking at you closely, you don't seem to be that young."

"*Chalo* what can I say? I'll take that as a compliment. At least from a distance I look younger. Haha."

"How old are you, Siri?"

She shook her head in surprise and smiled to cover it up. "Jay, don't you think before you speak?"

"I wouldn't have asked you if I didn't feel comfortable with you," I said.

Again she shook her head, with a subtle smile on her lips, she said, "I am 29. You don't look that young too. How old are you?"

Women are women. She gave it back to me. "I am 26," I said.

"Don't lie. Generally girls lie about their age."

"I am serious. I'm 26."

"You look older than that."

"I know I look mature for my age."

"Aha, looking older is not the same as looking mature. Don't try to manipulate with your management brain," Siri said.

"Did you work in India before coming here for graduation?" I asked.

"I didn't work in India but there was a gap between completing my engineering degree and coming here. That's a big story," she said.

"Cut the long story short like I told mine in one sentence, haha."

"Not now. And I cannot cut that story short," Siri said, with a tinge of seriousness on her face. After a small pause, she asked, "Shall we go? Did you finish your coffee?"

"I can have coffee on the way, let's go," I said. "Okay, you don't have to say that story, even the shorter version of it, if you are not comfortable, but don't be serious. That doesn't suit you."

"Generally people think serious face suits me, right?" Siri said.

"That's the impression of people who don't know you."

"You don't know me too."

"I know you better than them by one hour."

"Haha."

We resumed talking about IT as we walked back from Starbucks. I felt lighter having spent some time with a woman with absolutely no hang ups.

As we reached the guest house, Siri said, "Alright, Jay. Not that we didn't make any progress today, but we'll be more focused from tomorrow."

"Okay, let me take my book," I followed her into her room.

Siri took her coat off giving me the same tickling view of her back. Since I had developed some admiration for her by then my heart didn't support my eyes.

"Okay, bye. See you in the class," I said, taking my book from her room.

"*Chalo* bye," Siri said, un-tying her hair.

"What will you do now?" I asked.

"Follow-up with emails from vendors, evening walk, shower, and then class."

Shall I join you for the evening walk? I didn't ask. Instead, I said, "Okay," and walked out of her room. I didn't want to overload her with me on the first day itself.

As I walked up the stairs from Siri's room I saw Sumit sitting in the hall. Was he spying on me?

"What's up, hero?" Sumit asked loudly stressing and stretching the word "hero".

I knew what was coming.

"Nothing much. What's up?"

"I never saw this woman talking to anybody. Even if she has to talk to people, she comes out of her room and closes the door from behind and then talks to them standing outside. I guess she taught you in her room, correct? Dude, did you do some magic or what? How did she teach?" he asked.

Sumit made me realize the special treatment I got from Siri, which made me proud. "She is very knowledgeable but not a great teacher," I said, without prolonging the discussion.

"She is one of Rajiv's highly paid consultants. You know she rejects job offers for the sake of billing and location," he said.

Rejecting a job for billing and having a preference for

location were rare privileges in IT consulting, which were enjoyed by people with reliable experience behind them and confidence to roll in the market on their own.

"Anyways, be careful, bro, she is mad. Even Rajiv is scared of her," Sumit cautioned.

"Really? How do you know?" I asked.

"She once resigned from a job because her project manager insisted on something instead of requesting. The client requested her to take back the resignation and even promised to remove the project manager from the project but she didn't yield. She resigned from a job because of the tone with which the project manager talked to her, dude, just imagine."

"Really?"

"Yep. That's why I tell you to be careful with her."

"Haha, okay." Ironically, I was attracted to the same strong personality of Siri which intimidated people.

Sumit stopped talking about Siri as other guys in the guest house came to the place where we sat, and our conversation came to an abrupt end. He was mature enough to respect the privacy of our talk. The kind of self-restraint Sumit showed was instrumental in the growing friendship between him and me.

19

Within no time, the guest house had become my new home. Doing the same thing day after day and living in the same place day after day and seeing the same people day after day and not getting used to them is not human I guess. As the days passed, barring the university and MBA environment, I wasn't missing Austin that much.

Though my phone conversations with others reduced slowly after I left Austin, I kept in touch with Amy. She got too busy with her program in the second semester, which she said was lot tougher than the first one. She didn't have time for herself, leave alone talking to me. The number of things we could talk about also reduced after I moved out of Austin. Amy didn't have a clue about the IT world and the struggles Indian techies went through.

Most Americans thought we just bought a plane ticket and landed in the US and started working from the next day. If that was the case, half of India would have been in the US by now. Something that baffled Amy was how we could get jobs with a few weeks, sometimes just a few days of training when years of college education didn't help many others. What would happen to her if she knew that some consultants land a job somehow and directly learnt on the job?

I had a fixed daily routine in the guest house. I went to college on Tuesdays and Wednesdays. Unlike the college in Austin, I attended the college in Virginia with zero respect for academics. I didn't care to know who my classmates were.

The rest of the days I spent mostly in Siri's room. Her kitchen became my kitchen and I learnt the basics of cooking from her. Starbucks became a standard part of our daily routine. I started accompanying Siri during her daily evening walk as well. We talked about everything in the world during the hour long walk. Politics, which is my all-time favorite topic, was not Siri's cup of tea though.

With Siri's help, the training classes in the guest house also started making sense, but the feeling of an outsider didn't leave me entirely. I searched for profiles that didn't demand technical expertise. I wasn't sure if I would ever acquire the comfort of a computer engineer. I looked at IT more as a savior than a career option. Playing on the sidelines never interested me, but that's exactly what I was doing.

Over time my inner voice that confronted my compromising shift to IT became feeble. One day it might erupt forcefully exposing my guilt nakedly to myself but temporarily it got buried under the layers of new life experiences in Virginia. I drew my daily motivation from the assumption that I would get a job immediately after I complete my graduate studies and get out of the financial mess within no time and set my career straight. In all, I was on logically the best possible path though conscientiously a conciliatory one.

While I thought things within my purview were under control, the external environment grew increasingly uncertain.

Year 2008 was the time when the entire world looked at the US with conflicting perceptions—fractured economy on one side and the promise of the next president on the other. It was a foregone conclusion among the majority that the Democratic candidate would be the next president of the US. That was the time when Barack Obama and Hillary Clinton were lacerating into each other to win the Democratic party nomination.

The next president would inherit a shattered economy and an under-confident America. Open any newspaper or news website, burden of mortgages, housing market collapse, recession, auto industry collapse, rocketing gas prices, wars, debt, the list of problems went on. Ordinary people were fearful whether the macro-economic ordeal would end before the dreadful news of one of the worst recessions in the US history became real. Though there were diverse views on whether the US was in recession according to the economic parameters, the county was already going through depression emotionally.

The subject of economy dominated the discussion surrounding presidential elections both among the candidates and the general public. While catchy words like "change" and "fight against establishment" were present in every presidential election, in 2008 the American people craved for an honest leadership.

Indian IT folks also eagerly awaited a change in government as the economic downturn had already started hurting their careers. And people like me wanted the situation to improve as we wouldn't be able to afford to be jobless for a long time after completing master's.

The two incidents were too separate to be even called a coincidence, but at the time when the new US president was going to take oath in January 2009, I would be in the market scouting for a job after completing my graduate college. The new president will not have a magic wand but I was hopeful to benefit from the euphoria surrounding the change. I didn't have the time that the younger lot in the guest house had.

After Austin, I had a passing thought of moving back to India but after completing my master's, I wouldn't be able to even think of it without recovering the money I spent in the US. And why should I go back now? Don't Indians come to America to earn money? If I return to India with a debt, I would be the first NRI to do so. Did I go there to feed the US universities and pump money into the US economy? No way.

Even the stability of my life in the guest house didn't last long.

During one of our evening walks, Siri said, "One good news and one bad news, Jay."

"Okay, good news first," I said.

"How come? People ask for bad news first, right?"

"I don't want to spoil the good news by hearing the bad news first."

"Interesting. Okay listen. I'll break the good news and bad news same time. I'll have to move out of Virginia for a job in New York City," Siri revealed her new job confirmation.

"Good try. I know today is April Fool's Day," I said laughingly.

"Oh, I didn't even remember that."

"Very funny. You cannot fool me."

"I swear, Jay," Siri said, placing her hand on the head. I had to believe her now.

"Didn't you say that you are looking for a job in Virginia?" I asked her angrily, as if she was liable to be with me.

"Yeah, but nothing has worked out here so far. Things are getting delayed and looking at the market situation, I didn't want to let go of this offer. Also, somewhere inside I don't want to stay close to Rajiv, though I wanted a job in Virginia. He is a nice guy. He does a lot for me but I don't want to be dependent on him. I want to build a life of my own. I hope the move will be good for me in the long run," Siri said.

"Okay. When are you moving?" I asked.

"It depends on the date of joining. Most probably I'll leave on Sunday," she said.

"Today is Tuesday. Another four days?"

"Yeah."

After walking silently for a few minutes, Siri started the

conversation again. "I'll teach you as much as I can before I leave. I can help you from there also."

"Thanks for your concern," I said nonchalantly.

"I know you are not worried about the classes. Even if I worked in Virginia, what is the guarantee that you'll be here forever. You'll have to go wherever you get your first job, right? Sooner or later, this is going to happen," Siri said, slowing down her walking pace.

"Why didn't you tell me until now?" I asked. We almost stopped walking.

"Jay, you are the first person I am sharing this news with. I got the confirmation just before we came out for walk. The process had been going on for a few days but I wanted to tell you after I got the confirmation."

"Okay. Congrats!"

"What congrats? Why are you so formal? Cheer up. You don't look good with a disappointed face," Siri said, rubbing my back.

"Honestly, Siri, I am happy for you, but I am sad that you are going far away. I can't imagine this place without you."

"New York is not far, Jay."

I had heard the same words years ago from a girl whom I never saw again. Back then, I was mad after that girl for four years while what she thought about me is unknown to me even today. This time, it was an unexpected meeting with someone which turned into a friendship and both of us were conscious that we knew each other only for a brief time, in spite of our growing comfort with each other. It was a relationship between two people who had a mature approach to life.

"Jay, what are you thinking? Shall we walk back?" Siri interrupted my thoughts.

"Nothing. Yeah, let's go back."

For most of the time I was silent as we walked back to the guest house.

"Jay, don't be like that."

"I am not sad, Siri, really. Life has to go on. I heard the news just now. It'll take some time for it to sink in. Sometimes emotions takeover even strong personalities," I said, repeating the words she had once said.

"So you think you are a strong personality, huh?"

"Haha. No."

"I was just joking, Jay. You are a great guy. I was never so at ease with any man in my life so far."

"I feel the same when I am with you too. You take the burden of being cautious off me. Actually, most of the times, you tell exactly what goes on in my mind. And you choose better words than me," I said.

"Really? I thought you are like this with everybody," Siri said.

"Nope."

"Thing is that you hesitate to talk, but when you talk, you talk so nicely," Siri said.

"I learnt it from you," I said, making light of her compliment.

"Aha, now this is too much." After a small pause, she asked me, "There is nothing you don't like in me?"

"No. I even like your thick Indian accent when you speak in English."

"What the fuck?" Siri said, putting her hands on her hips.

What the fuck? Really? Did Siri just say the f-word without any hesitation? I like it when decent girls utter dirty words. Now I can confidently say that we have become really comfortable with each other.

"Nobody ever said to me before that I have an accent," she went on with the same visible displeasure on her face.

"Siri, relax. Before me, nobody had the guts even to talk to you, forget about saying something like that."

"Haha, very funny." Siri looked like she enjoyed what I said. I didn't know why scaring the shit out of people thrilled her so much.

"But seriously, is my English that bad?" she asked.

"Let me put it correctly. You have a great vocabulary and fluency and a fine choice of words. But when you pronounce words, your accent shows. That doesn't mean your English is bad. You really don't have to work on it. Honestly, that's one of the points of attraction in you, at least to me."

"Aww, really?"

"Yeah."

"Actually, it should be the opposite, right?" she asked.

"Right, but somehow to me odd is beautiful," I said.

"Okay, now you are saying that my English is odd."

"No no, I didn't mean to say that. Girls not so perfect in everything attract me."

"Hmm, interesting. So what other odd things you find in me?" Siri asked, with a playful smile.

"It's just your accent for now. Did you start looking for accommodation in your new place?" I tried to divert her to a different topic.

"Not yet. I haven't planned anything yet. I need to put an ad for accommodation. I didn't tell Rajiv also. I'll invite you to my new place once I am settled."

"Do you want me to accompany you there until you settle down?" I wasn't sure if I'll be of any help to her, but I asked anyway.

"No. . . I'll manage." It was rather a prolonged "no" like a musical note.

"This is my fourth job here, but still I am a little tense. I will be more comfortable if I handle things on my own. And by the way, I am your senior in every aspect. You might need me, but I don't need you," Siri said, laughing.

"Haha. Okay, senior."

Siri's laugh was growing on me. I laughed more than usual when I was with her.

As we reached the guest house, she said, "Jay, let's skip the class today. I have some paper work that I need to submit to the vendor by tomorrow. I need to go out to get some documents scanned. Why don't you join me? We'll go out for dinner also."

I didn't respond immediately though I didn't have a problem.

"What's there to think so much? Anyway you don't understand anything in the class. You don't have to show off because I asked you, okay?"

"No no. I'll be more than happy to go out with you."

"Then why didn't you say yes immediately?" she asked.

"My immediacy is slower than your normalcy, Siri."

"Aha. . ."

"How will we go? Cab?" I asked.

"No, I'll take Rajiv's car. Okay listen. We'll start around six, get the documentation work done, and then go out for dinner. Okay?"

"Are you asking me out on a date, Siri?"

"Yeah right, Mr. Jay. What to do, times have changed. Nowadays guys are showing off and girls are asking guys out for dates."

"Haha. Honestly I thought several times that we should go out for dinner but I didn't ask you," I said.

"You don't have to be that shy. You only said that you feel comfortable with me."

"That's true. With you, I am not shy."

"If you are not shy with me, then I can imagine your shyness with others. Get ready. I'll give you a call in thirty minutes. Okay?" Siri said, before entering her basement room, unzipping her jacket.

The proposed dinner that night with Siri was by no means a date. But dating is an interesting concept in America. How lucky those guys were to have such a convenient and spacious concept called dating that accommodated relationships ranging from meeting someone casually over coffee to meeting someone sincerely to know each other better to meeting someone haphazardly in search of a fucking partner. Generally it meant seeing each other but came with amazing riders and perks. And the level next to dating was what they called being in a relationship, which people openly proclaimed even on Facebook. Not sure about how much love involved, but being in a relationship was considered more sacred than dating, which had all the benefits of being with a partner minus the burdens of a marriage. The best feature of those arrangements was the naturally inbuilt and uncomplicated exit strategy. Just an internet connection and a Facebook account was enough to break up. The moment relationship status on Facebook was updated as single, people were ready to mingle again. Such socially accepted arrangements filled the gap between unfulfilled human desires and getting married. And that's precisely the gap in which Indians wasted considerable part of their precious youthful and adult years.

In spite of the open culture, as much as I knew, American women in reality were not as loose as they are depicted in Hollywood movies, just pulling up their skirts and pushing down their panties whenever, wherever, and with whoever. They were dedicated to relationships in their own way.

20

Call from Siri, exactly at 6:00 p.m. "Jay, are you ready?"
"Not yet."

"Get ready then. We'll start in fifteen minutes, okay?"

Siri's fifteen minutes was generally fifty minutes, sometimes even more. She didn't spend too much time taking shower or dressing up or putting on makeup. She took time to prepare mentally to go into the restroom for shower.

Surprisingly, she called me back in just fifteen minutes, "Come down."

I saw Siri already waiting outside her room as I walked downstairs.

"Nice shirt, Jay. Pink looks good on you."

"I used to like pink a lot in India. After coming here, I became a little conscious."

"Pink is not for everyone. Only real men wear pink. Okay, here is the plan. Let's go to Rajiv's house first, take his car, and then go out. We'll complete the paper work and then go to dinner, okay?"

"You go get the car. I don't feel comfortable coming to Rajiv's house," I said.

"With me?" she asked.

"Yeah."

"You shouldn't worry when I don't have a problem. *Chalo* lets go," Siri said, patting my back. I had an admiration for her non-pretense but that was bold of her.

"Okay," I said reluctantly.

"I called up Rajiv already. We'll go collect the keys real fast," she said, while walking to Rajiv's house, a few blocks away from the guest house.

I walked along with Siri, thinking what she might have worn inside the overcoat. Jeans, tank top and cardigan as usual? It didn't look like that. Below the coat, bare legs and black sandals took the place of her trademark jeans and red sneakers. As I tried to correlate the combination of her long vertical hair clip and her off-white clutch that matched with her off-white sandals to the dress she might have worn, Siri interrupted my thoughts.

"What are you thinking, Jay?"

"Nothing." Obviously I couldn't share the shit going on in my mind. A person should be entitled to a certain level of censorship.

"Something should be going on in your mind."

"Thinking of what I should talk to Rajiv," I said.

"Rajiv is cool, don't worry. You don't have to think so much. Come," she said, as we approached Rajiv's big single-family home.

Siri pressed the doorbell.

Rajiv's wife opened the door and looked at me in astonishment. Or did I feel like that because I was expecting something of that sort from her?

"*Bhabhi*, he is Jay," Siri said. It was not customary for people in the guest house to visit Rajiv's house, and Siri didn't mention it as well in my introduction.

"Please come in," Rajiv's wife invited us. "Let me get coffee for you," she said as we sat down.

"No, *bhabhi*."

"I'll make it real quick," Rajiv's wife went inside to get coffee for us anyway before Siri could resist further.

Siri didn't remove her long overcoat, still keeping me guessing about her dress.

As his wife got the coffee, Rajiv came and sat with us. He was mature enough not to show any feelings on his face on seeing me with Siri.

"Hi, Jay. How are you?" Rajiv asked me as he handed the car keys to Siri.

"I am good, Rajiv."

"How are the classes going on?" he asked.

"Initially I found it difficult to understand things, now I am okay. Siri is helping me," I said. Siri turned her head toward me with a jerk. I realized I had said something I shouldn't have.

"How come? I requested Siri several times to take classes for our new consultants but she never agreed," Rajiv said.

"I am just explaining some basics since he is new to IT, that's all," Siri said, smiling.

After we had the coffee, we thanked her cousin and his wife and got up to leave.

"Keep the car with you if you need it. You can park in front of the guest house," Rajiv said to Siri.

That was my first direct interaction with Rajiv, and it was not as suffocating as I thought it would be.

As we got into the car, Siri opened the buttons of her long coat revealing her light blue, plain, non-flashy, below the knee dress. Was she in a happy mood that she was about to start her new job or was she excited to go out with me or had she dressed up anyway because it had been a long time since she wore that dress? Whatever the reason, Siri looked adorable.

"Did I reveal too much to Rajiv? I could make out from the way you looked at me," I said.

"No, no, that's totally fine. I just looked at you involuntarily for being so frank. Rajiv is a great guy, he is cool. Otherwise I wouldn't be comfortable living in his guest house and using his car and all. And I wouldn't have confidently asked you to come with me. You can be frank with me, but you don't have to be that frank with people about me."

So what I said to Rajiv was not totally fine. "Haha, okay. Doesn't Rajiv ask you to stay in his house?" I asked.

"He does, but I insisted on staying separate. It's better to maintain some distance for healthy relationships. Rajiv pretty much keeps that basement open for me. Having personal space is better for me too. I can wake up when I want, I can eat and sleep when I want . . . you know?"

"Yeah, I know. You don't have to take shower every day, you can throw things all over the room, I know you really need personal space," I said.

"Shut up."

"Why didn't you buy a car?" I asked.

"I used to have a used car that I sold off recently. This time I'll get a new one, Mini Cooper. I was just waiting for my new job to begin. The used car market is pretty dependable here, unlike India. But still used cars are used cars."

"Okay."

"My documentation work will take about thirty minutes. Where shall we go for dinner? Don't say Indian please," Siri said.

"You suggest, Siri."

"Mexican?"

"Fine with me."

"You came from Texas, Jay. Mexican should be super fine with you. Haha." After a pause, she said, "They are asking me to join coming Monday."

"What difference does it make when I am prepared to see you off this weekend?"

"Listen. I am leaving this weekend, but I am telling them that I'll join on Wednesday so that I get some time to settle down in the new place."

"Okay."

"Rajiv said he will give me a ride. And I want you to join us."

"What? No way, Siri, please. How many hours?"

"About four hours."

"Four plus four, eight hours in Rajiv's presence. I wouldn't be comfortable."

"I know. Even I wouldn't be comfortable to talk to you when Rajiv is around. You need to push yourself into uncomfortable situations sometimes. This will be a good opportunity for you to get to know him. He will go to any extent to support you in your job efforts, filing for your visa and many things. Rajiv is not like other employers. He values relationships a lot and that's the reason he doesn't get close to his employees, so that he doesn't have to oblige whatever they demand," Siri said. Strategically, what she said made perfect sense.

"You are like that too," I said.

"Same family, sir. Same blood. So what do you say?"

"Sounds great theoretically."

"If it couldn't be practiced, there wouldn't be a theory, Jay."

"Hmm, sounds like correct," I said.

"What like correct? It is correct. Practice can be difficult, it might even seem impossible but it's not. If something is impossible why would it even cross a human mind?" Siri elaborated her theory on theory versus practice.

"Hmm."

"So you are coming with me to Jersey City?" she asked.

"Wait, give me some time. But why Jersey City?" I asked.

"I'll stay in Jersey City and commute to New York for work. It's expensive to live in New York. I'll think of moving to New York maybe later when I become a millionaire, haha."

"How can you plan everything from here?"

"I got hold of an ex-colleague of mine who stays in Jersey City, he gave me all these details. Otherwise how would I know? This is my first trip to New York, New Jersey area."

"I would be tense to go to a new place if I don't have anyone I knew there. You are a go-getter, Siri. You think fast, you move fast . . . and you walk fast, haha."

"Most of these things can be done online and over phone. It works the same way all over America. Once you get a job, you'll also get used to. And yes, I agree with you, I walk faster than you."

"I never said you walk faster than me. I walk slowly when I walk with you because I want you to catch up with me."

"Okay, let's see tomorrow. I'll beat you hands down."

"Okay, best of luck."

"But don't feel bad that you could not compete with a girl."

"Siri, let me tell you something you don't know. You think you walk faster than me because you sweat more than me. And at twenty-nine, you are not a girl anymore."

"I know, Jay, I don't want to be a girl too. I am a woman, not complete but a woman," she said, with pursed lips.

"You are a complete woman."

"No, Jay, you don't know me completely," Siri said in a serious tone.

Not to be too nosy, instead of asking "Why do you think you are not complete?" I said, "To me, you are complete."

Siri hit me with her fist on my shoulder, clenching her lower lip between her teeth without letting her smile surface on her lips.

After the paperwork, we reached the Mexican place Siri selected for the dinner. It was a huge restaurant with splashy paintings on the walls, colorful lights and loud Spanish music playing in the background. Groups of people waited outside for tables to be allotted. When we got our turn, we took the table in the middle of the big sitting place, not really the table of my choice but didn't have much option as the restaurant was packed.

"How do all these people know that you are coming here for dinner today?" I asked.

"Oh, it was on CNN," Siri said, spontaneously bursting into a loud laughter. "This place is always crowded. On weekends, you'll not get a table without advance reservation."

"Really? What's so great about it?"

"This is the best Mexican food in town. Margaritas are great here." With her finger moving up and down the menu, Siri mumbled for a minute. "Jay, can you drive?" she asked, suddenly without looking up.

"No. That's one of my goals, to learn driving soon. I'll practice on the car that Rajiv gave for guest house use."

"Get the license first. The longer you hold a driving license without any tickets, the lesser your insurance will cost. If you knew driving by now, I would have had a drink today. Mexican food and margaritas go well together."

"Really? Do you drink?" I asked.

"Very rarely, just margaritas," Siri said, winking.

"Do you also smoke? Rarely?"

"No, but in college I used to have a secret desire to try smoking."

"I'll order a margarita, you can have a sip or two. And after dinner, you can try smoking also," I said.

"I'll try margarita, but not smoking. It was just a small desire back then which I don't have anymore," she said.

"Is margarita a ladies drink, Siri?"

"Nope. Like real men wear pink, real men drink margaritas too." After a loud long laugh, she said, "People say that probably because margaritas are little sweet and light weight and colorful and served in stylish glasses."

"But none of those qualities describe girls appropriately."

"Shut up. What do you like?" Siri asked.

"You pick. I can pretty much eat and drink anything. Order something that has chicken. I can eat chicken in any form," I said.

"No, tell me."

"Seriously I don't have a specific choice, Siri. Go on, place the order."

"Okay, let me get a margarita first," she said.

We started with classic tequila margarita on the rocks with lemon along with the complimentary starters, chips, salsa, sour cream, and chili sauce.

Siri looked different that day with more than her usual dose of makeup.

"Why are you looking at me like that? Am I so beautiful that you are unable to take your eyes off me?" She caught me staring at her.

"I was thinking of something else," I said.

"So am I not beautiful?"

"I didn't mean that, Siri."

"Then? I was just joking, Jay. I know I am beautiful," Siri said, with a laugh.

Can any man contest that statement from a woman?

"Of course, Siri, you are beautiful. But I like you better in churidar and pony tail than this kind of dress. And I like you wearing glasses, not contacts."

"Oh, I can carry anything equally well, Jay. I am a total package."

"Really? That's why you wear pajama pants always?"

"I prefer comfort over fashion. You can talk while having chips also," Siri said, munching chips and making loud sounds that didn't go well with her attire.

To the waiter who came to our table to take the order for main course, Siri pointed to something in the menu with mouth full of chips.

"What next after dinner?" Siri asked, while still munching

chips.

"Home, sweet home. Guest house, sweet guest house. Haha."

"It's been a long time since I came out of the guest house. Let's go watch a movie," she suggested.

"We'll watch *21*," I said instantly as I had movies on my fingertips.

"What the hell is that? Is it a movie?" she asked.

"Yes, just released, reviews are good."

"No English movies, please. We'll go to a Hindi movie or a Telugu movie," Siri said.

"Okay we'll watch *Race*. Saif Ali Khan, Bipasha Basu."

"No Hindi movies, please," she said.

"Then why did you say Hindi or Telugu?"

"I didn't think you'll suggest a Hindi movie, haha."

"The only option left is Telugu, and there are no recent releases. I thought you don't watch desi movies at all," I said.

"Aha, is it written on my face? Anyway, I was just playing around. We don't have an option except that *21*, *41*, whatever. They play desi movies here only on the weekends. We'll see if we still want to watch a movie after dinner."

"Okay."

After dinner, we decided not to go for a movie in the theatre, instead watch some movie online in her room.

As soon as we entered her room, Siri asked, "Jay, are you sleepy?"

"No."

"Okay search for some movie online. I'll be back in a minute," she said, going into the restroom. "Telugu movie okay?" she shouted from the restroom.

Siri changed into her usual clothes—pajama and sleeveless tank top and hair tied into a knot at the top of her head and glasses in the place of contacts.

"When exactly are you planning to leave?" I asked as she

sat beside me.

"Sunday morning. You are also joining, right?"

"Let's see."

"What's there to see?" After a pause, Siri asked, slightly bending and looking into my face as I searched for the movie, "Jay, generally you are so cheerful and happy, but your expression changes instantly when something related to career comes into discussion, right?"

"Nice smell," I said, inhaling strongly.

"That's called fragrance, not smell. Davidoff Cool Water deo. I asked you something," she said, not letting me ignore her question.

"I shifted from management to IT and to this place reluctantly. I was not completely happy with my decision and found it difficult to relate myself to this field and the people around here. Slowly I am getting used to things. Yeah, your observation is right."

"You just have to take it into your stride, Jay, IT is not difficult. I am here to support you."

"Yeah, I know. But do you see that kind of frustration on my face?" I asked.

Siri let out a long loud laugh at that. I didn't know anyone who could stretch a laugh so long. I joined her with a little smile.

"Siri, you have beautiful teeth," I said, to stop her laughing riot.

"You don't have to butter me up to cover your embarrassment. I know you meant to say I have a beautiful smile," Siri said, after a good laugh. She molded the message the way she wanted to hear.

"But you never smile, you only laugh," I said.

"Shut up. Are you so concerned that your emotions are showing on your face?" she asked, again looking into my face.

"Now that you caught me red-handed, yes," I said.

Patting on my shoulder, Siri said, "Don't worry, it's just a matter of time. Don't look at all the stupid people around you and get disappointed. You might start with them but you'll reach a different height. IT is not all about coding and testing. There are some premium profiles in IT too which need smart people like you. Most people who make it big in this field don't know coding, and who knows you might be a big shot in IT one day."

"Honestly, after knowing you, I am little settled than before. But I never knew that the frustration was so conspicuous on my face," I said.

"Haha. Yeah, it is."

"Damn. I am not worried much about IT now. I am more worried about my inability to manage my emotions."

Siri started her laughter marathon again, falling on my shoulder.

"Siri, be careful. You might vomit the Mexican food we just ate on me. It was expensive."

"Do you think it's a blot on your manliness to show emotions on your face?" she asked.

"Yeah."

"Real men show emotions, Jay."

"Real men wear pink, real men drink margaritas, and real men show emotions. And what else do real men do?"

"They come with me to Jersey City on Sunday."

I didn't commit on that yet.

After watching the movie for a few minutes, Siri took off her glasses, started rubbing her eyes, yawning and falling on my shoulder often. We stopped the movie and called it a night.

For a change, I had met an original and confident Indian woman rather than someone who was either an over-confident feminist or an under-confident traditionalist. For a short and slender frame, Siri overflowed with confidence, minus the girly tantrums. Wherever and whenever possible, she made a strong personality statement to the extent of appearing overconfident and rude to unfamiliar people. Her inability to fit in made people like Sumit think of her as mad and strange. I wish she was a little more graceful in her handling of things, but seeing her being herself was better than seeing her trying to be elegant and not herself.

21

The next day morning I woke up to the phone ringing—something that I hate to the core.

I was about to cut the call when I saw Siri's name on the screen. Very rarely I answered a call when I was eating or sleeping but I did, spontaneously, and that call changed my life forever. From that day onwards, my days started with talking to Siri.

"Good morning, Siri."

"Good morning, aren't you up yet?"

"No."

"Okay, come down for a few minutes. Let's have tea. You can go and sleep later," Siri said, without even a trace of guilt in her voice for waking me up. "Come down fast. Your tea is getting cold. It's very nice outside," she said, while I was still contemplating how to say no.

"Umm… Siri…"

"Come outside the main door directly. I am sitting outside."

"Okay," I said lazily.

Very rarely I sacrificed my morning freshness for people. And very rarely I went out and met anybody without getting ready for the day. But I couldn't say no to Siri. I washed my face and went down without even brushing my teeth, a comfort which I never showed even with my guy friends. I went down putting on a jacket.

There I saw picture-perfect Siri from the back, wearing an

ink blue hoodie sitting on the entrance steps of the house in the morning mist with two cups of tea emitting hot smoke placed next to her.

Did she suffer from insomnia or what? And how confident was she to prepare two cups of tea?

"Hey, Siri, how come you woke up early today?" I said, sitting beside her.

"I woke up for bathroom and couldn't sleep after that," she said, handing me a cup of tea.

It was really a beautiful morning with bright orange sunshine that dominated the cold breeze and lit up the moisture over the grass. Not sure if it was worth foregoing my sleep though.

"I didn't know that you have so much appreciation for nature," I said.

"Why?"

I just passed a throwaway comment. I guess the public perception Siri carried played at the back of my mind when I said that. How could I think clearly before talking when I was woken up in the middle of a sound sleep?

By the time I framed my answer, Siri said, "I know people think of me as antisocial, Jay. But what can I do? I don't have tolerance for stupid people and their silly talk. I am very sensitive and probably more sensitive than many people. I take a lot of time to recover from a bad mood. I tend to protect myself a lot."

How come she heard what I was thinking? In fact Siri and I talked silly things too. But I guess her problem was to be around people who don't accept her as she was.

"Hmm, well said, ma'am," I said, sipping the tea.

"What's that now?"

"You call me sir too sometimes."

"Hmm, what is your complete name, Jay?"

"It took so long for you to ask me this question? Jayawardhan."

"And people used to call you Jay from childhood, right?"

"Actually people started calling me Jay as I grew up. My childhood name was Red."

"Red? They teased you because you are dark?" Siri asked, laughing so loudly that the reverberations of her laugh in the morning calm could wake up the community.

"Haha, no."

"Then?"

"Because of my love for red color."

"Really? You like red so much? You know red color symbolizes intensity?" Siri said.

"No. I don't like red because it symbolizes something, I just like it. What's your favorite color?" I asked her.

"Depends on the mood and season. I guess I have an inclination for white and blue," Siri said.

"And what do they indicate?"

"White is for purity and blue for trust."

"You also didn't like those colors after knowing what they meant, right?" I asked. I guess the hot tea kicked the sleep out of me, my brain started working.

"Shut up," Siri said, leaning toward me and pushing me with her shoulder.

"What's the plan today?" she asked.

"I have college."

"Oh, I forgot today is Wednesday. I thought of showing you some real project documents. We'll do it later then."

"Okay, shall we go now? I am feeling cold," I said, after completing the tea.

"Yep, *chalo*," Siri said, lifting her hand up for support.

I tried but I wouldn't be able to stand her up if she wasn't cooperating intentionally. Then I tried lifting her up with both my arms under her arms from behind. Though physical intimacy was not part of my relationship with Siri, I couldn't help control my provocation. Moreover I had come straight from bed without even wearing underwear.

The four days from that day passed in no time and the day had come when Siri had to leave for Jersey City for her job. On Sunday, March 9, 2008, Siri left Fairfax to Jersey City. I often forget birthdays of even close friends and family members but some dates get registered with no effort. I didn't feel much pain as I also joined her and Rajiv for Jersey City.

After about four hours of driving, we reached the hotel Siri had booked for a couple of days stay before she finalized one of the apartments she shortlisted. Though Rajiv suggested her to opt for shared accommodation for a couple of months, the fiercely independent woman that she was, Siri insisted on signing the lease on her own.

Siri assured that she was going to be with me for a long time by not creating an emotional scene when Rajiv and I started our drive back. Why would someone get emotional about something that was not going to end?

The drive back with Rajiv was not bad. I could strike a chord with him easily. Rajiv was like Siri, the conversation just had to start; both of them would keep talking non-stop. Rajiv was so protective about Siri that every now and then he slipped into talking about her. I listened to whatever he said without poking into their family matters. I didn't have to ask Rajiv about Siri, I could ask her directly. I was fairly close to her by then.

The trip to New Jersey was much more than just about dropping Siri, and it yielded the intended benefit. I had the opportunity to draw Rajiv's attention to my story. By the time the trip was over, Rajiv setup an internship job for me in one of his friend's office. He called up his friend during our drive itself.

I started my internship the very next day. At every step, I felt the pain of starting all over again, the same things I did in India years back at a much younger age. I wasn't really having fun but I sucked it up without complaining.

In addition to college on Tuesdays and Wednesdays, the internship on Mondays, Thursdays, and Fridays was a positive disruption to my routine and it happened at the right time. Otherwise I would have gone mad in the guest house in Siri's absence.

After about a month she had joined her new job, Siri invited me to her place. She showed kind of a reluctance to come down to Virginia. Suddenly the guest house basement was not hers anymore.

Not that I cared about social acceptance, but no eyebrows were raised about Siri and I being close to each other, and even Rajiv started asking me about how she was doing sometimes.

A call from Venkat one day suddenly reminded me that I was so much into Siri that my calls to him had drastically reduced.

"Jay, how are you? No calls these days? Looks like you settled down well there," Venkat said.

It has been more than a week since I had called him, which was very rare. Surprisingly he didn't call me too during that one week. I compensated for not telling the actual reason with a laugh. I didn't reveal anything about Siri to Venkat till then. Initially I didn't feel it was important, and as time passed, I don't know why but I couldn't. I didn't tell him anything about Amy either when I was in Austin, except that I got a ride from a girl in my class sometimes. Whenever we talked about girls, the only girl Venkat talked about was Jhansi. Once in a while, he revived the part of my heart crystallized with Jhansi's memories. But can people just survive on memories? I did. I lived with Jhansi's memories all these years, but what if someone disappeared beyond hope? What will the rest of my heart do? For now, it was with Siri. With Siri around, the frequency of Jhansi's thoughts had decreased. I guess America has not only made me belligerent about my career but also about how I thought about relationships.

"Listen, I have transferred some money to your account," Venkat said, bringing me back into the conversation.

"No, I don't need now," I said instantly.

"I received the tax returns. I wanted to send you some money before they disappear from my account," Venkat said.

"I am not earning but still I have a weakness for frivolous spending, Venkat. You know that."

"I know but you are my saving account, Jay. In fact, I should be thankful to you that you are helping me save some money."

"Hopefully, I'll give you some returns on the money I have borrowed from you," I said.

"Don't worry about returns. Just give me the principal amount when you have it. When your career turns around, I'll feel proud that I had a part in your success story. You have time until my daughter's wedding," he said, and laughed.

"Hopefully, I'll not take that long. But wait a minute. Do you have some good news?" I asked.

"Yep!"

"Congrats. And convey my wishes to Tulasi also."

"Thanks. Yeah, I will."

"But how do you know it's a baby girl?" I asked.

"We don't know yet, but hopefully. And how are things otherwise?" Venkat said.

"Going fine, Venkat. Actually I wanted to call you to say something."

"And you thought the phone would ring by itself?"

"Haha, no. I joined a desi company—"

"Joined? Joined as what?" Venkat asked, with a mix of

surprise and excitement in his voice even before I completed the sentence.

"Intern. This company does some federal projects. I'll be part of their team of business analysts. But they don't pay me anything," I said.

"Great. I was thinking that you should do something like that. Forget about pay for now. This is a great learning opportunity. Great great. How did you get it, by the way?" Venkat asked.

"Through Rajiv," I said.

"Your employer? This is interesting. You can work and get paid legally while you are in the university through CPT. You know that, right?" Venkat said.

"Yeah, curricular practical training, I know. I don't think they will pay me. It's a desi company."

"I know, Jay, but maybe they will in future. Make a plan to come down to Charlotte. It's been a long time since we met. Let me know the dates. I'll book the ticket for you. I guess now you can come down only on the weekends."

Except that I was not earning, I enjoyed a life more colorful than someone who had a job—college, internship, guest house, luxury to visit Siri's place and Venkat's place whenever I wanted, at their expense.

* * *

As the days and months passed, America plunged deeper and deeper into a financial mess. In the first half of 2008, economists, politicians and media had mixed opinions on whether technically the country was in recession or not. The general public took it easy because the contradiction between the voices of concern from the experts and the voices of placation from the government existed all the time. When Lehman Brothers filed for Chapter 11 bankruptcy protection in September 2008, not just Americans but the entire world started believing that there was something seriously wrong with the US economy.

What was thought to be sub-prime housing market crisis blew up into the worst recession in the US history since the Great Depression of 1930s. The effects were felt not just in the US but across the world. There were widespread reports that the recovery would be long drawn out.

Indian IT folks on the bench started complaining about declining job opportunities and billing rates. After a certain time, billing rates stopped being an issue because more and more people were going out of jobs. Even people with credible work experience were happy to get any job with whatever pay. Preference for specific profiles and locations started disappearing.

Indian media exaggerated the situation more than what it was, and the families of the NRIs back home panicked, which was worsening the situation for them. Indian media in the past glorified the US job market when things were good, creating false hopes among people, and it was now doing the same thing on the other extreme.

That's when, for the first time in the history of America, a black candidate was poised to take over the White House, raising hopes not just among the American citizens but also among the Indian IT folks.

Every four years, the US presidential elections happen in the month of November. But in 2008, the country was through with its presidential elections on August 28 itself when Barack Obama beat the formidable Clinton juggernaut to win the Democratic nomination. The fight was over. The November elections were just a formality. The burden of Bush legacy and failing economy made that election a real bad one for the Republicans.

The Tuesday that followed the first Monday in the month of November is when the Americans elect their president.

In 2008, that day fell on November 4, the historic day on which, true to expectations, Barack Obama became the 44th president of America with a decisive mandate. By electing him, ordinary Americans felt they had sent their man to the White House.

I followed the US elections like I had never followed elections in India.

The best thing I liked about Obama's election night's victory speech, apart from the catchy one-liners, was that he tried hard to make people realize that change has not come to America yet and it has just begun. He tried his best to bring the country out of the trance and set expectations by saying that it might take more than a term or two terms to bring the country back on track.

But Mr. President, I don't have that much time, please do something to revive the US economy fast.

The good news for me about Obama's victory was that he repeatedly claimed on the campaign trail that economy will be his top priority which will directly boost the job market. It was widely expected that Obama would combine both short-term measures of jumpstarting the economy by pumping money into markets and long-term strategy to exercise restraint on financial recklessness. He was expected to play somewhere in between being a ruthless capitalist and an ardent socialist.

I called up Amy to release my hormones of political excitement. When she didn't answer my call in the first attempt, I was worried if she was angry with me for not calling her for a long time.

She called me back soon.

"Hey, Jay, I was expecting your call. Why do you always call me when I am in the restroom?"

"You should be taking your cell to restroom then."

"Haha, that's the only place I don't take it right now. I was

just thinking about you when Obama was speaking," Amy
said.

"That was a terrific speech, isn't it?"

"Yep. He has an extraordinary ability to rally crowds
around his ideas. I had goose bumps when the crowds were
cheering 'Yes we can.' I sat in disbelief for some time after
the speech." Amy couldn't suppress her admiration for their
president-elect.

"You donated for Obama's campaign and you voted for
him. How do you feel now?" I asked.

"Great. What Obama accomplished is extraordinary. He
showed extraordinary character throughout the campaign.
Hope he continues to do the same as the president also," she
said.

"You should feel proud to be a Democrat," I said.

"I am not a Democrat. I am a registered Independent," she
said.

"Really? Do you have to register even to be an Independent?"

"It's an option we have. But I can vote for a Democratic
candidate being a registered Republican voter also."

"Then what good is registration?"

"A registered voter can vote for anybody or choose not to
vote also. But, no registration no voting."

"Interesting."

"Party registration makes a lot of difference in voting in
primaries. In closed primaries, only registered party voters
can participate in the selection of candidates. I guess most
of the states have closed primaries," Amy went on with her
discourse on American election process.

"Okay, did you major in politics in your undergraduate
college?" I asked.

"Haha, no. You know about me. How are things at your
end? You didn't call me for a long time. What's going on?
Busy?" she asked.

"I have joined an internship here which is keeping me little busy these days. That's some good news I can share with you."

"Wow, great," Amy said.

"I don't get paid though. It's an opportunity to understand practically how this IT thing works."

"Getting industry exposure when you are in college is always great. The up side of not getting paid is you'll not have the pressure to perform. You can focus on learning," she said.

"Yeah, that's right." Actually, I didn't think about my internship from that angle.

"I don't see the worry in your voice that you used to have when you moved there initially. I guess you found some direction now," she said.

"Yeah kind of, Amy. How are things going with you? How is your job?"

"Very interesting. I am enjoying it. I will be traveling to other countries soon."

By other countries I hope she didn't mean India. And why not, when India has become an important outsourcing destination to the US?

"Good to hear. *Chalo* alright, Amy. Take care."

"What the fuck is *chilow*?"

"Oh, it's an Indian expression for something like 'okay then'."

"*Chilow* bye." She pronounced the word in the weirdest possible way.

Chalo was something Siri used frequently and I guess I picked it from her. I didn't even realize it until Amy pointed out.

After MBA, Amy joined a prominent electronic instruments company in Austin itself. Her job was to coordinate with a group of her company's vendors as part of managing its outsourcing efforts. International trade management should be renamed as outsourcing management for what's left in international trade other than outsourcing and some legal documentation?

Maybe I was trying to find a respite in grumbling about the lost opportunity. That was the dream profile I had in mind, managing a business on an international scale with which I stepped into the US. I constantly remembered the fact that I got drifted away from my original plan but the reasons behind it paled with time. What if I completely forget why I started over a period of time and get flushed out in the flow of compulsions? Even the thought was unpleasant.

For the time being, what worried me more was my OPT, optional practical training, the permission to work officially in the US after completing graduate studies. It was like a return gift from the US government to the foreign students for coming to their country and helping their universities survive.

My OPT would kick in at a time when Obama would take the office as president in January 2009. Any good that happens to the economy because of the new president would boost the IT spending of the companies and hence IT jobs.

I kept my fingers crossed.

22

October 2009: Obama was on the verge of completing the first year of his first term as president and I was on the verge of completing my one year OPT period. The job of searching for job was still on.

The stagnant external situation turned the environment in the guest house gloomy. While America went through the worst recession in 2008, the ripple effects were felt throughout 2009. The much debated Obama's economic stimulus package worth hundreds of millions of dollars didn't trigger the economic recovery immediately.

Like any other graduate student, I waited to walk into the job market on red carpet as soon as my OPT started, which didn't happen. Weeks and months passed. I continued to hang around in the same guest house. I drew some solace from the internship job which I started working five days a week since the beginning of the year, still without pay.

Without the internship, the guest house life would have been pathetic. Neither Rajiv nor his friend who I worked for talked about pay, and I didn't have the courage to ask for payment during a time when people were just happy to be able to go offices. Apart from the internship, getting the driving license, courtesy of Sumit, was the only progress I made during my guest house stay. He showed more confidence than what I had in myself when he taught me driving.

IT industry took one of its worst beatings during recession. Many Indian techies, even those who put up some real-time experience, were out of work. People with pending immigration status renewal were forced to wait or change into another legal status temporarily or leave the country. Even the H1B visa quota wasn't getting filled up completely. Worst news came when a few Indian IT employers were arrested for H1B visa irregularities. Employers who were not willing to sponsor for H1B visas became even more cautious, which was not good news for people like me.

I was immune to the effect of economic slowdown in 2008 since I was in college. I didn't pay serious attention to what people used to say then. I thought my case would be different, I just needed one job. I was optimistic to the extent of being unmindful of the macroeconomic facts. Not even in my wildest imagination did I think that I would be searching for job for one full year after completing the master's. During my two years in the guest house, one year as a student and one year on the bench, I tried my hands at several IT courses, but none of them helped me get a job. It wasn't easy for me to keep pushing forward but I chose that path, and I couldn't have given up in the middle of the road.

Returning to India at that point of time was out of question since it would take a lifetime to clear the debt I owed to people by converting Indian rupees into US dollars. That was the difference of pay between America and India for the same work. I was confident of coming out of the financial mess somehow, but I wouldn't get back the precious time I was losing unproductively.

As I reached the end of the year 2009, I was more worried about the expiration of my OPT since I wasn't a beneficiary of extended OPT period based on my major in master's. I guess that's what happens to fringe players. I was forced to register into another fucking, useless, cumbersome, depressing, painful, and most importantly money-sucking university program not to study but just to be able stay in the US. Where would I get the fucking money? I was already sitting on a large debt, the dollar amount I was scared to even to utter. Money poured into my bank account from friends even before the need arose, but I needed to pay them back.

My H1B visa application got rejected in 2009 and to be able to file the application again by April 1, 2010, the next deadline, and get it approved, I needed to find a job by the end of March. I had tough deadlines for the coming period, failing which would lead to serious financial ramifications.

There are universities that enrolled students to give out CPT status in lieu of money, sorry course fee. I heard about students who enrolled in such universities to maintain their visa status without even attending colleges, most times without even having a look at the college campuses. I wouldn't do that. I wouldn't push my future immigration status into jeopardy by resorting to such a foolish step.

If people said to me that what I was going through was a possibility when I was preparing to go to America, I would have laughed at them.

Sumit had already gone to India for good after his H1B got rejected along with mine. Being an engineering student, he was eligible for extended OPT but he chose not to stick around. Compared to his peers in India, who hadn't had the opportunity to visit the US, he was in a better position for having exposed himself to America. His financially strong family background prompted his decision, but what about his personal sense of achievement after spending so much time and money? Would he have left America if he had a job? Perhaps not that early but how does that matter? Life operates on facts and not hypotheses.

After Sumit left, I felt lonelier in the guest house. Job or no job, I thought I wouldn't get affected. But I was wrong. I was not calling people back home that much. I kept in touch only with Siri and Venkat. I hadn't lost my internal frame of confidence yet, but I didn't want uncomfortable discussions to take over the strength I was holding together.

Siri and Venkat invited me to spend Thanksgiving and Christmas at their places, since the job market would be real sluggish in the last couple of months of a year. I didn't want to disturb Venkat as he was busy with his new-born daughter. He was of the same age as me, but he was already married and had settled well. I had all the options like him, but I chose not to. Not that his life was bad, but I wasn't ready for a normal life.

***

December 31, 2009.

"I am not a good dancer," I told Siri for the hundredth time that day.

Siri had proposed that we go to a desi dance floor that night. Until she came up with that idea, I didn't even know that she liked dancing. In the past more than a year that I had known her, I didn't see a hint of a dancer in her body language.

"Do you think I know dancing?" Siri asked.

"How can you be so enthusiastic about it then?"

"There's a first time for everything, Jay. I just want to experience it. I have gone to the dance floor couple of times earlier, but I was terrified to go anywhere near. I want someone by my side to feel confident. I can fairly guess that you suck at dancing. I'll be comfortable showing you some moves."

"I don't dance but I appreciate people who are good at it. I don't want to lose my impression of you by seeing your stupid dance moves," I said.

"I am not worried about that. You'll not be able to judge me in that dim light anyway."

"Then what's the fun in dancing?"

"Fun is not in dancing, Jay. Fun is in letting ourselves loose.

It's not for others, it's for us. I want to do it once and who can be a better partner than you?"

"Whatever you say, Siri, I am not getting motivated."

"Okay, let me try in a different way. You get to drink there. Since you don't have to drive, you drink as much as you want, okay? We'll step on the dance floor just for a few minutes around midnight. That's all, okay?"

"I didn't think you enjoy so much noise."

"Generally, I don't. Once in a while it's okay to experience the other side, what we are not, to appreciate what we are," Siri said with a wink, to which I could only respond with an expressionless face. "Don't think too much. We'll just go there and see how it goes. I'll not ask you to stay even for a minute if you are not comfortable, okay?"

"Okay," I agreed reluctantly.

After shower, I went out for a smoke to give some time for Siri to get ready. And when I came back, she looked stunning in red sleeveless, above the knee dress. Was that because I told her that I liked red or was I reading too much into it?

My heart beat faster as we entered the hotel but I was relieved as we entered the big hall to see more people sitting on the tables and eating than on the dance floor. Food was arranged on one side and drinks on the other side of the hall. I got my favorite single malt and Siri orange juice, which she never even touched at home.

As we took a corner table, looking at the glass in my hand, Siri asked, "How does that taste?"

"Very nice, otherwise why would I drink?" I said, with a smile. "It tastes a little bitter and burns your throat a little initially, but if you mix it with water or soda it tastes good," I said.

"Why didn't you mix then?"

"I like it this way."

"Black coffee, raw alcohol, it affects your health, Jay."

"It's not raw alcohol. It's called on the rocks. It gets diluted as time passes."

"What's your favorite brand?"

"Glenlivet. Any single malt is fine with me."

"What's single malt?"

"Hmm, good question."

"So that means you don't know, haha." Siri laughed so loudly that people sitting around our table got distracted from their business and got attracted to us. Her interpretation was right to an extent.

"I guess both the ingredients and the manufacturing process differ. I only know that single malts are light and non-smelly and taste better, and usually they don't give hangovers."

"Is it really that good? Let me have a sip," Siri said, taking the glass from me.

"Yeah. I can dilute it for you in another glass," I said.

"No. I'll try from yours."

"Okay, this will be too much for you. You'll hate the taste initially, but after a couple of sips you'll love it," I said.

"So you are preparing me mentally, huh?" Siri said, and took a sip from my glass. She made all kinds of expressions holding the drink in her mouth.

"Don't spit. Just swallow. It's precious," I said.

She drank quickly in one gulp, closed her eyes tightly, and stretched her tongue in and out rapidly couple of times and drank the orange juice immediately.

"Jay, how do you drink this? Fuck!" Again she distracted the people around us. At least she could have uttered the f-word softly. After sipping the orange juice couple more times, Siri asked, "Do you want to eat something?"

"No, I am fine."

Siri went to get some food anyway and came back with a plate full of snacks. "What's your new year resolution?" she asked placing the snacks place on the table.

"Nothing."

"Quit smoking and drinking," she said.

"No, Siri. I'll quit at some point of time in future but not now. I'll be bored without smoking. It's my best friend."

"Nobody can smoke and drink forever, Jay. They quit at some point of time. Why not now?"

"Nobody will live forever too, Siri. People die at some point of time."

"But you need to live a healthy life as long as you live."

"I was just joking. I understand what you said. I don't think I have to quit drinking because I am never big on it. I am a very light drinker. But I'll quit smoking definitely. Maybe after I get a job and when my finances fall in place."

"I am not that religious, but I pray to God that you should get a job soon," Siri said. I could see her concern for me in her eyes, which looked more expressive that night without her glasses on.

"God listens to someone who has never asked anything. Now I am sure I'll get a job sooner," I said.

As we were absorbed in talking and laughing and enjoying by ourselves, there was a sudden frenzy and people rushed toward the dance floor as the clock neared twelve, as if the new year guaranteed something to everybody.

How different is change of year compared to change of month, change of week, or change of day? Isn't the change of date from December 31 to January 1 as good as the change of date between any two days? But still we hope for miracles on every new year eve. On the brighter side, some good things do happen to people who take resolutions and follow them, at least for a few days. And job aspirants like me wait for the job market to pick up with renewed vigor. It's a change of gear to put aside the past year and look forward to a better year ahead, otherwise we never leave the past as if it's a valuable possession that cannot be parted with. It's one more occasion to take a break from regular life and indulge in something different, like Siri was trying her hand at dancing that night.

Siri pulled me to the dance floor to join the crowd. I was shocked to see an otherwise conscious Siri dancing unmindful of the crowd. Her efforts to be elegant couldn't cover up her raw moves. I stood there for some time, moved my legs and hands a bit and escaped from the floor telling Siri that I needed to call people in India.

"Jay! Happy new year!" Madhu yelled. It would be difficult to decide who would win the competition for a loud voice between Siri and Madhu.

"Happy new year. When did you come?" I asked Madhu.

"Yesterday. Why are you so dull? Why is it calm? Didn't you go out?" she asked.

"I came for a party with friends. They were dancing like crazy in there. I came out to talk to mom," I said.

"Mom and dad are watching TV. How are you?"

"I am good, eagerly waiting the for the job market to be better in the new year."

"Can I tell you something, Jay, if you don't get annoyed?"

"Yeah tell me."

"I know mom might have told you this several times till now. Why don't you come back? Dad is willing to pay off your debt. How long will you wait for job? Mom is very sad. Dad doesn't say it, but he also feels bad. Your brother-in-law also wants you to come back."

"I'll give it another six months, hopefully something should work out. The market is picking up," I said comfortingly.

"It's up to you ultimately, but we don't feel good here if you are struggling there."

"I don't have a job but I am not really struggling. I have friends to support me," I said.

"But how long, Jay? Anyway we'll leave it to you. Mom is

also worried that your marriage is getting delayed."

"Marriage can wait, Madhu. What's up with you? When are you planning for a second kid?"

"Just like you have time for marriage, we have time for second kid," Madhu said, laughing.

"You should tell the same thing to mom," I said.

"She'll kill me."

"How is Chintu?" I asked about my sister's son.

"He is doing great. He slept just now. He is already three years old and you haven't seen your nephew yet."

"I know. I'll plan a trip to India as soon as I get a job. I need to go inside to join my friends now. Tell mom that I'll call her tomorrow morning. Bye."

"Bye, take care. Don't drink too much," Madhu said.

"Shut up." I hung up.

Siri was still dancing when I went in. She was so immersed even after many people had already left the floor. Looked like the drink I had intoxicated her.

Though I couldn't do anything until the end of January, when the job market was expected to kickstart, I couldn't motivate myself for the year end celebrations.

When will I learn to have fun one hundred percent without the rational side of me bugging from inside and nagging parallel thoughts bothering me constantly? Why was I so conscious? Why was I getting into long periods of silence even in the presence of people? Was it because I didn't have a job? If I have a job by the next new year eve, will I drink, dance, and party like mad?

Shouldn't this streak of disappointments end at some point? Shouldn't this seemingly unending ordeal end somewhere?

I entered into 2010 in a compulsive optimistic mode. I didn't have the childlike optimism that I had in the beginning of 2009 anymore. By then, I was a mature job seeker. I knew practically what it meant to be on job search. I knew what it meant when a vendor doesn't come back after the initial promising conversation. I knew what it meant when a client doesn't respond after the interview. I knew that I don't have a job until I physically step into the client's office.

The new year started for me with registration into another stupid university program with another stupid major for the sake of immigration compulsions. This time around, it was a program with classes on alternate weekends so as to accommodate my work when I get a job.

By the end of January there was visible optimism in the job market. Vendor calls started coming in as if somebody had switched on something. The change of scene was dramatic compared to the past couple of years. The recession was so impactful that even at the place where I worked as intern for free, I went through a reference. Those guys didn't bother to ask me to stay even for minimum pay. For companies and consultants who sustained with a hope that the ride through the dark tunnel would end and they'll see the light, the year 2010 gave a promising start.

Whether the economic hope that Obama injected into the peoples' psyche started working or the stimulus money that he pumped into market or it would have happened anyway irrespective of any political and economic interference because economies went into recession and came out of it just like that as a matter of natural cycle—how will I know when even experts were confused? I was happy that America had started coming back.

23

March 4, 2010: I couldn't believe my ears when I heard the vendor's voice on phone—confirming my first proper paid job in America as a consultant business analyst in Seattle.

I wasn't instantly elated. The fear of performance in my first job overtook the joy of getting to do something worthwhile and getting paid after living for such a long time unproductively on borrowed money. Consultants were paid more than full-time employees, great, but they don't get paid for just showing up in a nice dress. The payment comes with expectations.

I got the job when waiting was taking a toll on me. A couple of months more on the bench would have broken me emotionally, while financially I was broke already.

It was Rajiv's company policy to not pay for relocation expenses which was an overhead, without a guarantee on whether I would be able to keep my job in Seattle for a long time. I started recollecting all the stories I heard about consulting IT professionals losing jobs as soon as they joined, sometimes on performance related issues and sometimes just like that, which induced a strange fear within me. Was there a need for me to travel all the way to Seattle to join a job which I wasn't sure of? If the job doesn't last for at least two months I would be spending more money than I would have earned. But then, having spent so much time on bench, did I have an option?

I spent the entire day with conflicting thoughts and called Siri when I thought she would have come back from office, to share the good news and my dilemma attached to it.

"What's up, Jay?" Siri asked. I could hear the exhaustion in her voice. That's how people sounded at the end of a working day when they traveled from New Jersey to New York for work and back.

"You look tired, Siri," I said.

"Oh, you are able to see me then? Tell me what color am I wearing?"

"Blue."

"How do you know?"

"Blue has more probability."

"I don't choose blue consciously, Jay, it just happens that I end up buying more blue clothes without even realizing."

"That's when people say you like that color."

"Haha. Talking to you refreshes me. It was a really hectic day. What happened to you? You didn't call me all day. What were you doing?"

"I need to tell you something," I said.

"Don't tell me that you have decided to go back to India," Siri said.

"No. I am going to Seattle."

"Who the fuck do you have there that I don't know about?"

She didn't think even remotely that I might have got a job there. With someone who had been jobless for so long, people couldn't be anxious for every phone call. And with Siri, with whom I talked several times in a day, that was a distant possibility.

"Finally there is someone who is ready to offer me a job," I said.

"Yay! Awesome!" Siri screamed with joy like all her tiredness had magically disappeared.

"Wait. What do you think? Should I go that far?" I asked, trying to bring down her excitement.

"Of course. Wherever, Jay, for the sake of job. That's the best thing you have right now, and you should take it. By the way, which profile?"

"Business analyst."

"Perfect. Then you should not even think. Don't think about me, Jay. This will be a good opportunity for me to visit Seattle. I have never been to the west coast."

"I am scared, Siri. It's a new place. I don't know anybody there. I'll have to spend a lot on relocation, I am not sure how long this will last and I am worried about my performance. I'll have to fly here every alternate weekend for college until I get my H1B approved. Too many things running through my mind."

"Oh, I thought you were worried about leaving me," Siri said.

"I am worried about you also."

"Aha, if that was true, you would have told me in the beginning itself."

"Do I have to say that to you, Siri?"

"Okay, I believe you. But none of what you have said is a strong enough reason not to take up this offer. You are going to Seattle, and we'll work out things. All expenses until you get your first paycheck are on me. Okay? Even if you work for a week, all the time and money you are going to spend is going to be totally worth it, believe me. Don't think that you are new to IT and all that nonsense. You'll get enough time to settle down. Clients here do not have unrealistic expectations."

"Okay."

"I am sure you'll rock, Jay. I know you. People who cannot even frame one correct sentence in English are working successfully here. You are a brilliant guy. And you need to trust the timing. April first is the deadline to apply for your

H1B and you got the job now," Siri continued, with her sermon.

"Yeah, you are right. I didn't think about it from H1B visa angle so far. Now I don't have an option but to go to Seattle," I said.

"Send me the address and dates. I'll book the flight for you," Siri said.

"No."

"What no? I'll take all this money back from you with interest later, don't worry Mr. Business Analyst."

That's what Siri always said. My unwillingness to let her spend on me was because of the doubt that she wouldn't accept the money when I return her back. The time Siri invested to train me and the emotional support she extended to keep me going were more than enough for me to be thankful to her for a lifetime. Financial indebtedness will be a burden I wouldn't be able to carry.

After Siri's inspirational talk, I was fired up for my first job. I sent the confirmation email to the vendor the same evening. Other than my own unfounded apprehensions, I had no reason not to take up the job that was closest to my skill set.

Venkat's opinions echoed with what Siri said. He was already planning to send me some money to take care of myself until I settled down in Seattle. My job confirmation was cheerful news for all the friends who supported me. They wouldn't have supported me financially if they were so eagerly waiting for me to join a job and repay them, but after all, they had a stake in my career.

I had a lot of things to take care of before I joined the job. Most importantly, I needed to equip myself with some formal clothes. I wasn't sure the ones I had would fit me anymore. For the past couple of years, after coming from Austin I hadn't got a single opportunity to wear formals.

Any other guy in my place would have done some research on the Seattle Seahawks because Americans identified themselves with their states' sports teams. That's the starting point of forging friendships and getting into peer groups in offices, I had heard. With time, I might get attached to their sports and teams. I hadn't used that as a tool to be cool until then.

As I thought about my Seattle trip, Siri called me again. "Jay, when do you have to join?" she asked.

"Not sure. I asked for almost nine days."

"Okay. When will you know exactly?"

"Tomorrow, most probably. Why?"

"I am looking at the flight tickets. The fare is almost the same whether you fly from your place or my place."

"So?"

"Why don't you come to Jersey City this weekend after your college and spend a few days, and fly from here? The following weekend anyway you don't have college."

"Sounds good, but first I'll have to fly to your place with my entire luggage."

"No. I'll drive there Sunday morning, meet Rajiv, and we'll come back in the evening. It's been a long time since I met Rajiv also."

"Okay. . ."

"Why are you saying okay doubtfully?"

"I am just thinking if I am missing anything."

"We'll take care of it when something comes up. Don't stress too much. *Chalo*, see you on Sunday then. Drink Glenlivet and celebrate. Your time in America has started. The tough part is over."

"Oh you remember Glenlivet?"

"Of course."

I didn't go out and drink and party. I didn't feel like celebrating that moment. I felt more vulnerable than confident. I was hesitant to be happy and confident lest I should lose the one small good thing that was happening to me in a long time.

I missed Sumit that day. He had been a partner in my struggles but wasn't available to celebrate my success. I dropped an email to him about my job and saved the phone call for some other time.

On Saturday night that week, the last night of my stay in the guest house, Rajiv came to see off his longest staying consultant. From his guest house, either people moved out to client place by securing a job or moved to another employer. Nobody that I knew of stayed as long as I did. It might have bothered Rajiv, but never ever did he make me feel I was a burden to him. He did his best to help me succeed. That night too he gave me a couple of contacts in Seattle who could be of some help to me in the new place.

By Sunday morning, I packed all my stuff and was ready to go. Late in the morning, Siri reached Fairfax and called me from outside the guest house.

***

"Congrats, Jay! I am proud of you." Siri gave an enthusiastic hug on seeing me. She was in her usual attire—sleeveless tank top, sweatpants, and sneakers.

"Thanks," I said, holding her hesitantly and looking around feeling conscious about the PDA.

Sensing my reluctance to hold her in public, Siri said, "Don't worry. Today is your last day in the guest house. You'll not see anybody here anymore."

"No. I have to come here for college until October, until my H1B kicks in."

"From now on, you'll come here as a guest, a real guest," Siri said, laughing. To me, her laugh was an instant energizer.

"Things really started working in your favor, Jay. I am sure you'll get your H1B also this time." It was Siri's habit to say that she was sure about things on which she didn't have any control.

"Okay. Let's go inside," I said.

"No wait. Here is the plan. Let's go to Starbucks first and have some coffee, and I'll go to Rajiv's house for lunch. We'll start sometime late in the afternoon and drive back to Jersey City. Okay?"

"When did you start drinking coffee?"

"Starbucks is not about coffee. It is about spending time with you. I get to see your happiest version at Starbucks."

"No. I am happy when you are around, Siri. I just cannot put it in beautiful words like you."

"Beauty lies in speaking plain truth, Jay. You don't have to try to talk beautifully."

"I know but that's the difficult part."

"You have opened up a lot in the last couple of years. It still baffles me how you gathered the courage to stop me during the evening walk that day being such a shy person," Siri said.

"Me too. It just happened," I said.

Siri left for Rajiv's place after coffee. Our walk to Starbucks and back was something I missed so much after she left the guest house for her job. That woman had something in her. I tend to be someone who I like the most in her presence. There was probably a message in getting my first job in Seattle; it was time for some distance between us since Siri and I were increasingly taking each other for granted.

Sometime around 6 in the evening that day, my journey from Fairfax to Jersey City started. I felt sad to leave the place where I had stayed the longest in the US till then. At the same time, I felt happy to leave because that place was not meant to stay longer.

The fact that I had a job relaxed my facial muscles a bit and I started smiling more than usual. Irrespective of whatever

Bhagavad Gita said about karma, it makes a difference to be successful and it feels good.

"How much is Rajiv paying you, Jay?" Siri asked as we started our drive to Jersey City.

"Salary basis. Thirty dollars per hour."

"Not bad, he paid less than that for some consultants in the past. After three months, ask him for a raise. After another three months, ask him to move you to percentage basis, 70–30, and 80–20 another three months later," she said.

"And after another three months?"

"That's the max he can go, otherwise he'll have to sell his company. Haha."

"I'll not be comfortable nagging him like that," I said.

"Then he will keep you on thirty dollars forever. You need to do it whether you feel comfortable or not," Siri said.

"Rajiv is not like that," I said.

"Everybody is like that in this business. You can show as much respect as you want but keep asking for salary hike. That's your basic responsibility. You shouldn't feel shy about it," Siri said.

"Okay."

"I suggest you to be with Rajiv though. He is a great employer to deal with and he works hard to create a good reputation for his company unlike other desi employers. People often complain that he could have expanded his business far bigger than what it is now if he were a little more aggressive. He looks slow but I think he is a shrewd businessman. It's a pain for employers to manage consultants on the bench when the market is down. He understands it more than anybody else, and that's the reason for his balanced approach. That's precisely why he delivers more than what he promises to his employees," Siri said, bragging about his cousin.

"Okay, you sold your cousin to me successfully."

"Shut up."

After a small pause in the conversation, I extended my left hand on to Siri's right hand resting on the gear stick, stroking gently, I said, "Thank you so much, Siri."

She pulled her hand from under mine and put it on my hand, and said, "What for, Jay?"

"For being there for me always."

"Don't make me feel uncomfortable by being so formal. You don't know how content I feel whenever I get to do something for you. You are a great guy."

"What greatness you see in me, Siri, that I don't know of?"

"To me, you are great guy, Jay. I met you at a time when I was increasingly contracting into myself, away from the world. You make me so comfortable that I don't feel conscious when you are around. You are my alter-ego I should say."

"It would be unfair to say that you stole my feelings, especially when you said it so beautifully, Siri. But you really did."

"Aha. . ." Siri burst into her natural laughter—loud, long, and stretched with intermittent breaks.

"What I said is true, Siri."

"I didn't say you are not truthful. I never doubt whatever you say. I take it as it is."

"Me too," I said.

"Don't copy my words," Siri said.

"When we share the same feelings obviously we have to use the same words, right? And you pick the words better than me and faster than me. If I don't have to copy you, then I'll have to say it in a different language."

"You always have the last word in the conversation, Jay."

"You are just being modest."

"Haha. See? Again."

Throughout the conversation, I had my hand below hers and Siri appeared like she was in no mood to take it away until the car stopped. The cars there being automatic, most of them, she didn't have to unless she wanted to. Not that I was not enjoying it, but I was in a fix whether to continue the status-quo or do something to indicate otherwise for the sake of formality.

As a middle path, somewhere in between enjoying her touch and inability to acknowledge it openly, I asked, "Shall we stop for a coffee?"

"Yeah, that's what I was thinking why you haven't asked for a coffee break yet. Let me look for rest area," Siri said.

"Coffee is mankind's best invention, Siri."

Siri looked at me with an expression and smile that was not familiar to me.

"Why are you smiling like that?" I asked.

"Nothing."

"No, tell me. You just said that you don't hide anything from me," I tried to provoke her to get the answer.

"I didn't say that. I just said you make me comfortable," Siri said.

"What more do I need to do to make you comfortable to say what you are thinking right now?" I asked.

"Your liking for coffee reminds me of someone," she said.

"Who?"

"Leave it for now, Jay. I'll have to tell you a long story."

"You said that couple of times earlier too. What's that long story?"

"Some other time, Jay."

"We have more than two hours now to reach home. Is your story longer than that?"

"Okay, let me stop for coffee first." As the car drove into the rest area, Siri said, "I need to use the restroom real fast. I have been holding it in for a long time."

"Then why did you pretend as if you stopped for me?" I said, trying to tickle her.

"No, Jay, please. I'll do it here itself."

I let her go use the restroom.

I kind of had a hint about her long story. I wanted to hear from her though I wasn't really dying to know the details. Otherwise I would have asked her by then, several times. But was Siri yearning to share her past with me? Else why would she bring it up?

24

I stood there on the curb of the parking lot of the rest area waiting for Siri, from where the freeway was visible at a distance.

The interstate freeways in the US are an absolute marvel, dotted at regular intervals with perfectly maintained and secure rest areas with ample parking space, abundant place to relax, outlets to eat and shop, clean restrooms and easily accessible trash cans. In addition, most gas stations along the freeways also have enough parking place and attached coffee shops to grab something to eat and drink. In India, the entire highway is a rest area, people can park, pee, and relax by the road anywhere they want.

"Shall we start?" Siri asked, coming back from the restroom.

"Wait, let's get coffee and let me have a smoke."

"Quick. Tomorrow is a working day for me."

"Okay, ma'am. Just five minutes."

As I walked with Siri to the open place to have coffee and smoke, she asked, "Jay, can I tell you something?"

"Just go on, Siri, you don't need my permission. Don't even give a chance to your mind to decide whether to say it or not, just vomit."

"I hate smokers," Siri said instantly, laughing loudly.

"This one thing you have bear with me."

"I was just joking, Jay," she said. "That doesn't mean I like smoking. That's just not an issue between us. I'll be happy if you quit smoking as someone who cares for you," she quickly corrected what she said.

"Of late, I have been smoking a lot, Siri. I think I need to reduce."

"What do you mean by reduce? You need to quit. Any amount of smoking is bad."

I just nodded. I knew that, and so does every smoker. I guess nobody smokes without any fear about health risks.

"Shall I tell you something, Jay?" Siri asked as we started our drive again, looking across her left shoulder to check the blind spot while merging into the freeway.

"You already told, Siri."

"What?"

"That you hate smokers."

Siri burst out laughing. Infectious would be an understatement to describe her laugh. While she laughed, I was little worried about the driving part. I wanted her to be in control though I liked to see her laughing. My career was just about to takeoff.

"I have something else to say too," Siri said.

"Just say it, Siri. Don't make me anxious anymore."

"Okay okay." Siri took a short pause and a deep breath.

I didn't interrupt her. I didn't even look at her in order not to stress her out while she compiled what she had to say.

"That part of my life. . . I don't even like thinking about it, Jay. But for quite some time, I don't know why, I am feeling the heaviness in me. I have been feeling a need to share with you," she began.

I didn't say anything. I gave all the time Siri needed between the words she spoke.

"Let me say it straight. I am divorced and have a six-year-old daughter."

What the fuck!

Siri summarized the story in one sentence, contradicting

my assumption that she would struggle for words. A few moments of silence followed her revelation. Probably she anticipated some reaction from me but I was mum. We just looked at each other's blank faces.

I knew that she was married, but I was dumbfounded when Siri said that she was divorced and has a daughter. Her fresh face, her active lifestyle and her teenager-like enthusiasm for life wouldn't have let anybody even guess that Siri was a mother of a six-year-old girl. All the moments I had spent with her from the first day she gave me that weird look when I was smoking on the deck till the present moment flashed in front of me like fast-forwarded movie.

"Siri, I need to tell you something," I said.

"What? Are you married too?" she asked, with a superficial smile.

"Haha, no. Sumit once told me that you are married. Later I became so close to you that I even forgot what he said."

"Sumit? Your guest house friend?"

"Yeah."

"How does he know?" she asked.

"I don't know. Somehow he knows about everybody in the world," I said.

"Haha, okay," Siri laughed. I was both surprised and glad that she did not take it seriously.

"But I didn't know that you are divorced and have a daughter. I'll not ask anything more about your past, Siri. You tell me however much you want to share with me. Otherwise we can talk about something else," I said, patting on her shoulder.

"Are you not excited to know what happened?" she asked.

"Honestly I want to know everything about you, Siri. Not because the story is interesting but because I care for you."

She glanced at me with a smile, and said, "Jay, you tell me

always that I talk beautifully, but when you talk, it's an art, not just language."

I smiled. I didn't want to debate who had better communication skills at that moment.

After a small pause, Siri continued, "I don't want you to be prejudiced about me after listening to my story, neither sympathetic nor alienated, nothing for that matter. I want our friendship to continue like before."

"It will," I assured.

"I know you are not like that. Otherwise you would have asked me by now since you already knew part of the story. But you haven't. I'll cut the long story short. I got married as soon as I completed my engineering. I didn't think about marriage until my parents brought up the idea when I was in the final year."

She paused for a while. Taking such pauses was unlike Siri, but the situation was different—the heavier the emotions the tougher the choice of words.

"I let my parents decide everything for me about my marriage. For every concern I had about my career, they had just one answer—you can do whatever you want even after marriage. I really believed what they said because I was getting married to someone from our close relatives' family, and I thought I'll have the flexibility. Everybody in our family talked so highly about the guy I was getting married to. I really thought nothing much will change after marriage. How innocent I was," Siri said, with a sullen smile.

She paused again and continued with a heavy sigh, "And when it happened finally, my marriage was a huge ceremony. My parents spent a lot."

Pause.

"After marriage, people from both the families started pressurizing us for a kid, as if nothing else mattered in the world. My parents started saying that I could do anything I wanted in terms of career after having a kid also. I wasn't happy with their argument this time. The big issue was that I wasn't happy with my husband."

"What's his name?" I asked.

Siri looked at me seriously and shouted, "Is that important now?"

Maybe it was insensitive on my part to ask that question at that moment. It was not irrelevant though.

"Prakash," she said.

"Sorry, Siri."

"No, I am sorry." She extended her hand to hold mine, and continued, "He has brightness only in his name but not in his life. He was a good-looking guy, well-educated and well-settled. To anyone else, he would seem like a very nice guy."

Pause.

"In a way he is. But I never felt loved by him. He is too calm, lethargic, and dull all the time. His life was all about himself and his job, that's all, nothing else mattered to him. Kind of selfish. It didn't take much time after marriage for me to understand that he was not concerned about me or my career at all. He knew that I hesitated to get married immediately after my engineering for the sake of my career. He didn't even bring up the topic after marriage. I didn't interact much with him before marriage but after marriage it was like hell for me. He doesn't talk much. He doesn't discuss things. Most of the times, I was like why don't you fucking say something?"

Pause.

"I wanted an active life, an active career, and an active husband, not someone who is always into laptop and phone and books. I didn't want to be someone who just cooked for her husband and watched TV all day. Though he didn't say it, he was against me working. We had plans to come to America after marriage. He forgot that too. He had a knack for conveniently ignoring things. He might have thought I would calmly settle down as a housewife after marriage."

Pause.

"I lost myself with each passing day. When I looked into the mirror, I started seeing a totally different and under-confident and frustrated Siri. Even people started asking if I was keeping well. At a point when I couldn't tolerate my restlessness, I came to know that I was pregnant. I wasn't prepared for it. I wasn't sure how it happened, we didn't plan for it. I wasn't even sure if that was an accident or if he played some trick. I was so angry to know that I was pregnant but I could feel a distinct transformation within me in just a few days and I started embracing my pregnancy. And you know something? He had the same dull reaction to my pregnancy news also. I never really understood what motivated him to be cheerful in this world."

Pause. Siri looked straight at the road throughout the conversation.

"The next few months I lived in my own world with thoughts about having a child and being a mom. And then my little angel arrived. I named her Priyamvada."

"Why?" I asked.

"What why?" Siri asked seriously, turning toward me.

"I mean, why did you choose that name for your daughter?"

I feared another shouting from her but Siri smiled, and said, "Oh, this world receives people based on what they talk and how they talk. I wanted my girl to spread a good vibe around when she speaks. Priyamvada means sweet spoken."

"Oh wow, so much thinking into it?"

"Yeah, do you like the name?" she asked. Talking about her daughter brought a glow to Siri's face.

"Yes. It's beautiful and very thoughtful," I said.

"He didn't show any interest in naming our daughter also.

He didn't even suggest a single name. He just left it to me."

"Where does Priyamvada stay?"

"With my parents in Hyderabad. My parents live with my elder sister's family. I want my parents to raise my daughter the same way they raised my sister and me."

"What's your sister's name?"

Siri stared at me for a second, and said, "My sister's name is Kirthi, her husband's name is Teja, their sons' names are Vivek and Suman. My dad's name is Ranga Rao and my mom's name is Vimala. Do you want the name of the maid working in our house too?"

"What's wrong in knowing names, Siri?" I asked in a soft voice.

"That breaks my fucking flow."

"Oh sorry. It's easy to relate to what you say if I know a person's name, like how a database works."

"Aha, don't teach me the stuff I taught you," Siri said in a mocking tone.

"It's not like that, Siri," I said, caressing her shoulder.

"Even my daughter could not save our marriage. I grew even more impatient with him after Priya was born. And the divorce was messy. The way he and his parents handled the divorce . . . they resorted to cheap blame game. I was more convinced than before that I was right in getting a divorce from him. The divorce was more traumatic to my parents than to me. It was not their fault. It had to happen like that. That's all," she said in a subdued tone.

Siri took a fairly long pause this time. "That's the long story short, Jay," she said, looking at me with a constricted smile.

I didn't say anything. I placed my hand on her hand rested on the shift knob. If that was the shorter version of the story, I could imagine the longer version of it and the pain of going through it.

"It's been a long time since I saw Priya. I miss her a lot," Siri said.

"When are you planning to go to India then?" I asked.

"I was waiting for my H1B extension to go through. After that, I thought I'll wait until you get a job. Now I can plan my trip," she said, with a smile. I was touched to hear what she said.

"You shouldn't have waited for me, Siri. My struggle goes on."

"There is another reason too. If I visit India during summer holidays, I can spend more time with Priya. I didn't sacrifice anything for you, Jay. You are family too. You don't know your importance in my life and I cannot say it in words. You brought the cheer back into my life. I am glad that you stopped me that day during the evening walk," she said.

"I received much more than I can ever give you back, Siri. You are just trying to be humble. I would have gone mad without you in my life. I am a little egoistic to say it but I really owe you a lot," I said.

Her past, her marital status, and her mom status didn't immediately influence my feelings toward Siri. I didn't want to let sympathy overtake the original impression I had about her. Any expression of sympathy from my side would be a turn off for a strong woman like her. In fact, I didn't feel sorry for Siri, instead, I was awed by her strength to push forward in life in spite of her volcanic past.

Except for the scars left by the mess of her divorce, visible only when she talked about it, Siri looked like she had gotten over her past. I guess the divorce had liberated her and made her even stronger.

We had dinner on the way and reached home.

"Jay, do you want to have a drink? I kept the bottle you left last time."

"No, not after dinner."

"Okay, *chalo* we'll sleep then. It's already late. I'll get you blankets."

Siri kept extra blankets for me to sleep in the living room whenever I visited her place. I followed her to the bedroom and as she pulled the blankets and pillow from the closet, I held her shoulders from behind.

"What?" Siri asked, without looking back.

Sympathy for her past or admiration for her courage or thankfulness for being there for me, I don't know exactly what prompted me, I pulled her back, turned her toward me, and said, "I would have been in India by now if I didn't know you, Siri. I owe this job to you."

Siri rested her hands on my hips, and said, "This is not the time for emotionally charged dialogues, Jay. You have gone through a lot. But you never lost the smile on your face. You are a strong man. Don't give all the credit to me. Now I want to see you successful in your job. It might take some time for the world to recognize you, but I know for sure you'll be a great achiever in life. *Chalo* let me get the bed sheets for you," Siri said, patting my hips.

But I didn't let her go. I moved closer and hugged her, and said, "I like you a lot, Siri. I am blessed to have you in my life."

Siri also held me which she didn't until I completed what I had to say, she said, "This time you said it first, Jay. You literally robbed my feelings."

"It's not Davidoff today," I said, collecting the blankets and pillow.

"Haha, yeah. I knew it would be a long day so I used a roll-on. Can you still smell it?" Siri asked, bending her head a little toward left and lifting her arm. "Oh yeah. *Chalo* good night," she said, waving her hand.

"How many times will you say *chalo chalo?*"

"But still you are not leaving, haha."

"I know it has been a long day and tomorrow is a working day for you, but I feel like being with you for some more time," I said.

"Tomorrow I'll be home early. We'll go out somewhere," she said.

"Okay, good night."

"Good night, Jay," Siri said, blowing a kiss and laughed out loud.

"Stop laughing. People might call the cops for the noise pollution you are creating."

Her laugh became even louder. I left the bedroom and closed the door behind me, which was the only way to stop her laughing.

Siri played a big part in my successful comeback though I didn't have the right word for her place in my life—friend, or mentor, or alter-ego as she said, or much more than all of them put together.

25

March 13, 2010: Siri gave a tearful farewell at the Newark International Airport.

The anxiety of my job after a long gap, in a relatively new field, in an unfamiliar location superseded the sadness of moving away from Siri. I was about to step into a formal work environment after a gap of three years, practically starting my career all over again.

Siri hugged me, and said, "You are going far away, Jay. Even the time zone is different."

I was so filled with thoughts about the job that I couldn't feel the hug. The standard rhetoric between any two close people getting separated by distance—it wouldn't make any difference—almost came out of my mouth but I resisted. I held her and kept quiet. It was not easy for me to console someone who has been my strength all along. In fact that was a moment when I needed some consoling from her.

"On one hand, I want you to build a successful career, and on the other, I don't want you to leave, Jay. I'll let you go this time. Once you get comfortable with your work, you should come back here. Your next job is in New Jersey, New York area. I have decided," Siri said, with a smile on her lips and tears in her eyes.

"Okay, Siri. I need to go now, it's time. Wish me luck."

"Take mine too, Jay, if I have any reserve luck left in my account."

"Bye, Siri. Thank you."

"I don't want to hear you say fucking thank you again. Bye," Siri said, pushing me.

"Okay," I said, and stood there still unable to leave.

Siri pushed me again, and said, "Go now. Don't make me cry any more. Go."

I walked up to the security check and looked back and waved to Siri from a distance long enough to stop us from falling weak again and run toward each other and hug and get emotional.

On the first day of my job, I was scared like a rabbit to face my manager. I couldn't sleep well the previous night. I couldn't eat breakfast that morning. Seattle's damp weather added dullness to my dread.

Years back, after my MBA in India, companies flocked around our campus to attract us with competing packages. We dominated in our negotiations with the companies with more than one job for every student. What I saw then had no comparison to what I was going through now. When I joined my first job in India, the company booked the best hotel in the town, arranged pickup and drop, and even chalked out a sightseeing plan for me. And in Seattle, I opted for shared accommodation for financial reasons. I shared a two bedroom apartment with three other people. I wasn't sure if my life was moving forward or backward. I felt like breaking something real costly like a TV to bring down my frustration.

But I was happy that I had started earning instead of depending on borrowed money for everything. Compared to the recent past, I was moving forward.

My boss, a bearded gigantic guy, met me in the lobby on my first day and suggested that we go to the café and talk. I heard about bosses who loved to screw the team members over coffees and lunches. I hoped he was not one of them. His handshake almost crushed my shaky hand. My armpits were sweating. I was really not at ease but tried not to let it show.

"I found it difficult to pronounce your name. Can you please say it once for me?" My boss asked as we sat in the café.

"Jayawardhan. You can call me Jay."

"Jay is better. Most Indian names are tongue twisters to me," he said, smiling.

Oh, really? If you guys came to India for jobs, your names would have been tongue twisters for us too.

My boss looked like a cool guy despite his intimidating physique. But you never know. The frightening stories I heard from the folks in the guest house about work environment made me doubtful.

After a few trivial questions about my travel and accommodation, my boss came straight to the main topic—my project.

"There is some delay for your project to get started. In the meantime one of our business analysts needs some help with her project. Do you mind working with her?" he asked, as if I had an option.

"Sure. I'll be happy to do that," I said, as if I obliged him.

"I'll introduce her to you, and you can get started right away. I'll also introduce you to your project manager so that you get the updates on your project directly from him. Once your project starts, you'll work full-time on that."

"Yeah, okay." No matter how much I controlled, "yes" never came out of my mouth in the place of "yeah". However, I backed it up with a smile to cover any rudeness "yeah" might carry.

I was glad that I had some time to settle down and understand how things worked at the client's place. For the first time, I felt I was lucky. Otherwise luck was something that eluded me always.

I looked around the café which was full of desi folks. Even after 9, they were chatting over breakfast as if they had come for a breakfast party. The sight brought me kind of an unknown relief.

Day two was better than day one and day three was better than day two. My comfort level with the job grew every day. Opportunity to work with an experienced American lady, the other business analyst I was helping, was a tremendous learning opportunity. She had great attention to detail and was brutally honest even in the review meetings. With such a fair approach, it would have been impossible for her to survive professionally in India, except as a kindergarten teacher.

My joy knew no bounds when I received my first salary. The money I was earning was hardly anything compared to other desi IT consultants, but considering my financial status a few weeks back, I was in a much better position. I treated my roommates at Buffalo Wild Wings to celebrate by first paycheck, hoping to start clearing my debt from the next pay. I feasted on the chicken wings so wildly that it upset my stomach for the next couple of days.

A business concept solely based on chicken wings? With American football, basketball, and baseball leagues running one after the other every year, plus several local and college-level competitions, a sports bar and restaurant like Buffalo Wild Wings had customers throughout the year. When they could create a business model worth billions of dollars around a savagery called American football, they can create a business around any damn thing in the world. It's funny that they had restrictions on pit bull fights but not on American football.

The best part of my first job was that I was earning by doing something close to my skill set. As of 2010, I was lucky to enjoy the aura surrounding the role of a business analyst, though the job had its own demands. Non-technical roles like business analyst and project manager, in which expectations were more on business understanding, personality, and communication and coordination skills than on what people did sitting in the cubes, were yet to be attacked by the Indian masses in a big way. With the kind of reputation we had for mass-customizing things, even that day was not far behind.

The American work environment was a delight—the way people got things done respectfully, the way they helped out readily, the way they respected others' time, the way they listened before they talked, the way assessments were done objectively. I felt I was more productive there than I was in India. There was something called personality that did the trick in the US that forced many Indians to refine themselves. Consultants who got the contract extensions were not always top performers but those who showed the right temperament.

After six months on the job, Rajiv started paying me on a percent basis which was the fastest for any consultant in our company. The power of the trip to New Jersey with Siri and Rajiv worked well for me. First off, the exposure I got through the internship helped me in my job. And then a faster pay hike without having to beg for it.

As a contractor I was supposed to complete my job in Seattle in twelve months as per client regulations. Toward the end of my contract, my boss called me to the same café where I met him on day one to break the news that I was getting another three months which would be my last and final contract extension, the other option being converting into a full-time employee. Apart from not being able to identify myself with Seattle and yearning to be closer to Siri, the latent aspiration to move back to India in the near future didn't allow me to accept the full-time job offer.

After that conversation with my boss, I spent the following three months pretty much winding up my stay in Seattle. I updated my resume with my current work experience and started looking for jobs in New Jersey, New York.

Having acquired the job experience enough to back up my negotiations for a better pay and preferred location, I started flexing muscles.

Looking back, I couldn't believe the transformation that had happened in a span of little more than a year. During the fifteen months that I worked in Seattle, I regained my lost momentum professionally.

The images of my fearful face on day one were still vivid in my memory. For the first one month, I had Siri and Venkat ready at my disposal for whatever help I might need. Toward the end, I gained the strength to laugh at those initial days when I used to over-confidently promise my boss about what I would accomplish to come across as a promising consultant. In order to abide by my promises, I used to work on the weekends and afterhours. I never charged for the extra hours I spent working, because I put in all those efforts to compensate my lack of experience for which I didn't want the company to pay. In fact I didn't want my boss or anybody to know about my extra efforts.

The fifteen-month work experience in Seattle gave me an opportunity to take a peek into the professional environment of Indian techies in the US. I knew Indian consultants who went home early just because they ate lunch in the cube which counted as their productive time. I knew consultants who came late to office and spent another hour in the café eating breakfast but left the office promptly on time only to charge the company eight hours per day. I knew consultants who worked extra hours just because of their incompetency but charged the company for the extra time they worked. I knew consultants who quoted a timeframe to complete a task that was several times longer than the actual time it would need and enjoyed the leisure time while getting paid by the client. I knew consultants who lobbied to push their computer illiterate spouses into jobs and worked for both of them. I knew consultants who logged into work laptop whenever they woke up in the middle of the night to pee just to create an impression that they worked day in day out for the company and probably charge extra time. And I knew the worst category of Indians who after settling down well there, tried to keep a distance from fellow Indians who were new to the country or to the work place, and move closer to the Americans as a matter of pride.

Isn't it funny that all those enriched NRIs blame India for its corruption? Isn't the difference between them and the corrupt Indians in India just a difference of place and opportunity?

On the other hand, I knew Indian consultants who took responsibility for the entire project and not just their work and drew pleasure in contributing more than what they were paid for though they knew they wouldn't stay with the client forever. I knew consultants who weighed their contribution in terms of value addition to the client business rather than the number of hours they logged in. And I knew consultants for the sake of whom the clients even changed their policies in order to be able to retain them. Those were the real torchbearers of Indian IT prowess.

The flexible work place dynamics in the US accommodated all kinds of people.

On the personal front, I got my H1B visa approved by the time I completed my first job that saved me some money since I didn't have to visit the weekend college in Virginia to maintain my immigrations status. Not having to go to Virginia also stopped meeting Siri, I missed her. Except the disappointment that Siri wasn't able to see west coast before I left Seattle, everything went well for me.

My job did some good for Siri also. She visited India twice during that period but was still caught between bringing her daughter to the US and allowing her to grow up with her parents and sister for some more time. Moving back to India was not an option for Siri because of the aversion she had developed due to the divorce and the trauma that ensued. Every time she visited India, her hatred toward the country doubled.

Many parts of India hadn't grown up to accommodate liberal and authoritative women like Siri. If I had met her in India, she would have been a different person with a veil that covered her originality and I would have not had the same impression as I had about her now. I wonder sometimes if the society-centric environment in India suppresses individuals from blooming to their fullest. Lot of value is placed on sacrificing individual self for the sake of everything else— family legacy, parents, relatives, friends, culture, and societal expectations. On the positive side, it's the family structure of India that kept the country progressing in spite of all its aberrations.

I booked a one-way ticket to Siri's place since I was hoping for my next job to be around there, and that was the first time I booked my flight ticket after landing in the US. It was either Venkat or Siri who did it for me every time.

It would be easier to make friends in train journeys in India than at work places working as contractors in the US. Life was real volatile for them. They got hired, they got fired, they left jobs for better pay, they moved places, they frequently sold and bought cars, they broke apartment leases, and they never carried more luggage than whatever they could carry with them in a car or in a flight since anything more than that would be a non-productive overhead. In spite of all the difficulties of a makeshift life, the better pay aside, consulting job compared to a full-time job had its own charm. It was kind of an expensive fun to be a contractor. I probably wouldn't have said this if I was married.

My attachment with Seattle was minimal, even after fifteen

months, I felt like a stranger there. Given its dull weather, it was difficult to fall in love with the place. I tried my best to adapt to it. When I started out for Seattle, a friend hinted that it was okay to forget carrying underwears but not an umbrella, so I was mentally prepared for its tough, sunless, rainy days. Otherwise, I would have drowned in its depressing weather. I would miss its greenery and fresh air though.

Seattle deserved the credit for making me habitual of checking the weather constantly, almost on an hourly basis. Such was the unpredictability of its weather. Before going there, I was concerned about weather only on a daily basis. And before going to the US, I don't remember weather being a concern to me at all. Everybody in India have their own predictions with just one look at the sky.

With a small farewell from colleagues and roommates, I left Seattle on a high note.

26

June 17, 2011: I flew to Siri's place from Seattle on a Friday night so that I had a full weekend to spend time with her before I got serious with my job search.

Not having a job in hand didn't worry me. Having survived one of the worst recessions in the US history and a lengthy bench time, a small jobless break wouldn't really hurt me, especially when the job market looked promising. Though I wasn't financially stable, I was in a confident phase of life. Since America had just recovered from a financial mess, the expectation was that there wouldn't be reckless decisions from the new administration that could push the country to the brink of economic collapse again. I acquired enough stamina to sustain any minor disruptions.

Like a kid who runs to mom after school, I dropped my bags on the ground and almost ran to Siri as I saw her at the airport. It was noticeable and I felt it clearly when I hugged her that she had gained weight. Six months back, I could easily hold two Siris in my hands but now one and a half Siris probably. She almost slept in my arms. The airport security guard had to remind us that we were not allowed to park the car for a long time at the terminal.

On our way to her apartment, I asked Siri, "Shall we have dinner on the way somewhere?"

"No."

"Why?"

"Surprise for you. I cooked dinner at home," she said, excitedly.

"Really? Then I'll pick my dinner."

"Shut up." She slapped on my leg.

That was a real surprise since Siri was fond of eating out often than cooking at home. But when she cooked, she did the job well.

"I see you a lot happier after your India trips," I said, actually asking how her trips went.

"Yeah, I still have the hangover, Jay. This time I spent more than a month at home with Priya. All those images are still running through my head. And the real reason today for my inability to hide my happiness is seeing you after so long."

"You don't have to hide," I said.

"That's why I am not hiding, haha. When I am here, I regret not being with Priya. But when I went to India, I was very content that she is in better hands. I wouldn't have been such a great parent for her compared to my parents and sister. They treat her like a princess. My dad says they see me in her."

"Priya looks like Prakash, right?" I asked.

"Yeah she is more like him in her looks and more like me in her personality. We both are Leos."

"What's Priya's date of birth?"

"August first." And I knew Siri was born on August 13.

"What is Prakash's sun sign?"

Siri looked at me seriously, and said, "This is your last question about him, okay?"

"Okay."

"Cancer. That's why he is selfish."

"I don't know much about sun signs but I asked about Prakash's just like that," I said.

"Even I don't care much but one of my friends in college was very fond of this horoscope and palmistry stuff. I picked up a few things from her," Siri said.

"What's a Leo woman like?" I asked.

"Exactly like me," she said, and laughed. Going by the intensity of her personality, whatever horoscope Siri's was, she should be representing it holistically.

New Jersey was like coming home for me. As soon as we entered the apartment, I put my luggage in the living room and glanced around eagerly, nothing had changed.

Siri went into the kitchen, and said, "Go, freshen up. I'll arrange dinner for us. And keep your bags in the bedroom." That was unusual. Generally my bags stayed with me in the hall whenever I visited her; rarely did I enter the bedroom.

"Jay, don't you ever wear shorts?" Siri asked, looking at me top to bottom as I came back after changing.

"I am not used to wearing shorts. I am not comfortable in shorts, probably because of my thin legs."

Siri looked down at my legs, and said, "You don't look like you have thin legs."

"Haha. How do you know?"

"I have X-ray eyes, you know?"

"I know. You can see the color of my underwear also."

"Shut up, don't you know X-rays get only black and white images?"

"Okay, tell in the first place if. . ."

"Stop it!" Siri shouted, closing her ears.

While we laughed, Siri pulled a Glenlivet bottle from the cabinet and held it in front of her face, and said, "Surprise for you."

"What the. . ."

"Complete the sentence, no problem," Siri laughed.

"How did you get it?"

"Liquor store."

"I know that, but did you go there on your own?"

"Yeah."

"We would have got it after I came here."

"I wanted to surprise you."

I took the bottle and pulled Siri closer, and said, "Thank you, Siri. I am overwhelmed, not because of this one but because you took the pain of getting it for me."

"Come on, don't be silly. You have another bottle also with some leftover. You always leave some stock in my room. But go ahead and open the new one today. I'll give you company with orange juice."

As I prepared my drink, Siri said, "The desi guy at the liquor store looked at me surprisingly. And I looked at him confidently as if I can drink the entire bottle in one night. He might have thought how much desi girls change after coming here."

"Situation in India is no better. You should try scotch today at least for the sake of the look that guy gave."

"Nah, I enjoy watching you drink. Sometimes I feel you like Glenlivet more than anything and anybody else in the world."

I enjoyed my drink with the chicken curry Siri had prepared while watching the movie *No one killed Jessica*. The movie just played on her laptop while we talked. By the time the movie finished, it was past midnight and both of us were sleepy. I followed Siri to her bedroom to get my blankets and pillow.

As Siri pulled the blankets from the closet I held her shoulders from behind. Before a word came out of my mouth, she said, "Stop saying it if you are about to say thank you."

"No, why should I say thank you? You did your part," I said.

Siri turned and punched my stomach and we both burst into laughter. There was no stopping Siri when she started laughing.

And as she turned back and started to pull the blankets again, I placed my hands on her shoulders again.

"Now what?" Siri asked, without turning toward me.

I hugged her closely from behind, and said nothing. Placing her left hand on my hands resting on her abdomen, Siri lifted her right hand around my head which she couldn't completely. The view of her open underarm and the smell of the deo added essence to emotion. I moved my hands on her abdomen on the tank top and turned my head toward her. As my lips reached the fold of her neck, I could feel her heart beat all over her body. Perhaps she felt the shiver of my hands moving on her abdomen too, the grip of her hand on mine tightened.

"No, Jay," Siri said.

I heard: *Yes, Jay.*

I slid my hands inside her top, nuzzling into her neck. Siri ran her fingers through my hair synchronizing with the movement of my head. The tremble in our bodies died down gradually.

After several minutes of caressing and kissing, Siri interrupted, "Jay, wait!" Turning toward me and wrapping her hands around my waist, she said, "I always forget to apply body moisturizer. Why don't you take a little into your hands? I am sure you can do it well." We burst out laughing in the middle of something where words had no place.

What appeared as a jittery attempt from my side, ended in a complete consensual act. After a long night, we woke up only for lunch the next day.

When we woke up in each other's arms, the warmth that we had shared the previous night disappeared. I used the restroom first and prepared morning coffee and went to the patio. Siri joined me later and took the coffee cup from my hand, had a sip, and said, "Yuck! How can you drink such strong coffee?"

I just smiled.

After a few silent moments, she said, "It's almost twelve, Jay. What's for lunch?"

"You tell me," I said, without looking at her.

"Let's eat something light. We'll go to Subway," she suggested.

"Okay." I didn't look at her this time again.

I could feel Siri looking at me steadily as she talked to me but I couldn't look into her eyes. Not looking at her was not a plan, but I just couldn't for some reason. After a brief moment of silence, she stood up from her chair, took the coffee cup from my hand and put it down, and sat on my lap. She took both my hands and placed them on her abdomen and her hands on top of mine. Resting the back of her head on my left shoulder, and gazing into the open she said, "Jay, I am not guilty of what happened between us last night. In fact, I am happy. I feel every moment we shared with each other so far culminated into this."

She paused as if it was my turn to say something.

"Even I am not guilty, Siri. Until now we shared a beautiful—"

"And it'll remain beautiful. We didn't sleep with each other on the day we met. I feel closer to you after last night than ever before. I am sure you are feeling the same since you are my alter-ego," she said, turning her head toward me, smiling, and kissed under my chin. Siri and gentle smile was a rare combo.

This time I didn't fill the pause and let her continue. "What happened last night was not an important part of our relationship, Jay. If that was what we wanted from each other, it would have happened long time back. Even if this is not part of our relationship from now on, I don't think it'll affect us in any way. To me, the bonding we share is above everything, it's special, it's not a conventional man–woman relationship."

Relieved from her assuaging talk, we started making out on the patio. What Siri said relaxed me for that moment, but sex added an important dimension to any relationship. I hoped what she said will hold true in our case.

After the situation had eased a bit between us, I asked her, "Last night when I asked about protection, you said we don't need it. Why?"

"You are asking now?" Siri asked with a constricted face, and her voice reached the normal decibel since the emotional part of the conversation was over.

"Haha, I didn't have the patience to wait last night. I just went by your words."

"You shouldn't trust people so much. By the way, congrats!" she said.

"For what?"

"For becoming the father of my second child," she said, laughing.

I pulled my hands away from her suddenly.

After a good laugh, Siri took my hands into hers and placed on her abdomen, she said, "I got that surgery done . . . for birth control . . . whatever they call it in medical language."

"So that you don't have to use protection?" I asked.

"Shut up." Siri pushed her elbow into my stomach. "I had a strong conviction from my college days that I'll have only one child, and I'll give my everything to that child. I got the surgery done immediately after my first delivery."

"And people agreed?" I asked.

"Who people?"

"Your parents, Prakash's parents, and Prakash."

"He didn't have a strong opinion, as usual. Others objected but I went ahead and got it done."

"Oh wow! It's not easy not to yield to people's pressure," I said.

Siri laughed sitting straight and putting her hands on her hip as an acknowledgement to the praise. I took back my hands from her abdomen as soon as she lifted her hands, not that I was not enjoying.

"Why the fuck do you take off your hands again and again?" Siri yelled.

"Siri, because of you I got used to using the f-word frequently."

"Aha, as if you are an innocent kid otherwise."

"Not innocent but not as spoilt as you."

"Shut the fuck up. Actually, f-word adds a lot of weight to words. It helps in conveying the message with effect. Can you think of any other word in English more versatile than the f-word? It can be used in any fucking context," she said.

"You are fucking right, Siri. Did you get a fucking Ph.D. on the f-word?" I asked, mocking her.

"What a fucking joke, Jay, what a fucking joke," Siri said, thrusting her elbow into my stomach. I'd have peed then and there if she did that harder, I was that full.

"Is it paining?" Siri tried to stand up from my lap in the middle of a cheery laughter.

"No no," I said, pulling her back.

Siri got off my lap anyway after a moment and sat on the other chair.

In her usual style, she started running her fingers through her silky hair holding the hair clip between her teeth. She became conscious as I looked at her and brought down her hands suddenly.

"No, I am not looking there," I said, smiling.

"Whatever," Siri said, smiling, and clamped her hands tightly to her body. After last night, she knew well about the points of my fascination.

"But, Siri, please don't stop wearing sleeveless tops. You look good in them."

"Whatever."

"Let's get ready and go out. I am hungry. I am already craving Subway," I said.

***

With my job search running in parallel, I spent about a month at Siri's place. I started feeling the time lapse. I had been getting calls from the west coast since my resume was with recruiters in that area, but I wasn't interested in going there again. Sometime toward the end of July 2011, I got an interesting job offer but not in the New Jersey area. The profile and pay were so attractive that I couldn't ignore the offer even though it was not in my preferred location.

On the day I got the job confirmation, I told Siri as soon as she returned from office, "One good news and one bad news."

"Tell me both at the same time."

"Job confirmed in Louisville."

"Congrats!" Siri said, hugging me. She moved away suddenly, and said, "The bad part is greater than the good part in this news. If it were your first job, I would have considered it a hundred percent good news. Louisville should be around eight to ten hours from here. Let's see. You should start driving long distances now."

We didn't talk much about my new job that night. The next day evening, as soon as Siri came back from work, she said, "Everything is good about the job, Jay. I thought about it. The pay is very tempting. The only concern is that you are going far again. But how long can we wait for a job in this location? I am saying this very reluctantly, I feel you should accept the offer."

Siri's words reflected exactly what was going on in my mind. She relieved me of the burden by saying it first. I fell for her non-possessiveness.

Finally, I accepted the job offer in Louisville. On August 14, 2011, the day after celebrating Siri's birthday, I took the flight to Louisville to join my second job in the US. From that very moment, with the possibility of clearing my debt completely in sight, I couldn't stop thinking about moving back to India—the thought that has been deeply suppressed for a long time. The entire time I travelled from Siri's place to Louisville I thought about it. I could clearly sense that the day was not far.

My trip to America was not supposed to prolong for so many years. I got muddled in unforeseen circumstances and my own inconsistencies. All these years, I waited for the right time to leave, which would have been when I was successful. I didn't want to be booted out by circumstances and carry the burden of failure with me to India.

To me, staying in America or moving back to India was never a matter of debate. It was just a matter of working out when and how. I had been making all the choices in favor of returning to India in the near future. I didn't buy anything that would increase my living expenses. I maintained a distance from paying mortgages. I didn't accept a full-time job offer from my first client. I didn't pursue my green card. "I might not stay longer in the US" had been my answer to my friends all along and their standard response, "Everybody says that. We have seen several people like you. Just apply for the green card first, and you can still go back to India."

People who stayed back in the US had their own reasons. But every NRI doesn't have to run after green card and citizenship. My calling was more important to me than established thinking and entrenched way of doing things. Even I was curious about how my life would unfold as far as returning to India was concerned. I had the determination but not the details yet.

The difference in the confidence level between the first

day of my first job and the first day of my second job was immense. While I was scared like a rabbit for my first job, I went to the second job like a lion. I had to remind myself time and again to not to lose my humility so as not to lose the opportunity to learn. While surviving on the job was the motto during my first job, I set out for my second job with an anticipation of some professional gratification.

As the days progressed, I was stressed at times with workload and struggled once in a while for proper direction but was never short of confidence. The frequency of my calls to Siri and Venkat didn't reduce but our conversations were not confined to my work anymore. My relationship with the client was an equal partnership in which I enjoyed contributing my best and the client viewed me as a promising resource. More and more challenging projects came my way. The repetition of same kind of duties bored me though.

Within a few weeks of joining the job, I could see that I'll have enough work to continue at the client place for the maximum period a contractor could work for them, which was two years. By then I'll have saved some money for myself in addition to clearing the debt.

I started exploring places, started eagerly waiting for the weekends, started going out in the evenings after work, started reading books, started talking to more friends, started thinking about money from not just clearing the debt perspective, started living on my own in an individual apartment, started talking to people back home more and more, started opening up to the world.

As Siri said, I overcame the phobia of driving automatically after I bought the car. I got used to driving so much that I felt like I was driving since I was born. On the first day I took my car on the road, I stopped at the traffic signal crossing a little into the pedestrian zone. Scared by the cops who wouldn't be bribed, unlike in India, I reversed the car hastily. A few seconds later, I saw a white guy knocking on my glass window. As I rolled the window down, he said that I had forgotten to change the gear; it was still in reverse. He didn't do it because I could hit his car. He was not from the car behind mine but from a car in a different lane and a couple of cars away. For several hours that day, that whole night, for several days later, and even today, I couldn't stop appreciating him. I wouldn't be able to do something for that guy since I didn't know who he was, except that he was a good Samaritan. That incident made me feel guilty whenever I didn't rise to the occasion for people around me. If he hadn't run to me, I would have hit the car behind mine on the first day I took my car out, and probably dreaded driving for a long time.

After I started driving in the US, I appreciated more than ever, their roads, freeways, traffic control, maintenance of vehicles, and general traffic sense of the public. Never did I feel threatened on the road when I followed traffic rules. And the credit should go to the country for putting its people on the right track. America would have been another India if its people were left of their own accord, or even worse.

What people would think as theoretical propositions in India practically existed in the US. They used technology and systems appropriately to add quality to public life. India supplied manpower to IT industry in the US more than any other country, probably more than the US itself, but lagged behind in the adoption of technology for better society back home, exposing the huge gap between its potential and progress.

When I thought about what had contributed to such a vast disparity between the two countries—America was blessed with visionary leadership in the initial years of the birth of the country which set its course in the right direction. Being a country of immigrants, it had a distinct advantage of building everything from the scratch and the country's leadership didn't fail to seize the opportunity. When the country was literate the leadership couldn't have escaped from its responsibility toward its people. Probably that's the reason why Indian politicians do not make any efforts to alleviate illiteracy in India. But what has literates like me done to our motherland other than living in America and earning dollars for ourselves?

There's so much for India to learn from America, both from its government and its people.

27

While I was actively thinking about returning to India, I didn't feel good about keeping Siri in the dark. It had come into our casual conversations several times in the past, but I wanted to tell her that I was serious, and I wasn't one of those crazy NRIs who claimed at every opportune time that they would move back to India.

Siri's part in my life was not so insignificant and the topic was not so trivial to take it up over phone. I waited until I met her personally to talk about it, which was during the Thanksgiving break that year. Siri succeeded every time in inventing some reason for not moving out of Jersey City but not this time. Very reluctantly she came to Louisville.

For the four days Siri stayed with me, we ate at the choicest restaurants of Louisville and covered as many historical and natural sites as we could in and around the city, since both of us preferred time together in quiet places than vigorous activities. I struggled hard to cover up the internal pressure to reveal my return to India plans, throughout her stay. Because of the anticipation of an unfavorable reaction from Siri and the fear of disappointing her, I postponed bringing up the topic every day until I couldn't anymore.

The evening before she was about to leave Louisville, while walking in the open meadows and woods of Cherokee Park, I gathered the strength to talk to her.

"Siri, can I tell you something?"

"Just vomit, Jay, don't even give your mind a chance to

think, haha. That's what you tell me always, right?"

"Right," I said, but I didn't start.

"Go on, what are you waiting for?" Siri said, holding my hand.

"This job I am sure will go on for two years, and that's the maximum time they can keep a contractor."

"Okay. . ."

"And the two-year period ends in August 2013."

"Okay. . ."

"And my first leg of H1B visa ends by the end of September 2013."

"We are lucky, Jay, some people are not getting H1B visas for three years nowadays. Okay, tell me, sorry."

"After completing this job, sometime in September 2013, I am planning to go back to India." My voice quivered as I said those words.

"We'll see then, Jay, 2013 is far way," Siri said, kissing on my hand and leaning on my shoulder.

The weather was so romantic that evening that it made me feel guilty for bringing up such a serious and stressful topic with Siri.

"I am serious, Siri. Why don't you come back to India too? Don't you think you'll have to come back at some point for Priya?"

"I can bring her here. In fact I am planning to do that, hopefully by the beginning of next academic year. I am not coming to India. Tell me why you want to go back. If you have made up your mind, you might have a compelling reason also."

"More than one reason, Siri. I don't talk about it often but not even a single day passes for me without thinking about India. That's our country and our people there. I am sure I'll not stay here forever, then why not leave sooner? I feel I am responsible to my country and my parents."

"What the fuck do you mean by responsible for your country? Do you think you are some kind of Mahatma Gandhi? Even Gandhi cannot save India. Responsibility toward parents is a valid reason, but you don't have to rush right now."

"I am not rushing. I am planning ahead. You only said 2013 is far away. I have almost two years from now. Responsibility toward the country doesn't mean that I'll do something of the magnitude of Mahatma Gandhi. I can contribute something to the country while doing something for myself there. It could be in a small way, to the people around, to the neighborhood, to the society."

"Jay, whatever you said is good in theory."

"You only said once that if something is not possible practically, it wouldn't even cross our thoughts," I said.

"Shut up and let me complete. And don't repeat the same shit I told you. I was about to tell you that you need to have a fucking plan in place to back up your ideas. Do you have it?"

Going by her choice of words, I could gauge the gravity of the conversation we were having. In a way, Siri was testing my premise which was good.

"I have a direction on how I want to spend the rest of my life, Siri. My first priority would be to set up a stable income source and then slowly increase the amount of time I spend on social causes. I'll work out more details by the time I go. If I am not seeing the path clearly right now, that doesn't mean that the path doesn't exist. Plans can be worked out as we go if we have a sense of direction. I know for sure the life I am living here is not what I want," I said.

"India is so fucked up and the people are so fucked up there. Why do you want to waste your time?" she asked.

"Exactly, Siri. That's happening to India because good people like you and me are here, not there. Too many people sacrificed too much to earn our independence. India is too precious to be left to assholes. That's our country."

"There are good people in India too. There is a reason why they just mind their business. There is a reason why most people here don't go back. There is a reason why people don't talk patriotic shit like you," Siri said in a serious tone.

"Majority is a misconception, Siri. I cannot identify myself with the people you are talking about."

"Instead of working there, work here, stay here, and do something for your country from here," Siri said.

"I am not talking about doing charity to our country living here. That's like satisfying a guilty heart. I am talking about being there physically. With this move, I'll get to try something on my own. It has been a long pending dream too."

"Why can't you do the same fucking on your own thing here?" she asked.

With each sentence, my voice became softer and Siri's louder.

"Of course, I can. To do that I need to get hold of a green card holder until I get my own and start a grocery store, or a gas station, or a consulting company. As far as I know, Indian entrepreneurship in America is limited to these three options. To become a full-fledged citizen of this country, I'll have to wait another ten or fifteen years, or maybe more than that. Until then, do what? Rot in the same job and sleep every night with the same rotten dreams? I cannot keep pushing here with a constant outsider feeling and draw happiness in counting my savings. Can we ever integrate completely here? Entrepreneurship is not about making few extra bucks, Siri. It's about creativity, creating value, giving back, satisfying the inner hunger. It's about leaving a positive footprint on the society. It's about leaving a legacy."

"Jay, I just don't want you to go, that's all. You haven't visited India after you came here. It's been almost . . . how many years?"

"Four years."

"Four years. You don't know the reality there. How much savings will you have by the time you leave? Do you know how costly India has become? Oh sorry, I forgot that you are the son of a rich dad," Siri said sarcastically.

"I know I'll not have much savings, but where is the limit for money? I might make more money in India than here if that's what I really want in life. And again, if dad's money is something I take pride in, I would have left America long back. You know that well."

"But why do you want to destabilize your life here and start all over again, Jay?" Siri asked, her voice trembling. She stopped walking and turned to me. Her moist eyes looked straight into my eyes. I didn't even realize when had Siri left my hand during the conversation and started walking a little far from me.

"I hope this will be the last destabilizing decision I take," I said, trying to pull her toward me.

"Fuck you. Don't touch me," Siri yelled, pushing me aside, drawing the attention of the sparse crowd walking in the park.

Siri was right. The f-word adds weight to words. I understood how difficult it was for her to maintain her composure until then. It all came out in a sudden splash.

Would I have done the same thing if a young, unmarried girl was in Siri's place? Hundred percent yes. Wouldn't that young, unmarried girl have figured in my plans? Even Siri figured in my plans and I probably figured in her plans too, but our outlooks for our future were way apart. If she was ready to come back with me to India, was I ready to marry her? Yes, if I choose to get married. But getting married and settling down in life somehow was not my goal. How could I jeopardize her life when I was not ready yet? How could I hook an angel like Siri to my not-so-foolproof plans? But that's something I wanted her to understand. If I had to express in words how will I make her believe?

After rather a long pause, I asked, "Should we go back?"

"Yeah," Siri said, rubbing her moist eyes.

As I tried to pull her toward me again she pushed me aside, and hit me, not once but several times. From that moment, Siri didn't talk to me. She didn't have dinner that night either, and the following day, she took a cab to the airport, not allowing me to drop her.

Are there only two possible next steps for a relationship, either to end or go to the next level? How beautiful would it be if there was a middle path for us to continue to be there for each other just like we have been all these years? I didn't want to lose Siri but I couldn't hold on to her. When I was not ready to stay back for her, I didn't have the moral courage to insist her to come back to India with me.

That day when Siri left my place, I didn't do anything in the office except drink coffee and stare at the monitor. I called my mom during the lunch break partly to inform her about my plans and partly to get over the sadness of disappointing Siri.

"Jay," Mom said in a sleepy voice.

"How are you, Ma? Are you sleeping?"

"No, just lied down. How are you?"

"I wanted to tell you something," I said directly. I didn't have the mood to prepare her mentally.

"What?" Mom asked, nervously. She takes no time to become nervous.

"Nothing serious, calm down. After this job, I am planning to come back to India."

"What do you mean after this job?"

"Toward the end of 2013."

My mom started laughing, she said, "That's two years from now, Jay."

"I know, Ma, but I am serious."

The moment I said I was serious, my mom's voice turned serious too. "You left everything here and went to America. You struggled a lot to find a job there. And when we all are thinking that everything is going good, you want to leave America. What are you doing, Jay? We asked you to come back when you were without a job but you didn't. Now we want you to continue there, get married, live happily for a few years, save some money for yourself, and come back later if you want to. But you want to come back. For now, your dad and I don't have any health issues. You don't have to be here for us."

"Ma, I am not taking the flight tomorrow. I am talking about two years from now. Take marriage off your mind completely and listen to what I say, okay? Marriage can wait."

"When do you want to get married then? See your friend Venkat." Mom almost shouted without letting me complete what I had to say.

"I'll get married when I come back to India for good, okay?"

"Why don't you come here once on a vacation and then decide?"

"Ma, I already told you. There is no guarantee that I'll be able to come back to America if I come to India now. There are lots of visa rejections nowadays. I don't want to take a risk until I clear the debt completely. And I don't have to see India to make a decision."

"If that happens, dad will help you out. Why are you so adamant about taking the debt burden on your head?"

"I had that option from the beginning, but I'll feel good if I clear this mess on my own. I am earning good money here and I can do it. I just wanted to tell you that I am not going to stay here for a long time. You should be happy, Ma."

"I'll be happy when you get married and settle down."

Mom needs something or the other all the time to be worried. First it was my job that bothered her and now marriage.

"We'll talk about that later. How is dad?"

"He is fine. Do you want to talk to him?" she asked.

"No. You tell him what I told you," I said.

"Why don't you tell him?"

"Okay, bye. I'll call you later." I cut the call before she handed over the phone to my dad.

∗

August 13, 2012: To surprise Siri on her birthday, I took a week off from work and flew to her place hoping that she was still living in the same apartment.

I could have called her but I wasn't sure if she would take my call. Last Thanksgiving, which was almost nine months back, was the last time we saw each other and talked to each other. From the day she left from Louisville angrily, wakeup calls every morning, cozy calls at night, update calls several times in between, all calls stopped. My messages and emails were ignored.

I stood in front of her apartment in the evening waiting for her to return from work. Standing there I thought how dull those nine months had been and how lonely I had felt in Siri's absence. Every act of her is a zest that lightened me up. I tend to take some of it when I was with her. Netflix to some extent filled the time but not the joy she brought to my life.

And there she was, walking from the parking lot with her head down. She walked slowly compared to her usual speed. Not many changes in her in the last nine months, she looked same. Siri lifted her head as she approached her apartment and stopped suddenly on seeing me. I thought she would pick another fight then and there; instead she came running and hugged me.

"Where is my gift?" she asked.

"I am the gift."

"Give it to me." Siri almost snatched the shoulder bag from me as we both walked up to her apartment. "How many days?" she asked.

"I resigned," I said.

"What the fuck? Why?" she exclaimed.

"I want to be with you," I said, unable to control my smile.

"How will I believe that someone who has decided to go back to India leaving me has resigned from his job to be with me?"

"Siri, please."

"I am joking. Come," she said, pulling me by my hand and shifting the shoulder bag to the other hand.

"I took a week off," I said.

"Really?" Siri asked, with excitement.

"When you are so happy to see me why didn't you answer my calls and messages?" I asked.

"Don't start again. You just called me for a week or so and sent me a couple of messages, that's all."

"Oh, that hurt your ego? That I didn't continue to chase you?"

"Shut up. How is your job?" Siri asked, unlocking her apartment door.

"There is nothing much to talk about the job. I just feel like I am pushing forward for the sake of money," I said.

She threw my bag in the hall, and pulling my hand, she said, "Okay, come."

"Come where? We are already in the house," I said.

I took a cursory look at the house, absolutely no changes in the last nine months. Siri dragged me to the bedroom and there I saw, hanging on the wall, a huge collage frame put together with pictures of her, her daughter, her dad and mom and her sister's family. Her daughter didn't look like her but she has the same soulful eyes of Siri. Until I completed seeing the pictures of her family closely, I didn't notice that a picture of me was also part of it. I was pleasantly surprised.

I looked at Siri pointing at my picture in the collage. She hugged me without saying anything.

"I felt really sad not seeing a message from you at twelve last night. I thought you were still angry with me. I didn't think you planned such a big surprise for me on my birthday. You don't know how happy I am. I can't even express in words," Siri said.

In spite of all the affection, she couldn't overcome her ego to call me or text me even once. I didn't know how long she would have continued like that if I didn't take the drastic step of dropping in front of her apartment unannounced. I could have shown the same stubbornness Siri had shown or I could have assumed she no longer cared about me, but somehow I couldn't.

We didn't sleep that night, catching up with the lost time. Siri decided to show her anger on me by not revealing about her India visit after she came back from my place. She visited India like she went to some nearby city.

"You go to India so frequently. Why do you hesitate so much to come to my place?" I asked.

"I came once, and you know what happened. Not anymore. It doesn't matter anyway, whether I come there or you come here, I just love to be with you."

"Yeah, I know it doesn't matter but you always want me to come to your place."

"Shut up."

Siri was right. She and I could keep talking forever without doing anything extraordinary, so place didn't matter.

It was almost morning by the time we went to bed. I fell

asleep in no time only to be woken up by Siri. "Jay? Jay, did you sleep already?"

"Yeah."

"It's not even a minute, Jay, wake up. I am having a vomiting sensation."

I sat up suddenly, and said, "Let's go to the restroom."

"No. I didn't mean that, I want to tell you something,"

"Okay, tell me." I fell on the bed again.

"I am sorry, Jay."

"Siri, sleep now. You don't have to say that," I said, pulling her to the bed.

"No, please let me say it. I am sorry for being so egoistic," she said, resting her head on my chest.

"No, Siri—" I said, stroking her hair.

"Shut the fuck up and listen. I am not done yet."

"Okay, go ahead."

"I should have been happy for you if I truly liked you, instead I was selfish. It was over-ambitiousness on my part to expect to be part of your life forever. I kind of got carried away. I couldn't take it when you said you were planning to go back," Siri went on.

I didn't realize that she wept silently while talking to me until I felt her tears on my chest. The situation was not conducive to sleep anymore.

I carried her to the kitchen in my arms with great difficulty, thinking she should never visit India. With every India visit she gained weight. I prepared two cups of coffee, one with full of sugar for Siri, and we both went to the patio. It was morning already but little cold. Siri quickly got a comforter and wrapped around us sitting on my lap.

"Siri."

"Yeah."

"You need to take back what you said. It's not over-ambitiousness on your part to expect to be part of my life.

Maybe you are referring to your past which has never been an issue between us. You hurt me by saying that."

"I didn't mean to say that, Jay."

"You are precious to me, Siri. I honestly think you should come to India too but I am not confident enough to ask you. When I go back, I'll be at crossroads working through things. If I am on my own, I can confidently take risks and start all over again even if I fail. But I cannot afford to make you part of that uncertainty. In any case, it doesn't matter since you said point-blank that you hate India."

"I don't hate but India sucks, Jay. People are so disgusting there. I don't want you to go there too. I can't imagine you dealing with assholes. I don't want you to waste your life. You have just started settling down. You don't have much savings also."

I didn't feel like presenting a case in favor of moving back to India one more time and losing Siri for another few months, so I let her speak.

"I want you to be happy wherever you are. I can't believe someone has such ideal goals in life in these days. I am just scared that someone so close to me is taking such a bold step. I don't know how but I'll do my best to support you in this journey," Siri said.

That was a reassuring message from her.

"Will you miss me when you go back?" Siri asked, after a small pause.

"Will you not kill me if I don't miss you? You are the second best thing that happened to me in America."

"Who the fuck is the first?"

"Ask what, not who."

"Okay, what the fuck is the first?"

"Dental floss." I didn't know why I remembered that suddenly. Maybe because it was morning already and it was time to brush teeth.

"That green thing you left in the restroom?"

"Yeah. I was joking, Siri. Maybe you are first and dental floss is second."

"What's so great about it?"

"Until I came here, I didn't know that a cool thing like dental floss existed. But I'll not miss it because I can carry it with me. It doesn't hate India."

"Shut up."

"You never used it?" I asked.

"Nope."

"Doesn't the food between your teeth bother you?"

"What's the big deal about it? Food doesn't stay there forever. It goes away," Siri said.

"*Chi. . .*" I tried pushed her away.

"Okay I'll start using it from today," Siri said, laughing.

I was anxious when I had set out on the trip to Siri's place. But I was relieved by the way it turned out. With the honest conversation we had, the emotional burden on me eased and Siri turned into a dear friend who got involved in my preparations, so much so that she even booked my flight ticket to India later.

Barring the internal conversation I had within me, the longest debate on my return to India happened with Siri, followed by Venkat. With other friends, I played it down, talked only about my parents as the reason but not the country. The sense of responsibility toward motherland has become such a joke amongst Indians in the US that I stopped talking about it despite my honest commitment. Not everybody had to know the finer details. When I didn't apply for my green card and was not even willing to extend my H1B visa beyond September 2013, they knew well that my intentions were genuine.

28

Almost one month after completing my job in Louisville, I was all set to return to India on September 19, 2013.

After Siri and I came to terms with my moving back to India, she was involved in every step of my preparations. She did a large part of my shopping, both for me and for my family and friends who I was seeing after six long years. I had a long list of people and long list of things to buy. The Thanksgiving and Christmas of 2012 were completely dedicated to my shopping.

I was so immersed in my preparations in the last one year that my favorite hobby took a back seat. Except knowing about the events superficially, I didn't closely follow what was happening with the US presidential elections in 2012. My curiosity about politics shifted from American to Indian. I thought about everything from the perspective of moving back to India. I started spending more time on what was happening in India, in my state, and in my town, and catching up with people here.

The scene of Siri's tearful farewell to me at the Newark International Airport haunted every minute of my last days in the US. I spent a week at Siri's place in the first week of September which could be the last time I ever saw her. Or maybe not. After checking-in my luggage and before the security check, Siri and I sat there listlessly. Though we were prepared mentally, when the day actually arrived we were in disbelief. I was returning to my world in India but Siri will be on her own in the US, away from her world in India.

Should we have planned not to come so close to each other? But again, do people have so much control on relationships?

Siri looked outside silently, with tears rolling down her cheeks. I took her hand and tried to say something when she turned to me, and said, "I am sorry, Jay. I really wanted to see you off with a big smile. See, I wore a red top also for you. I didn't plan to make these moments special by being sad. But. . ." Siri cried so loudly that people around us had started staring at us. I put my hand around her shoulder and pulled her toward me.

After a while, I said, "You have been my strength from the day I knew you, Siri. You were there for me all the time. I cannot see you like this."

Even in such an emotional situation, she suddenly pulled away from me, and said, "I am still strong. I feel good to have found someone for whom I can cry. I never went through these kinds of emotions earlier."

I just had to keep Siri talking. She was good as long as she talked. It was in those silences in between the words that she wept.

"I wish we had a life together, Jay. I don't know if our paths will ever converge. I am sure we'll be born again to complete this story. You love India so much and I can't imagine living in India. I am happy that you are pursuing something so passionately. My wishes will always be with you. Maybe I can give you my blessings also since I am elder to you," Siri said, rubbing her eyes and nose to my hoodie. I let her do it this time.

For the purpose of rhetoric what she said was fine, but one life, whatever we do and whatever we don't do, just one life. Siri and I had used up the time that was meant for us to be together in this one life. Or maybe not.

I wasn't sure if I deserved so much positivity from her

about my return to India. I was definitely fired up but was not totally certain about the consequences, which I guess is part of any big decision. Things go according to plan only in schools and colleges, not in the outside world, and that's why schools and colleges are failing to prepare people for life.

Siri broke my streak of thoughts, she said, "I am not really good at saying emotional things, Jay. I feel like I have a lot to say, but I am unable to speak." That was Siri's style—saying whatever she has to say beautifully, and backing it up with humble words. "At least today let's not be under the belief that nothing will change. I know everything will change. With the kind of determination you have, I don't think you'll ever come back to America. When I visit India, I don't think we'll have the same privacy we had here, and I am not sure we'll keep up the same spirit we shared all these years."

"That's the problem with you, Siri."

"What?"

"You just don't stop at acknowledging the truths. You call them out loud."

Siri hit on my shoulder, with a smile on her face that overran her tears for a moment. She held my hand closely interlacing my fingers with hers and rested her head on my shoulder. She kissed my palm and placed it on her cheek.

Siri pulled herself back with a jerk and hit on my thigh and gazed at me for a moment. "Do you think you'll change India? I hate you for what you are doing. I don't want you to go, Jay," she said in a harsh voice, and started crying again.

I pulled her closer to me again, extending my hand around her shoulder.

When it was almost time Siri and I went up to the security line together. We parted with great difficulty from each other with a long tight hug. The tears I struggled to hold for so long came out running.

I didn't like the fact that I was the reason for an otherwise strong Siri falling so weak emotionally. I was sure I'll not find another woman like her in my life ever. I guess I learnt from Siri to be sure about things I don't have control on. While it was a one-sided love with Jhansi in college, with Siri I was totally me—no inhibitions, no pretense, and no nonsense. In a way, I could come out of my fix for Jhansi because of Siri. The only credit Jhansi still held was being my first love, but the hangover was gone. If I could put Siri aside, Jhansi doesn't even have a place in my newfound purpose of life. I guess all college loves will just disappear if they were time-tested.

Unmindful of the passage of time and unwilling to part away from Siri, I got delayed to my flight. I was sure I was going to miss the flight if I had to the follow the long security line. When I requested the guy standing in front of me to allow me to jump the queue, he grew more concerned than me that I might miss the flight. He not only allowed me to bypass him but took the lead to convince others to give me the way to the security point. Not in a million years will that happen in India. When people hardly give way to ambulances, forget about giving way in a queue. Was that a hidden message against my decision to leave America? It doesn't change anything even if it was.

On my way back to Louisville, I traveled back to the memorable time Siri and I spent together. I was totally engrossed with the feelings I did not and could not express to her. The thought of returning to India and leaving Siri behind had given me nightmares in the past few months. I woke up from sleep suddenly out of breathlessness innumerable times.

I knew it should have come out from my mouth first or she wouldn't insist on taking our relationship forward because of the predicament she was in. I knew she stood by me all along genuinely and not with an eye on a long-term relationship. But I didn't take the lead. I didn't use her past to get out of the relationship but I didn't want to be liable for tagging along an adorable woman like Siri to the vulnerability of my plans. Love is such a sacred relationship which I didn't want to initiate when I wasn't sure I could back it up with an unwavering commitment.

In spite of not seeing the possibility of taking our relationship to next level and being together forever, I never wished I had not met Siri. I will look back fondly at the affection she showered on me. They say never say never, but I would rather say it in her case—I might never get to meet Siri again—with a hope that this never of not seeing her will not be a never.

If she had been on her own navigating the highs and lows of life in the past, I hoped she will do it successfully one more time to recover from the vacuum I created. I'll carry with me the guilt of promoting her dependency on me though. I had not seen such a wonderful relationship in the offing when I had gathered the courage to stop her during the evening walk that day. And as the relationship progressed, I was too clouded by her magic to think through it rationally. I could only wish she'll surprise me by coming out even stronger.

After returning from Siri's place, I just had one week left in Louisville which I spent wrapping up things.

I had left for Venkat's place on September 15, 2013, with a few days left for my flight to India. It wasn't painful for me to leave Louisville though I had stayed there for two years. By then, I was a seasoned contractor. Moreover, the thought of leaving America overshadowed the thought of leaving Louisville.

Venkat was involved in my return to India plans as much as he was involved in my preparations to go to the US. He was not completely convinced with my idea of going to the US back in 2007 and he was not completely convinced of idea of leaving six years later. He felt I should have stayed for some more time to make money, applied for my H1B extension, and looked for a job in India.

I understood his concern for me as a friend but if "just in case" was part of my plans, I wouldn't have forgone a full-time position at my client place in Louisville at a package that many would consider a lifetime achievement, I wouldn't have declined vendors who offered me jobs in their offices in India. I wasn't obsessed with carrying a baggage of safety options anymore. India, to me, is not a test drive to have a Plan B, it is my destiny.

If I had to figure out things in India from the US itself, I would have done that based on what I heard from people, based on what I read in newspapers, and based on my understanding of the country six years back. I chose to return to India with an open mind and take a fresh and firsthand look at India after six years. In the process, I was prepared to lose some time which I would consider an investment in the name of proactive exploration.

***

I came back to my senses when the flight landed at Chennai International Airport.

I was so absorbed in my flashback the whole time that I didn't even recollect what I did during the layover time in Abu Dhabi. I had even forgotten to buy my favorite Glenlivet, which I would have to get at the duty-free shop in Chennai airport. I didn't remember where Mr. X and his wife disappeared; they probably took a connecting flight to Hyderabad. I was glad that I didn't miss my connecting flight in Abu Dhabi.

I read the news about airports in many cities in India getting upgraded to international standards but Chennai was clearly not among them. I couldn't spot restrooms until I reached the baggage claim. While I waited for my bags at the crowded baggage claim area, I regretted several times not pissing before

I got off the plane. With so many people around, I didn't dare to leave the place until I collected my bags.

The jostling crowd which I wasn't used to in the past six years made me uncomfortable. Finally, when I collected my bags there was a tough competition for the carts. The porters hoarded the carts, forcing people to use their services. The game had started—a desperate fight for anything and everything.

I didn't want anybody from my family to come to the airport to receive me. I wanted to be on my own until I reached home. Venkat had arranged their family car and driver to pick me up at the airport. As I got out of the airport, I spotted Venkat's driver from the placard he was holding with my name—first of all it is Jay, not Jai.

I excused the driver for a couple of minutes and pissed in the open air. What a pleasure. My adaptation to India was quicker than I anticipated.

"Rafi, where do we get cigarettes here?" I asked.

"You know my name, sir?" he exclaimed.

"Venkat gave me your name and number," I said.

"I have been with Venkat sir's family for the last four years, sir. How is Venkat sir?" he inquired.

"He is good. He sent dresses and chocolates for your children. I'll give it to you when we reach home, I'll have to open my bag," I said.

"They treat me like a member of their family, sir," he said, overwhelmed with Venkat's gesture.

"Do we get cigarettes here?" I asked again.

"It's too late to get cigarettes here, sir. I have a cigarette packet," he said.

"I need Gold Flake Kings," I said.

"I smoke the same thing, sir," he said, surprising me.

"Do we have public telephone here? I need to call my mom and make a couple of US calls," I asked him, lighting a cigarette.

"After these cell phones came, public telephone booths disappeared, sir. You can call from my cell," he offered.

"Can I make a US call from your phone?" I asked.

"Yes, sir. I give missed calls to Venkat sir sometimes." He surprised me again.

I called up Venkat and mom and informed them that I had reached Chennai and was on my way home, and then I called Siri. I was worried when she didn't pick up the first time. She called back immediately without letting me worry for a long time. It's customary and cheap for people in America to call people in India.

"Siri, Jay here."

"What's up Mr. India?" Siri asked, laughing out loud.

She took me by surprise by not being sad. I hoped she was not faking it to not let me down.

"Did you kiss your motherland as soon as you stepped out of the airport? Haha."

Same originality. I couldn't have asked for more.

I lit another cigarette and deeply inhaled thinking that the dilly-dallying with "let me figure out things after reaching India" had ended and the actual figuring out part started.

Two cigarettes in the polluted air and a piss in the open air brought me back to India completely. The good old days when I didn't have to worry about polluted air or people watching me when I smoked were gone.

Physically exhausted by the journey, mentally drained by reliving my America sojourn during the flight, and emotionally relieved by hearing Siri's warm voice, I slipped into sleep as soon I got into the car, only to wake up to the new reality called, India.

My name is Jay, and that was my story.

Epilogue

Anonymity was good when I was struggling but for how long? I was bored of living a life of confinement in America—days confined to job, lifestyle confined to salary, aspirations confined to safety, reach confined to immigration compulsions, social life confined to NRIs, and happiness confined to comforts.

If life was satisfying in the US, why did the guilt of living just for myself constantly bother me? Why didn't my conscience allow me a peaceful stay? Why didn't my heart always smile as much as my lips did? Why didn't the sense of underachievement leave me? Why did my mind turn blank whenever I tried to recollect the last time I jumped out of bed even before I completed my sleep to start the day to make a difference?

I yearned to break free from mediocrity and go all out. And what could be a better place to realize the meaning of my life than my own country and around my own people?

Is life all about flying higher and farther with the wings I acquired? At some point, don't I need to use the same wings to fly back to the place and the people who made me who I am, to give them back something? Don't I have the responsibility to leave my country a better place for the next generations than what I received from my forefathers?

On my deathbed, it would be a great sense of relief to remember that I chose to let go off many things and chose a few things close to my heart to which I dedicated my life and hopefully made a difference. Therefore, I chose to be neither a paranoid Indian in the US nor a US-obsessed Indian in India. I chose to be a complete Indian in India.

The images of continuing to live in the US were so dreadful that I wouldn't have been able to do so any longer without remorse. It was a collage of missed family time, failed moments to catch up with friends at the places where we grew up together, dread of letting parents grow old on their own and probably hear the news of their death in the middle of a sound sleep one night, cut off from a generation of India, lost out on being part of India's progress, lost opportunity to give back to the society that shaped me—lost in soul and lived in luxury.

There were several internal calls in the past that I haven't attended, either I totally ignored them or kept them pending until they became irrelevant. Eventually they disappeared only to reappear at a point when I couldn't go back and correct them. Not this time, I pledged myself. The result of ignoring the inner voice could lead to letting life drift with the flow oftentimes. Not anymore, I assured myself.

If I waited until I saw a clear path, I would have waited forever, and if I returned in a fit of emotional rage, I would have invited potential regret in future. When the balance in my heart shifted toward moving back to India vis-à-vis staying back in the US, I took a call with belief in myself and faith in God. My return to India was neither impulsive nor compulsive, nor was it strategic. It was a conscientious return.

My India calling was quieter when I was drowned in debt and started resonating heavily as my life firmed up, like an alarm reminding me of the time. When I had a clear inclination within me, what was I scared of? That I'll not make so much money in India? That I wouldn't be able to buy the comforts of the US in India even if I have money? Isn't the basic premise of moving back to India after I earned so much a failure in itself? And if it was about lifestyle then how would I be able to sleep comfortably every night in America when my people in India are living a life to which I think I'll not be able to adapt to? How could I despise my own country and my own people just because I had the good fortune to be exposed to a better world?

It was a choice between a comfortable America which was not mine versus a chaotic India which was mine. It was a choice between what the best country in the world could offer to me and what I could offer to my country to strengthen it to compete with the best in the world. If I stumbled at forgoing a convenient life, what was the fun in harboring such lofty ideals in life? How could I have it both ways?

Like any big decision in life, my return to India was not devoid of internal turbulence. I cross-checked myself a million times if I chose to return to India under the influence of another false inspiration to do something other than what I was doing in the present to escape the burden of action. I questioned myself a billion times if I missed something in the whole equation. While I left the validation of my decision to move back to India by general worldly parameters to time, personally my choice was beyond a simple gain or loss, or a success or failure equation. If at all there was something I needed to make sure before I left America, that was whether I was happy or not, and I was upbeat though I was little nervous.

My decision to return to India wouldn't have been so unsettling to my family and friends if in the name of citizenship I had a free pass to enter the US whenever I wanted. But again as an American citizen, don't I belong more to the US than to India? For my well-wishers who thought I should have taken more time to plan it well instead of moving back in a hurry —yes, I was in a hurry, nobody ever guaranteed me a leisurely time in life. For others who thought I must have had a strong rationale or I must be mad to return to India at the time when my career was settled in America—the answer is both, India is both my rationale and my madness since I cannot think of scripting my story alienated from India. Whichever part of the world I lived in, ultimately my future wouldn't be any different than India's future.

To be fair, the reasons that kept NRIs glued to America were beyond dollars, which Indians who never visited there would never be able to fathom—structured life, progressive work culture, opportunities for kids, competitive education, quality healthcare, equal opportunity, equal under law, clean weather, communal safety, public civility, and lot more.

America as a country does not draw pleasure in making its people constantly engage in desperate fights even to live a normal life. It's a country with sensible laws and encouragement for people to adhere to them and a penalty for not doing so. There is a defined way of doing things without much confusion. Some of the things might sound utterly basic but they acquired prominence among the Indians there because of their denial in India.

I thought I was different. I thought I would say goodbye to America with a big smile on my face without any pull back but I was wrong about myself. To me, living in the US was a mix of diverse and lasting experiences which will continue to influence the rest of my life. Compared to six years back, I was a changed man in many ways. I'll be especially proud of the fortitude my America stay instilled in me as a result of the tough turns my life took there. I'll miss America.

But my personal gratification would have diminished if I stretched my stay any longer, which I experienced partly toward the end of my days in America. I wanted to protect it forever. I was already lucky that I was not forced out of the country because of immigration issues or joblessness. Was it not important to exit when I felt was the right time and on my terms? Was there a better time than when I actually left?

The moments I cherish most in my life are those when I stood firm with my instincts. Unfortunately those moments were not many. My return to India was one step in the direction of correcting that statistic. Why the fear of unknown when I couldn't think of a worst case scenario that could jeopardize my life in the process? After all I was coming back to my country.

I tried being a guy on the sidewalk repeatedly, holding back my desire to jump onto the main street and fight it out in life, and I was tired of it.

For once, I wished to be true to myself. . .

For once, I wished to be fearless. . .

For once, I wished to test my tenacity. . .

For once, I wished to beat myself. . .

For once, I wished to pat myself on the back. . .

For once, and forever!

Acknowledgements

To my family, friends and colleagues: I owe you a debt of gratitude for your unending support that goes beyond words and expression. So I will simply say thank you from the bottom of my heart.

To my publishing team, editors, beta-testers, and freelancers: The depth of my appreciation for your hard work and expertise knows no bounds. When the next story burns its way into my heart, I will not hesitate to call upon you—the most excellent team in the world.

To my readers: By adding *Guy on the Sidewalk* to your reading list you've given me a gift beyond compare. Thank you for becoming a valuable part of my journey as an author.

About the author

Bharath Krishna's debut novel, *Guy on the Sidewalk*, is a reflection of his passion for writing woven through his life like the golden thread of a rare tapestry. As a child, his flair for writing was ever present, but it wasn't until he started blogging on topics close to his heart that his talent was fully realized and appreciated, which ultimately led to his novel.

Bharath's resume reads like a kaleidoscope of sorts—a bachelor's degree in agriculture, double master's degree in management, and years of professional experience in marketing, teaching and IT in India and the United States. To know more about and connect with Bharath Krishna, visit www.BharathKrishna.org.